"YOU'RE TREATING ME LIKE . . . AN ENEMY!"

Jocelyn ran at him, her heart twisting in her bosom. She'd fooled herself to think things had changed between them.

Hammond tried to draw Jocelyn toward him, his hands on her upper arms.

"Do you think I want to leave you here? You know what's at stake. If I can accomplish my mission, I'll come back. I promise you."

Jocelyn meant to hurl herself out of his embrace but found her hands instead entwined in his lapel. She raised her chin defiantly.

She felt a whispered chuckle against her cheek as he kissed first it, then her mouth. . . .

Gentleman's Folly

Cynthia Bailey-Pratt

JOVE BOOKS, NEW YORK

GENTLEMAN'S FOLLY

A Jove Book / published by arrangement with
the author

PRINTING HISTORY
Jove edition / December 1991

ISBN: 0-515-10716-6

Jove Books are published by The Berkley Publishing Group,
200 Madison Avenue, New York, New York 10016.
The name ''JOVE'' and the ''J'' logo
are trademarks belonging to Jove Publications, Inc.

PRINTED IN THE UNITED STATES OF AMERICA

10 9 8 7 6 5 4 3 2 1

CHAPTER ONE

RELAXING IN THE DEEPEST, MOST COMFORTABLE ARMCHAIR in the upstairs salon, Jocelyn sewed at a shirt, a present for her youngest cousin's thirteenth birthday. Every so often she looked up from her work and sighed happily. Outside the open window the day was bright, clear spring, the first of the season, with neither rain nor bluster. A lively little breeze flirted with the white muslin drapes, bringing with it the smell of growing things. Best of all, the priory was completely quiet. Her aunt and uncle were in the library, working on their presentation for the London Preservation Society. The two boys who still lived at home had taken advantage of the weather to go away.

On the floor below, a door slammed with a startlingly loud report. Jocelyn jumped in surprise, then hurriedly bundled the shirt into her workbasket to hide it from Arnold. A drum-beat of excited footsteps came up the stairs. Jocelyn wondered if it would be mud, or rabbit's blood, or syrup she would have to remove from the hall carpet this time. Their most recent housekeeper flatly refused to clean up after Arnold any more. Though only the Luckems' niece, Jocelyn played a daughter's part in looking after her two cousins.

Rather than passing the salon door, the footsteps paused. Jocelyn stood up, bracing herself. It opened.

"Granville!" she exclaimed, having expected not him but Arnold. "What has happened?"

Her sixteen-year-old cousin was never seen without the most extreme attention having been rendered to his toilet.

1

Now he stood before her, a sweating, dust-smeared disaster. His cravat, pride of his life, had evidently been used to wipe a streaming brow, and his coat hung as if half-torn from his back. The boy gulped. "I . . . uh . . . nothing whatever, cousin."

"Come now," she said as she poured him a tumbler of water from the carafe on the table. "Drink this, and tell me what is wrong."

Gratefully he drank but hesitated before fulfilling her second request. "Do you promise not to tell Father or Mother?"

"I can't do that."

"Oh, please. Their speech to the society must be finished before tomorrow, and they've lost so much time already this week thanks to that hubble-bubble brother of mine. Curse him! Why couldn't my parents have stopped breeding with me?"

"Now, Granville," Jocelyn said mechanically, though to herself she admitted he had a point. "What has Arnold done this time?"

"Why, nothing in the world except commit a hanging offense!" He sank into her armchair.

"Hanging!"

"He was fishing in Lord Netherham's lower stream. Again! In plain daylight with Handsome Foyle. Constable Regin came along with his big feet, and they never heard him until he clapped hands on Arnold. Foyle avoided capture and found me at Winston's."

"Dear heavens! We must tell your parents this. At once!"

"No!" Granville clutched at her arm. "Arnold didn't give his right name, thank the Lord, and Regin's new enough that he doesn't know my dear brother's face as yet. If we can get Arnold back, Mother and Father will never have to know."

"How can we do that? I can't walk into Libermore gaol and ask the constable to release Arnold without bringing the family into it. Regin is not Constable Phillips. Perhaps if Phillips had been firm with him, Arnold would have stopped getting into these ridiculous scrapes years ago."

"He's not the only one who has fallen into a bumble broth before now." Granville looked at his cousin slyly. "Do you remember stealing Mr. Nicholson's peaches?"

"Oh, no," she said, her gray eyes widening in alarm. "No, Granville, absolutely not!"

"Oh, come on, Jocelyn. It's not much of a sacrifice. Any way, we've no choice. It's either you help me or I ask Mr. Quigg. And his rheumatism has been kicking up since you told him to dig the garden. He'd be no good if we have to run. Somehow, I'm sure we'll have to run. It's the only thing to do when Arnold gets into trouble."

Seeing that she still hesitated, he pleaded, "Come on! We can't let Arnold be hanged."

"They don't hang twelve-year-old boys anymore," Jocelyn said, attempting to sound confident, although she wasn't entirely certain of her facts.

"Then he'll be transported. They'll do that sure as a gun. His age or Father's status won't matter in a poaching case. And I'd have to go with him, and bang! go my chances at Oxford. You must do it, Jocelyn. You must!"

"I'm not even sure where any of those clothes are. Or if they'd fit. I was seventeen then. I've grown."

With a glance at her figure Granville said, "You could still pass for a boy."

"Thank you so much." She shook her head. "Absolutely not. I won't do it."

Granville tightened his grip upon her sleeve. "We're wasting time! We've got to get there before Regin takes Arnold to gaol. Once he's there, we'd never be able to rescue him."

The very real agony in Granville's voice decided her. Although she felt a good fright would do wonders for Arnold, she could not allow him to be entangled in the law's merciless web without raising a hand to help him. "Oh, very well," she said, stamping her foot with frustration. "Look in Tom's room for the clothes. I'll go change."

Within half an hour two youths could be seen racing toward the riverside town of Libermore. One ran rather awkwardly, as if unused to the freedom of trousers. And such trousers! The boy looked as if he'd dressed in the dark, with a ragbag for an armoire.

The faded blue coat had been retrieved from her eldest cousin Tom's wardrobe and still smelled of the stables, though Tom had been away at Oxford for two years. Her inexpressibles were Granville's patched and thus disdained property.

Her waistcoat, once gloriously embroidered with whitework, now threadbare, had been caged from a former housekeeper's quilting bag. The grubby shirt belonged to Arnold, as did the shoes. The disreputable hat that Jocelyn anxiously held clamped over her short and curling hair had been found by Arnold last spring on a riverbank.

The gaol in Libermore was in the oldest part of town, near the river. Jocelyn kept her eyes on Granville's back as he moved confidently through the teeming streets. He seemed to know his way, and Jocelyn was glad not to be alone. She'd never been down there before. It was not a place for a respectable girl. At least she could be certain no one who knew her would see her in her eccentric costume.

Granville paused on the pretext of inspecting a fruiterer's barrow. "Just ahead," he said out of the corner of his mouth, like a naughty schoolboy. "Do you see them?"

A strangely assorted pair came toward them. The parish constable was as massive as a castle tower. He scarcely picked up his enormous feet as he lumbered forward. His dark head was the shape of a pistol ball, with about as much expression. The contrast to the youngster beside him could not have been greater. Arnold Luckem was small and thin with a sunny blond head. Despite the rope around both wrists, he bounced along the street as if out for an afternoon's pleasure. He paused frequently, smiling at people in the street and looking with interest at wares displayed for sale, until, with a jerk at the rope, the constable towed him along once more.

All Jocelyn's anger at her heedless cousin was transferred to his captor. Obviously, the constable possessed no tact whatsoever. Tying Arnold up like an animal and parading him through the busy streets? A more decent man would have brought the miscreant to Mr. Luckem and likely received a tip for his trouble. In disgust Jocelyn looked away. Her eye fell upon a vegetable marrow on the cart before her. Though exposed for sale, the gourd was far from ripe. Curving her fingers around it, the heaviest part of the bulb stuck up like a club. She looked down the street at Regin, a troubled furrow between her dark brows.

Granville took his lucky half crown from his pocket. "Crown, you grab Arnold and I trip Regin. Spade, I take my brother." The coin spun. "Spade. Damn. Two of three."

Jocelyn reached across and took the coin from him, handing it with a smile to the fruiterer. Granville protested wordlessly.

His cousin said, "It's not much of a sacrifice." She took the vegetable marrow. It was hard as stone when she tested it against her palm. "Spade it is. Let's go."

Pausing only to collect his change, Granville went after Jocelyn. They waited about forty feet from the town's lockup. Granville whistled shrilly. Beside Regin, Arnold turned his head as he searched the crowd. Spotting his brother, he merrily waved both hands.

"What's you lookin' at?" Constable Regin growled.

Jocelyn stepped forward. Taking a deep breath, she raised the vegetable high. As though she'd practiced for years, she brought the hard gourd down on the parish officer's pate. At the instant of impact, Granville grabbed his brother, lifted him bodily off the ground, and ran like the devil, Arnold shouting something over his rescuer's shoulder.

Dearly as she would have liked to, Jocelyn could not follow at once. Regin turned his eyes upon her with a questioning frown. Jocelyn looked at the remaining half-gourd as if uncertain how the thing could have thus grown to her hand. It slipped to the ground as she smiled sheepishly.

Even as the massive parish constable reached out his large hand to arrest her, his eyes rolled up in his head. He rocked backward and fell with a noise like a hundredweight of brick falling onto cobbles.

Guiltily Jocelyn looked around. She met no eyes. It was almost like a conspiracy to ignore what happened to the constable. She wondered how many of these street merchants, living hand to mouth, suffered from Regin's strict enforcement of parish regulations and fines. Jocelyn walked away. Little by little her pace increased until she ran toward where Granville and Arnold had disappeared. They were nowhere to be seen. And she, looking about her, found that she was lost.

Scooting rapidly out of the path of a hustling drover with a sheep on his shoulder, Jocelyn ran full tilt against a man who suddenly emerged from a shadowed doorway. Looking past him, she murmured an apology and continued on her

way, only to find her arm seized in the enormous hand of an
army officer in a coat nearly as scarlet as his face.

"I beg your pardon, sir," she stammered. She tried to
wriggle loose as the man clapped his other hand to his uniform pocket.

Hoarsely the officer demanded, "Stealin' my purse, is it,
or my kerchief? Ye're fer the Newgate, my lad! Here!" the
man cried lustily, attracting the attention of passersby. "Call
me the watch. I've been robbed!" Her captor tightened his
grip.

"No, indeed, sir," Jocelyn protested, fear rising in her
throat. Regin would soon be back in the running. Who knew
how long so hard a head would remain unconscious? Looking
back the way she'd come, Jocelyn said, "I'm not a thief!"

"A liar, too, by hell! Give me my purse, or I'll thrash
ye!"

"Come now," said a stranger, pausing as he walked by,
good humor quirking his black brows. "Let the boy go. This
isn't London, my good sir, where every chance encounter
may lead to unpleasant end."

Pleadingly, Jocelyn looked at the stranger. She thought his
open face and clear gaze were those of an innocent curate or
clerk, though he was perhaps thirty-five, older than such men
usually were. His shoulders, too, were perhaps rather straight
for him to belong to either crouching profession.

A curate might feel it his duty to stop to aid someone
falsely accused. Certainly, no one else seemed interested
enough even to stare. "You're no thief, are you, my lad?"
the man in black asked cheerfully, fixing her with his deep
brown gaze.

"No, sir, I'm not. I swear I'm not," she said, her voice
quavering up and down an octave.

"There, you see, sir?" Jocelyn's friend said, smiling with
great charm at her accuser, giving him the opportunity to
admit his mistake. "An honest lad, if ever I've seen one.
Besides, not even the meanest thief would in these days steal
from one of England's gallant defenders. Congratulations on
Wellington's elevation to a dukedom. Tell me, were you at
Pampeluna, or perhaps San Sebastian?"

Something in this pleasant speech enraged the officer. His
face grew purple with rage, and his thick neck overflowed its

stock. "I have it now," he said, spatulate fingers nearly meeting in Jocelyn's arm as he shook her as a dog shakes a bone. Her hat fell off.

"I have it now! Ye're in league, the pair of ye. A fiddle-stringer and his pup, I'll be bound. Have ye both run in." As the man swelled his lungs to shout again, a silver-headed cane whistled down with a crack across the man's forearm. He roared out in pain, his fingers opening, no longer obeying his will.

Jocelyn found her arm grasped anew as "Run!" was shouted in her ear. She was towed along behind this unusual clerk as he ran. The rising ruckus behind her lent her feet unaccustomed speed, her hat remaining, a sorry prize, at the feet of the officer in the scarlet coat.

An alley opened to the right, and she followed the bobbing back of her rescuer. She splashed through a muddy puddle. Jocelyn's heart beat thunderously in her throat, and she could hardly catch a breath. She seemed to have been running for years, forever chased. They dodged down many dark and stinking ways until all sound of pursuit was lost.

Behind a shed of rotten planks, the gentleman's arm pressed across her, Jocelyn waited until he decided all was clear. Her rescuer was taller than she had first thought, so that she had to lift her head to see his face. He smelled clean, something she would not have expected from a man whose clothes were so obviously old. Muscles moved in the arm around her, and Jocelyn realized she might have misjudged his place in life. His breath in her ear was labored and rasped faintly when he inhaled.

When he let her go, she started to thank him. He stopped her with a sharp, "Nonsense! I was watching you. You've never committed a crime in your life. But you'd never have made him believe it. Officers are selected for their stupidity, it seems." The man laughed shortly. "I should not have teased him with the glorious defeat of Soult. Quartermasters don't fight."

"I . . . I wouldn't know, sir," she said. "I do thank you for your assistance. It would have been terrible to be taken up for stealing."

Too late Jocelyn remembered her voice. She coughed and

said, much more deeply, "My mother wouldn't have liked it."

A gleam of sunlight from overhead caught the man's face, and she saw a slight smile come and go on his lips, though the brim of his hat shaded his eyes. She glimpsed only a liquid gleam throwing back the sunlight.

"I'll be off then, sir," she said, unnerved by the unseen eyes.

"No, I think not," he said. "Such men very rarely let an offense pass so easily. He'll probably report you to the constabulary. You'd better lie low for a bit."

He paused, while the silver head of his cane, no poor man's, massaged the jaw of his lean face. She could feel his hidden eyes studying her, and a blush leapt into her cheeks. She noticed that he kept his other hand hidden inside his coat against his left side, like in the engravings she'd seen of Napoleon before his exile to Elba. The stranger expelled his breath in a long sigh. "Have I done you a good turn, do you think?"

"Yes, sir. I'm very grateful."

"I wonder if I could ask you to return it so soon. I think I have a use for a likely lad, such as yourself."

Was there or was there not the slightest hesitation in his voice as he claimed her as a male? Jocelyn could not quite tell but knew it was best to be wary. His eyes seemed to take in more than those of ordinary men. Perhaps he might be some sort of criminal.

No matter what his station, it would be basest ingratitude to refuse to do him some small favor. He had, after all, extricated her from a charge of theft that would have led to a worse charge. Her hand still tingled from the vegetable marrow's contact with the constable's head. It would have been impossible to free herself from gaol without calling in her aunt and uncle and revealing her shameful costume and behavior. Her reputation would be worthless if word of today's escapade got out. The stranger had saved her from all these consequences.

Jocelyn said manfully, "I'll do whatever I can for you, sir, of course."

His long fingers rested on her shoulder for an instant, as

if gauging her moral strength. "Good," he said, nodding as if he approved of what he found. "Come with me."

As they emerged into a wider street with more light, Jocelyn inspected him still more closely. Despite the elegant touch of the beautiful ebony and silver cane, Jocelyn now noticed that his coat was so old it no longer looked black, but rusty brown. He wore knee breeches quite out of style and baggy at the knees. The points of his collar drooped above a ragged cravat.

He noticed the unfavorable impression his clothing made and smiled with cheerful unconcern, revealing white, well-formed teeth. "We seem to make a matched pair, you and I. Neither of us can be said to be in the first stare of fashion. By the by, do you know where we are?"

Jocelyn looked from the stranger to their surroundings. They'd emerged into a wide pleasant street that looked familiar, yet Jocelyn did not think she'd ever been in it before. Fewer people walked here than down by the river. They dressed more elegantly and strolled with pleasure as their aim, not bustling along in the interests of commerce.

Jocelyn and the man went on a few steps, and then, as she looked down another avenue, she cried out in recognition, "Yes! There's the chemist and just beyond that is Mr. Yalter's shop. That big gray building is the Groat and Groom."

"That, I take it, is some sort of inn."

"Yes, sir."

"Is it popular?"

"Yes, sir. Many people visit it of an evening."

"Then it is not what I want. Can't you take me someplace . . ." He looked around and then finished his sentence. "Someplace quieter?"

Now that her feet were on a road she knew, Jocelyn almost felt as if she were in her proper clothes, thinking her usual thoughts. She knew it wasn't right for her to be alone with a strange man, although she sometimes went in mixed parties on longer walks than this. But on those excursions girls remained with girls, and the young men congregated even more closely. Then, too, on those occasions she had always been decorously dressed. Jocelyn said, "Well, sir, if I knew why—"

"If I wanted you to know why, I would have told you already!" he snapped. At once he seemed to regret his bad temper and said more gently, "Now, please, a quiet inn where a man might rest the night undisturbed."

Looking past him toward the top of the street, Jocelyn saw someone she knew, but she did not go to him for help. Grim Cocker, the vicar's new manservant, seemed to be searching among the passersby, his ugly face tense. His reptilian eyes passed over her and her companion, passed over and returned. He began to come toward them. Two ladies with open parasols blocked the pavement.

Jocelyn turned casually to walk away from Cocker, the man in the old coat following her. Jocelyn shivered as though with cold. Ever since she walked home alone from church three Sundays before, her two cousins being confined at home with the grippe, Jocelyn had done her best to avoid Cocker. His bold comments on that occasion might well be repeated if she were glimpsed in a tight pair of breeches and a boy's coat, doing the best it could to hide the feminine contours of her figure.

The stranger said, "Do you know that man?"

"What man, sir?" she said, keeping her voice low. "I'm taking you to that inn you asked for."

She could not help looking behind her. Cocker was not yet at the opening to the alley. She knew the man she led noticed her anxiety, but he asked no more questions. Jocelyn thought that was fair of him, as he would answer none.

Jocelyn led him down Stone Alley, through Vetter Lane, and into Spenser Court. A hostelry stood there that her oldest cousin Tom and his friends condemned as "too dull." She'd never been there, knowing only its general location. Jocelyn felt both surprise and pleasure at finding it so easily. Perhaps, she thought, I know Libermore better than I believed.

The inn was a small wooden building squeezed into a dark corner. Dilapidated balconies hung in front of the second-story windows. The buildings on either side of the alley were also old and seemed to lean over them, cutting out the sky and all save a little light. The sun seemed dimmer, and a thin wind blew down the cracks between the buildings.

"There, sir. Is this all right?"

He surveyed the inn carefully before approaching any closer. "Yes, it may serve." He gasped suddenly and lurched as his feet slipped in the mud. When he brought out the hand that he had held to his side, Jocelyn was horrified to see a stain on the handkerchief he held between his fingers. There was too little light in the narrow alley to see the color, but Jocelyn's eyes grew wide as she guessed what the stain was.

"Go along, boy. And thank you," he said in a faint, gasping voice that Jocelyn did not like the sound of at all.

Though it was growing late and she felt she really ought to find her cousins and return home, Jocelyn could not make herself turn away and leave him in this dark and lonely place. "Sir? Let me help you." She stepped nearer to him and put her white hand on his arm.

The man's breath was more labored now than it had been after their frantic run. He nodded, accepting her help with reluctant gratitude or, she thought, as if he lacked the strength to force her to leave.

He leaned against the rough brick of the wall, saying, "If you would, go in and ask them to give me a room. It must be on the second floor, one . . . one that faces this way. Can you do that?"

She found it difficult to understand him, for now every sentence was accompanied by long sighing breaths, and the ugly rasp in his voice increased from moment to moment. Jocelyn said, "Yes, sir. Gladly."

"Go on, then." He slowly drew a soft wallet from his breast pocket and handed her two or three coins. "Pay my lodging for . . . a week. Yes, a week."

She took the coins and half-turned away, hesitant to leave him. Full of questions, she wetted her lips and said, "Sir . . . ?"

His clean hand darted out with the same speed that had taken the officer by surprise. He gripped her by the arm, his fingers biting with terrible strength. His dark eyes burned into hers as he whispered, "No questions."

Jocelyn could do nothing but nod. He seemed to take her response as a promise and let go. She looked back once to where he leaned against the wall, hunched over, his eyes closed.

The landlord looked at her suspiciously and scratched at his unshaved chin as Jocelyn tried hard to imitate the brusque manners of the street boys who picked up pennies by running messages. It wasn't easy to answer the man's natural ques-

tions, and she wondered what lies she could tell if her stranger
faltered before safely in his room. Jocelyn knew that the landlord would pitilessly turn the man out if there was the slightest
chance of his dying while in the inn. At last the landlord
agreed to accept the money, and Jocelyn turned to bring the
man back. She regretted leaving him so long. What if he had
fainted—or worse?

As she went out, Jocelyn was pushed aside by the gentleman, who swaggered in, rapped his stick on the dirty table,
and loudly said, "Coming to get me, lad? Knew you were a
good boy!"

She blinked to see him come in through the inn's door as
if he were a lord when ten minutes before he had been
hunched over, hoarding every bit of his strength. Even his
coat seemed smarter when the back that bore it was so ar-
rogantly straight and his old hat seemed more an affectation
than the possession of a man who owned no better. But Jocelyn noticed the light sweat shining on his forehead and thin
cheeks and understood the effort behind this masquerade of
perfect health.

He turned to the landlord, who now nodded and smiled,
all his worries at an end, and said, "A glass of ale, my man.
And will you join me? Can't be sure of good drink unless the
landlord drinks with me, what?" He downed the golden liquid in three long swallows and then rubbed the empty tankard
between his hands with a satisfied sigh.

"That's what I wanted. No, thank you, one's enough for
now." His eye fell on Jocelyn. "Are you thirsty, boy?"

"No, sir. Thank you."

"No?" She could see his surprise at this refusal of a street
boy to drink free ale. "Then a meal perhaps. You're too thin
for your height. Isn't he, landlord?"

The landlord obviously had never before considered the
question of a ragamuffin's stomach. However, he saw that the
gentleman was willing to pay for a meal, so he agreed heartily.

"No, truthfully, sir," Jocelyn protested. "I'm not the least
bit hungry." He couldn't be a criminal, she reasoned. Why
should a bad man care for another's hunger? For that matter,
why would he have helped her in the first place? Surely a

wicked man would be happy to see an innocent person suffering.

The gentleman shrugged and only Jocelyn saw the look of pain cross his face. He said, "Thank you for your help, boy." He put his thumb and forefinger into his breast pocket and brought out a half crown, weighing it with a glance at Jocelyn.

With a change of mind he said, "No, I may need you again." He spun it in the air, a golden glitter in the dark taproom, caught it, and restored it to his pocket in what seemed a single motion. He smiled at the landlord. "Show me up, if you please."

Jocelyn and the landlord followed him as he bounded up the narrow stairs two at a time. She watched while he poked vigorously into all the corners of the small chamber and peered out the thick glass in the heavily leaded windows. A streamer of late-afternoon sun struggling to enter was the only light in the room.

"Perfection, my dear sir. I could not ask for a more salubrious site!" He thumped the landlord heartily on his broad back and told him a wicked story. Jocelyn sniggered at it obligingly, after a glance from her stranger, though she did not really understand it.

However, when the landlord had gone, rejoicing that God at last had sent a generous man to his inn, the laughing face and overwhelming manner faded. The gentleman felt behind him for the bed, misjudging the distance. Only a hasty grab at the solid bedpost saved him from sliding to the floor.

He swore in a jagged whisper. "Damn Frenchies," Jocelyn heard him mutter. "Never do clean their knives." She saw his eyelids flutter and remembered the time she saw her cousin Tom's arm broken by a kick from the pregnant mare.

Jocelyn was just in time to catch the stranger as he slumped over, his silver cane tumbling. She staggered on the uneven floor. He was heavier than he looked. Her arms seemed to lengthen from the effort of supporting him. However, she managed to maneuver him so he lay more or less on the bed, though his arm insisted on flopping over the edge. She walked around the bed and covered him with the half of the blanket he did not lie on. Only the rising and falling of his chest reassured her that he lived.

The muddy soles of his boots peeked out, but Jocelyn decided against removing them. She thought, I've done all I think I need to. I'd better go. The boys will be wondering where I am. In truth, Arnold was probably so angry at being tricked out of a journey to Australia that Granville had not yet had time from defending himself to think of her.

Jocelyn looked at the man on the bed. His thin, brown face looked younger, relaxed, and unaware. She noticed the deep, bruise-colored circles beneath his eyes and the way his nose seemed sharp as a peak above the hollows of his cheeks. It came to her suddenly that this man had not eaten very well of late. Without knowing why she did it, Jocelyn reached out to brush the lank black hair off his damp forehead.

Blood. Blood on her hand. She stared at it for what seemed a long time while her mind raced with panic. She had often comforted the small wounds of her cousins' childhood. However, when she saw the rich red smear on her palm, she felt shaken, sick, and stupid. The blood seemed to burn like a cinder on her skin. It was all she could think about.

Careful to avoid getting the blood on the lining of her coat, she stripped it off and laid it across the end of the bed. Lifting the water jug, she mechanically noted that it was empty and went out to fill it, not caring if anyone saw her clad in shirt and waistcoat. She wanted to wash the blood away, from her hand and coat sleeve, and she wanted to do it now.

Used though he was to sleeping in strange places, it had been a long time since he lay on a bed with a sheet that smelled of . . . The man had a sudden vision of his father's house. Not as he last saw it, with the storm clouds overhead echoing the storms within, but shining, the cream-colored towers rising at the foot of hills, his family's as long as time itself.

To him, his father's house stood for the England he fought for, even when barred from the company of Englishmen. He supposed the chateaux he'd seen during the last ten years stood for France to the sons of the families that held them, yet those ancestral seats had been destroyed, trampled under the galloping feet of the steeds of war. He thought of Graycroft with shattered walls and smoking fields, the people he still considered his lying dead among the ruins.

The thought stabbed him, and he sat up, ignoring the sickening swirling of the room around him. He opened the strings of his shirt under his cravat and reached inside. His fingers closed around a piece of heavy paper while his dark eyes searched the room for a safe hiding place.

The boy's coat lay near at hand. Nothing closer suggested itself, and he felt somehow that he did not have sufficient strength to get out of the bed. His heart pounded painfully just from the effort of sitting up. He reached for the coat, and a loose thread on its shalloon lining caught his eye. Slowly he pulled the thread. It came free, unstitching itself. Hearing the boy's footsteps on the stairs, he thrust the paper between the lining and the blue wool.

When Jocelyn came back with the jug, he lay in the same position as when she left, but his eyes were open. "What's your name?" he asked dully.

She began to say her own name, bit it off, and said, "Joss."

"I'm Hammond. It must have frightened you, my going off like that. I'm sorry." His breath still came in long sighs, but his voice seemed steadier if not strong. She did not like his color. Jocelyn saw his hand move beneath the blanket and a grimace contort his tired face.

"Well, Joss," he said with a sigh that seemed less involuntary and more like that of a man prepared to face a painful ordeal. "This looks pretty rum, eh?"

"Oh, no, sir," Jocelyn said brightly and then felt like a fool. "I mean, I suppose so."

"Do you turn sick at the sight of blood?"

She looked at her coat lying on the edge of the bed and shook her head with her eyes shut. "Not very."

"I only ask because I need your help. You can see I've been hurt. I don't think it's too bad. I can't bandage it myself, though, and . . . I'd rather not have a doctor."

Despite his evident exhaustion, Jocelyn realized Hammond was trying to encourage her. His voice was bright and bracing, though not very loud. Lifting his arm with an obvious effort, he threw off the blanket.

Although she wanted to run away, Jocelyn fought down her fear and approached the man on the bed. Surprised by the steadiness of her hands, she set the jug of water on the floor. Tenderly she helped him remove his old coat. His sim-

ple woolen waistcoat came off easily. Underneath, a wide
rusty stain on the left was plain as only blood can be, fresh
red glimmering in the center of the stain. His shirt stuck to
the long wound under his chest, and Jocelyn thought she'd
never find sufficient courage to pull the material away.

"Do it quick," Hammond said before setting his teeth,
but he could not stop a cry of pain as she tugged. Jocelyn
thought he should have cursed her for being such a clumsy
idiot. Her head spun, and she sat heavily on the bare floor.

When she looked up, Hammond was peering down the
length of his body at the sluggishly bleeding wound. "That's
not bad at all. Just sliced along a rib. If it went in as far, I'd
be waking with the angels by now. As it is, I'll never know
it happened in a day or two."

He looked at Jocelyn and smiled with a sweetness she did
not expect. Her own lips curved in answer. "That's the worst
over, my boy. Now if I can ask for the loan of the bottom of
your shirt . . ."

Jocelyn knew her face was hot and hoped it might be passed
off with her dizzy spell. "I would be glad to give it to you,
sir, but it's my only one." She was amazed by how quickly
she learned to lie, never having practiced.

"Well, then, we'll have to sacrifice the bottom of the bedsheet. I'll pay the landlord for the loan, if he ever discovers
it." The linen at the inn appeared to have been recently
washed, a thing Hammond said he'd scarcely expected.

"Is there anything of my shirt that isn't such an unbecom-
ing shade of red? No, don't tear anything higher than the
middle; I still have to wear the upper half in public. Tear off
a piece. Dip it in the water and give it to me."

He demonstrated cleaning his wound, and when Jocelyn
took the makeshift sponge, Hammond lay back and stared at
the wall. Though she went as slowly and carefully as she
could, once Jocelyn thought she felt him shudder, and she
whispered an apology. He shook his head and continued to
stare at nothing.

"Good lad," he said when she finished and put down the
pinkish cloth. "I'm afraid this isn't very easy for you."

"No, sir," she confessed.

"We're nearly done. Rip the bedsheet." Jocelyn turned
back the bottom of the blanket and tried to pull a seam on

the sheets. The landlord's wife was too good a seamstress and her stitches defeated Jocelyn.

"I can't get it started, sir."

"There's a knife in my left boot. Use that."

Timidly Jocelyn took the knife from the dark leather against his shin. The knife was long and thin with a dangerously sharp edge. It looked more like a wicked weapon from some melodrama than a knife a gentleman might use for slicing fruit. Jocelyn half-expected to see some dark stain on the blade and relaxed when she saw no such mark. Somehow, ripping the coarse linen into strips made her feel better about her squeamishness.

"Good," Hammond said when a small pile of bandages lay on the bed. "Make some of that into a pad, and then I'll show you how to bandage such an unwieldy thing as the human torso. It'll be useful to you, no doubt, should you ever join the Army."

Jocelyn thought that the bandaging went fairly well. At least, Hammond's face wasn't set into rigid lines, and he didn't seem to sigh as much as before. She tried to touch him lightly. Although she'd often seen her cousins without their shirts, she felt the considerable difference between their thin, unformed chests and the smooth muscularity of the stranger's body. She had to look at him to bandage him, but she tried not to let her eyes wander away from her work.

When she finished, she asked, "Is there anything else I can do for you, Mr. Hammond?"

"It isn't mister. Just Hammond." He grasped the blanket and settled himself beneath its itchy warmth. He sighed again, but with contentment not pain. "Do me one more favor before you go, Joss. I'm sure your mother must be growing anxious."

"Yes, sir, I'll do what I can."

"Look out into the street. No, not that way, you ass! Cross to the wall, lift the curtain out slowly from the side, and then, showing none of your body, look out."

"There's nobody, sir."

"Are you sure?"

"Yes," Jocelyn said, looking a moment longer, just the same. The alley's darkness had deepened since they were in it an hour or so before. Now the lengthening shadows ob-

scured all but a small square in the middle. "There might be
. . . no, it's only a stray cat."

"That's all right, then. Take that coin out of my pocket.
You've more than earned it." Hammond shut his eyes.

Jocelyn came over and picked up her coat from the bed,
noticing the blood still upon the sleeve. After what she had
been called upon to do, a small smear like that hardly seemed
worth noting, and she felt ashamed of her earlier foolishness.

Looking down at him, she thought he slept, but he said,
"Joss?"

"Sir?"

His eyes opened slightly, like a child awakened in the night.
His voice was softened by approaching sleep. "Don't . . . don't
say anything to anybody, will you? I can trust you, yes?"

"I won't say anything," Jocelyn promised.

A frown passed over his brow, slowly vanishing as if he
could not concentrate on his worry. "I'll come see you, when
I'm better. Meet your mother and reward you properly. Where
do you live?" She almost missed the last word.

"Um . . ." What had become of the facility she boasted
of in learning to lie quickly? She could think of no falsehood,
so she settled for half a truth. "We live on the Luckems'
property. Anyone can tell you where that is, sir. You rest
now. And thank you again for saving me from that officer."

Hammond did not speak. She didn't know if he even heard
her. Jocelyn stood by the door for a long minute, her hand
on the latch, watching the rise and fall of his breathing. She
didn't want to remember about her cousins or the duty owed
her aunt and uncle. She wanted, with an intensity that surprised her, to be there when Hammond awoke, to be able to
reveal herself as a girl. Perhaps he would be glad of it. Jocelyn remembered and went down the stairs.

CHAPTER TWO

―――――

"OH, OH, YOU DO LOOK FUNNY! GRANVILLE SAID YOU DID!"
With a haughty glance Jocelyn passed Arnold by, trying not to limp on legs and feet sore from the day's exercise. "I'm not the least bit interested in talking to you, Arnold Luckem. How can you fall into such scrapes? Poaching with Handsome Foyle! A more ill-named man never lived."

Arnold slithered down from the stone fence that ran along the lane. "Don't be that way. I was waiting for you to say how grateful I am to you for saving me."

"I suppose Granville made you wait for me."

"Well, yes. But I would have thanked you anyway."

If asked, Arnold Luckem would have admitted that his cousin was by no means the worst girl he knew. That honor belonged to Clarissa Rogers, who never failed to make sheep's eyes at him in church. Even Jocelyn, however, had ideas about cleanliness and truthfulness that a fellow could not be expected to admire. Arnold prided himself on his fairness, and to be fair, his cousin acted like a brick in coming to rescue him from Constable Regin. It had taken Granville two hours of earnest conversation to make his brother see cause for gratitude.

Jocelyn turned suddenly on Arnold. "What makes me angrier than even your poaching, Arnold, although you should know better by now, is your leaving the house at all. Didn't Mr. Fletcher send you to bed until supper for not knowing your declensions?"

"Yes, but—"

19

"Please, Arnold. Spare me. You always have an answer for everything."

"I know." Despite the expression of solemnity on his triangular face, Jocelyn knew laughter sparkled in his sharp blue eyes. If the evening light were a little stronger, she would have seen it clearly.

Haughtily she walked away from her cousin. She was glad Arnold was not in truth a mind reader, though at times he seemed to have the facility. If he had been, he would have realized Jocelyn was not as angry with him as she seemed. In a way his ridiculous arrest was responsible for her having met Hammond. A man in his sort of trouble would never have asked a girl to help him.

She could not help wondering what his reaction would have been if he had found out her true sex. Jocelyn thought of his pleasant smile and imagined how it would deepen when he realized . . . she sighed. Hammond would more likely feel trapped by gratitude than appreciative of her efforts. He would not find her worth smiling at, a girl with hair that would not grow long and a figure like a boy's even without a costume. No one, she reflected, ever found her very attractive.

Jocelyn's mind flinched away from considering his actual wound, its brutal appearance sickening her even in memory. Yet, before reaching her home, she began to feel proud of how she kept her hands very gentle and of how little sick she felt while actually washing and bandaging the wound. And he did seem to be a deal better, falling into a natural sleep instead of that horrid faint.

After a moment in which he watched a bat diving after a moth, Arnold came up beside her and took her hand, peering up at her face with a look of impish comradeship. Jocelyn struggled against giving in to his blandishments, as she well knew he calculated them with cool precision. But Arnold's personal charm overcame the remains of her anger.

"Oh, stop that," she said. "We're going to be late."

The garden at the rear of their house was deserted. As they came closer, a sweet breeze full of the scent of earth and new growth rushed down upon them. Jocelyn stopped and inhaled deeply. Spring was coming at last. She'd seen the green points rising up for a week, but all at once she felt spring blooming in her heart. It had been such a long and difficult winter.

She warned, "We'd better be careful. Anyone looking out of the windows can see us now."

The boy sniffed at this girlish timidity. "The housekeeper's too busy getting supper, and Granville's fussing in his room. I've never seen him look so . . . so normal as he did today. Come on." Arnold went first.

Warily they slipped around the hawthorn bushes to the old chapel, through the priest's stair, and up to their rooms. They saw only Mr. Fletcher, the boy's young tutor, who was pacing the upper gallery with his eyes fastened upon a book. Jocelyn shrank against the wall, waiting for him to turn his back.

Arnold walked boldly past him, saying "Good evening" in his most piercing tenor. Mr. Fletcher never looked up, only grunting vaguely under his breath. He had obviously forgotten his earlier decree of punishment for his youngest student, as he often did.

Jocelyn scuttled along behind Arnold. He could afford to behave so high-handedly. If caught, he'd only be sent once more to his room. Though Mr. Fletcher held no jurisdiction over her, a glance from him or anyone and she would feel forced to give an explanation of her boyish attire. She snuck rapidly down the cold corridor.

The Luckem family lived in an old house that had been a priory before the Dissolution under Henry the VIII. Jocelyn's maternal grandfather had purchased it from the Duke of Carnare. Though much thought and effort went into remodeling and decorating the house, it still felt as if one might meet a cowled brother around any corner, the long galleries and high ceilings of the common rooms and huge kitchen much as they were when the house was still a religious one. The bedrooms were once two or three cells, the walls now knocked out to make large single rooms.

Jocelyn liked her room, with its tall, narrow windows that looked out toward the hills. The walls were white plaster, hung with rubbings from ancient carved axes, and the rosewood furniture had feminine curves. Though cluttered with needlework on the table, piles of books in the corner, and objects no monk would have recognized littering the dressing table, something recalled the room's previous use to mind.

Jocelyn shut her door behind her and immediately started stripping off the male clothing, kicking it, for now, into an untidy heap. Her arm hurt as she pulled off the shirt, and she paused. Black circles stood out like footprints on the snowy skin. The angry officer's strong grasp came back to her in memory. That moment now seemed so long ago, she was startled to find fresh bruises.

As swiftly as she could, she washed off the dirt of her busy day from wherever it showed, and hustled into clean shift, petticoat, stockings, garters, and book muslin gown. Only then did she feel as if she could draw a full breath. She tied a scarf the faint blue of the spring sky through her short dark brown hair. It would do no good to comb or brush it. Nothing made any difference to the thick springy curls covering her head.

Jocelyn picked up the coat and spent a few minutes removing the bloodstain from the sleeve with the cold water in the bedroom jug. When the mark faded enough to be indistinguishable from any of the coat's other, varied stains, Jocelyn gathered everything together. Clutching the bundle to her chest, she peeked around the jamb of her door. When she saw no one, she walked quickly to Tom's room. She hung the coat on a hook and lay the other things in the bottom of his wardrobe for now.

Having only worn boy's clothes once before when teased into accepting a bet from Granville, she could judge how much she had grown up by the extent of her embarrassment today as compared with that of four years ago. She vowed that she would never be wheedled into such nonsensical behavior again. Her entire body shook when she considered how close she'd come to ignominy and disgrace.

To her shame, she realized she felt worse over dressing as a boy than she did about striking down a constable in the performance of his duty. That had felt splendid, now that she took an opportunity to reflect upon it. Opening a window to air the room, Jocelyn took a deep breath before going down to bid good evening to her aunt and uncle.

In the library every surface including some of the floor was occupied by objects of almost unimaginable use. Jocelyn's uncle sat behind his U-shaped writing desk, staring out the windows, the end of his old-fashioned quill pen curling around his balding head like an angel's wing. Unnoticed, Jocelyn kissed his cheek.

His wife raised her faded blue eyes from her work. Jocelyn's uncle and aunt avidly collected Saxon artifacts, specializing in those items made just after the Romans departed from the British Isles. Arasta Luckem pushed the fine fair hair off her face, grubby from the soft lead she used to record the surfaces of ancient objects. Thus begrimed, she bore a startling resemblance to her youngest son.

She had been a pale, pretty girl when she married Gaius Luckem twenty-five years ago, but many of those years had been spent on open hilltops searching for evidence of ancient life. Her face, like that of her husband, was browned by the sun and roughened by the wind, with many small lines around her eyes from squinting at the things they found.

Mrs. Luckem said, "Phew, my dear, I cannot believe how far behind we are. I knew we've been terribly slack of late; I hadn't realized the extent of the work still to be done." Wiping her face with a handkerchief, she only spread the blackness farther down her neck. "You kept Arnold so quiet. I never even knew he was in the house."

Jocelyn flushed guiltily. Mrs. Luckem did not remark it. Having lived with her uncle and his wife for most of her life, Jocelyn knew their blind spots. They were in another world when evidence of early people was before them. Chances were good that Mrs. Luckem would never hear of Arnold's poaching. She certainly would never know that Jocelyn connived with Granville to aid Arnold in an escape from justice, unless some unhappy circumstance brought it forcefully to her attention.

Jocelyn wished she could have told her aunt all about her day's adventures. The air of mystery about the man who called himself Hammond intrigued her almost to the exclusion of worrying about Arnold. However, to tell about Hammond would mean betraying not only Arnold's escapade but also revealing her shameful behavior.

"It must be getting near the dinner hour, Aunt Arasta."

"Is it?" Mrs. Luckem looked vaguely at the clock ticking cheerfully above a cold fireplace. They believed the influx of hot air and smoke would damage their specimens, as the damp spoiled the books. Even in February's Great Cold, when it snowed for six weeks without stopping, they worked con-

tentedly in coats and gloves, rather than expose their treasures
to the hazards of a fire.

"Go and see if dinner is ready, will you, Jocelyn? I can't
spare even a moment. We must get away tomorrow. I can see
that this and the packing will take half the night." Her gaze
was drawn irresistibly down, as she covered the shield on the
table with paper, and began to rub lightly with her stick of
lead. Her husband, with an expression of enlightenment,
wrote three words of his speech, to be delivered in London
at the great Preservation Society dinner in three days.

Leaving the library, Jocelyn crossed the Great Hall and
passed down the nine wide steps behind the screen in the
dining room. Entering the kitchen, she found no fire, no
smells of cooking, and no cook.

Jocelyn sighed and squared her shoulders. She opened the
door to the pantry and found a cold joint of boiled beef and
most of a salmon pie (without lobster), as well as some preserved asparagus and a large spice cake. She would serve the
boiled beef reheated, with her own mushroom ketchup.

On the back of the stove sat a kettle of what appeared to
be hotchpot, stone-cold and with a thick skin on top. Whether
their most recent housekeeper stayed long enough to put in
all the ingredients could only be told when it warmed. After
setting the beef down on the scarred table in the middle of
the kitchen, Jocelyn went to collect kindling to light the iron
stove, huge in itself but looking very cowed in the center of
the cavernous mouth of the monks' old fireplace.

A pile of sticks and larger pieces of wood was stacked
handily outside the door. She paused to look around the
kitchen garden. Snow had hidden in the shadowed corners
until almost the last week in May. Although now the second
week of June, spring seemed determined to have its moment
before summer came. A green haze covered the garden as
though the plants were eager to escape their over-long im-
prisonment in the ground. At the end of the garden the line
of cedars screening the back of the house seemed fresher and
greener than they had for months.

Jocelyn caught the scent of a pipe and looked for the
Luckem family's gardener and man-of-all-work. "Good evening, Mr. Quigg," she said when she saw him standing beneath the old elm by the garden gate.

"Good e'ening, Miss Burnwell. Can I be bringin' in that little bit o' wood for ye?" Even as he asked, he stooped, his smoke-colored pipe never varying from its outthrust position between his teeth.

Jocelyn found it difficult to tell how old Mr. Quigg might be. He had been there when her grandfather bought the house. His hair was of no particular color. His skin was smooth and red-flushed, though she did not know whether this enviable condition was due to his outdoor life or the private bottle he kept by him in his little stone house near the orchard. During the winter when the wind cut coldly through the chinks of the best-built house, he complained of his aching back.

On days like this, though, it was as if the years dropped away. Last spring a housekeeper left after complaining that Mr. Quigg pinched her in the dairy house. Why she had been there, since Mrs. Luckem kept no cows, she had not volunteered.

"I've smelt the wind all the day and I still be here," Mr. Quigg said in response to Jocelyn's question about his health. He bundled the wood into the stove and set it blazing with a chip lighted from his pipe.

"Time was, in my young life, such a wind would have blown me clear away. Did, too, more than once." He chuckled. "Except that's what happened to Mrs. Who-sit. She opened the door and blew right 'way."

Jocelyn smiled at a vision of the heavy-figured woman flying away like a peeved angel. They came and went, these women. Mrs. Luckem insisted on their using only Saxon cooking utensils, and one woman did make the effort, until caught using a fork. During another's stay, Granville turned away in disgust from anything other than boiled eggs and toasted wheat bread, because some London dandy suggested this diet to cultivate a pale and interesting complexion. Mr. Luckem shouted at one for dusting the library, and she left, muttering imprecations. Arnold, too, contributed to the parade of departing housekeepers by keeping a live snake in the kitchen, the warmest part of the house.

The stove heated well. Jocelyn took down a large cast-iron pot and filled it with settled water from the bucket that stood beside the dry sink.

Mr. Quigg warmed his hands a moment longer at the stove

and then said, "Don't you mind putting out a place fer me, miss. I been eating boiled beef too long to relish it much."

"I'm going to give you a piece of this pie I made just two days ago, Mr. Quigg."

"Give it me now, then, miss. I'll eat it under the trees." He held out his large blue-spotted handkerchief, none too clean, and Jocelyn cut him a wide slice. He thanked her and left, knowing she did not have the key to the cellar. The drink that went with his pie would have to come from his private source.

Sliding the slab of beef into the hot water, Jocelyn tried to remember how long to heat preserved asparagus. Was it to steaming or to roiling? She supposed that if she made enough white sauce, no one would notice if the timing was off.

She could scarcely wait until her own fresh vegetables were ready for picking. Jocelyn had grown tired of last year's produce in March, when it seemed as if spring would never come. She felt she should not complain. Some of the older and poorer people perished in the midst of the interminable snow. The Luckems had been very fortunate. Only the one week had been very bad, when the firewood gave out and they'd burned the old game table. Putting her cool fingers against her hot face, she recalled the recipe for white sauce with an effort.

Cooking made Jocelyn irritable. She thought of Arnold reading or messing about with one of the animals in his room. She entered the servants' stair, where steep steps lead straight to a tiny closet on the next floor. The acoustical properties of this hall were well known. Anything said in the kitchen could be clearly heard at the top of the stair.

Jocelyn called, "Arnold!" loudly and impatiently. She knew summoning Granville was pointless. If he was not lying down with a cloth over his eyes after his difficult day, he was undoubtedly trying new ways of tying a cravat to amaze his family at dinner. Arnold, however, would not be able to resist finding out what was happening in the house.

Arnold appeared, clattering down heedless of his limbs. He grinned as he said, "Another one gone, eh? Good, I didn't like her; mean eyes." He puffed up his face and squinted his bright eyes in imitation of the vanished housekeeper.

But Jocelyn didn't care to be amused. "Watch that pot," she said sharply. "Don't let it boil." With fair meekness, for he knew well cooking did not improve his cousin's temper, Arnold did as he was told. He began to tell her about his plans for the week, something about a river he'd been meaning to explore.

"I would have thought," she replied, "that you were planning to spend the next week or so at your books."

"Huh?"

"Don't grunt, Arnold. I mean, of course, that you cannot go out for . . . yes, for two weeks. Until your parents come home, I'm responsible for you. How would they feel if you were hauled off to gaol? Again."

"You can't restrict me to the house! I was going . . ." He mumbled the rest of the words.

"Poaching? Thieving? Or some other activity that will once again bring Constable Regin's hand down on your shoulder? He's going to be watching for you, Arnold. I don't think he's the kind that forgets quickly."

"He won't forget you bringing that vegetable marrow down on his head. Constables ought to wear helmets or something, don't you think? Like Roman soldiers, or the Coldstream Guards."

"Constables' headgear aside, Arnold, you are staying indoors until our constable finds something else to think of. Remember, if you please, that he took a long look at me just before—"

"Crash!" Arnold shouted jubilantly. The sight of the massive constable falling was evidently one of the high spots of his young life.

Jocelyn's lips tightened. She could not possibly reveal to Arnold that she had been accused of another crime within moments of assaulting the parish officer. He would find it too funny.

Her concern for her cousin, to her surprise, mingled with worry over the stranger, Hammond. If Arnold were once more arrested, surely Constable Regin would come to the house to inform Mr. and Mrs. Luckem. And, should he see her, he would undoubtedly recognize her as the "boy" wanted in two street crimes. A boy who went off with a man in black.

Jocelyn had heard reports of Regin's determination not to let any suspicious circumstance escape him. Hammond's behavior could certainly be considered suspicious, and Jocelyn somehow knew it would be fatal to have a large and implacable constable prying into Hammond's affairs. She was convinced that keeping Arnold within tight boundaries would be best for him, herself, and Hammond.

For once all six members of the Luckem household sat down together. As Jocelyn came in with the salmon pie, Mrs. Luckem said, "I forgot to tell you that Mrs. . . . what was her name . . . left. I'm dreadfully sorry."

Granville left his seat and took the serving plate from Jocelyn's hands. She smiled at him and forgave her aunt for overlooking the housekeeper's departure. She couldn't be angry while the family prayed over the meal she prepared. It would be hard in any case not to forgive the Luckems their faults, even if she didn't owe them all the happiness she knew.

Not even Tom had yet been born when Jocelyn's father died at sea and her mother came to live with Arasta and Gaius Luckem. Julia Burnwell did not live long, and her child was absorbed into the household with little fuss and less worry. Jocelyn sometimes wondered if she had inherited some stability of temperament from her father, about whom she knew nothing beyond the bare facts of his name and rank. Certainly, she did not possess the single-minded determination of the Luckems, who did what they pleased without reference to other people.

That quality, however, did not belong solely to the Luckems. Jocelyn knew from childhood the story of her paternal grandfather, who refused to acknowledge either his son's marriage or the birth of his only grandchild. She'd seen the letter her gentle mother wrote to the unknown man which had been returned with his reply, stinging as cold rain in the face. There would be nothing, neither money nor affection, for a brat whose relation to his son could not be proved, no matter how many "marriage certificates" were produced. Julia Burnwell never wrote again. First anger, then death, made re-approachment impossible.

Jocelyn passed the asparagus to Mr. Luckem. "I suppose," he said, coming reluctantly into the present century, "we'll have to advertise again."

Granville laughed at him. 'Really, Father, I'm sure all the housekeepers in England have heard of us. We won't find another for love or money.''

"What's wrong with us?'' Arnold wanted to know as he flipped a bun into his pocket for one of the creatures in his room. Only Jocelyn saw, and though she pursed her lips and shook her head, she said nothing.

"Oh, you wouldn't understand." Granville's gaze passed over his family, taking in all the evidence of their lack of interest in the important matters of life.

The chairs in which they sat matched neither each other nor the long rectangular table, spread with a much-stained cloth. The pictures on the wall were all drawings of Anglo-Saxon objects. His cousin, were Granville's life part of the novels he was fond of reading, should have been a perfect beauty with classical features. Instead, she was thin and snub-nosed with ridiculous hair, the curls tightened by the heat of the kitchen. Arnold never had been told to be "seen and not heard." And his parents were hardly the remote, cultivated persons of consequence who deserved such a son as himself.

Granville longed for the day when he would go to Oxford, to mix with the notable and noble, and to have all the advantages lost upon his elder brother, Tom. They seemed all the more precious as he realized how close he'd come to losing them today. While fixing his cravat, he'd decided that resolving any further adventures of Arnold's would be someone else's responsibility.

The tutor, Mr. Fletcher, read silently at the end of the table throughout the meal, a habit none of the Luckems would have considered worth mentioning to him. He did help to clear the table, using only one hand, the other employed in holding his book before his well-shaped nose. Mr. Fletcher seemed to operate like a bat, avoiding objects without seeing them.

After his task he disappeared to spend the time before bed with more reading. Jocelyn had reason to think he might spend a few moments dreaming about one living person, her friend, Helena Fain. If he did think romantically about Miss Fain, it didn't affect his work. He was an excellent tutor and was Granville's only hope for entering university next year.

After supper, Jocelyn pressed Arnold into washing the dishes by a glance of implied blackmail. Granville refused to

ruin his hands with the coarse soap and only took up the
dishtowel after his younger brother promised harm to his best
coat if he didn't agree to dry.

Later, they helped to pack their parents' collection carefully in straw. The cousins were well used to handling the
fragile objects and to swaddling them well against bumps and
crashes. Arnold actually owned the lightest touch of any of
them, save Jocelyn.

Mr. Luckem oversaw the packing of the artifacts into the
three small barrels Mr. Quigg had picked up in Libermore.
One smelled strongly of pickles, and Mr. Luckem even made
a joke, saying how he hoped the smell would "preserve" his
treasures. Only the larger pieces, such as pots and the bits
that were determined to be of military use, were packed in
this fashion. The most delicate were carefully wrapped in Mr.
and Mrs. Luckem's own clothing.

Jocelyn helped with this task, while the boys loaded the
carriage under Mr. Quigg's supervision. Picking up a rare
and beautiful enameled clasp, Jocelyn felt it would crumble
to dust in her hand, no matter how gently she handled it. She
cushioned it securely in her uncle's quilted dressing gown and
feared again when she took up another piece, an elaborate
brooch of twisted gold.

Mrs. Luckem came in, her arms filled with some of Tom's
clothes. Jocelyn recognized the blue coat she had worn that
afternoon. She thought of Hammond's eyes flicking over it,
and she suddenly felt too warm.

"Tom asked me for this old coat; there's some sort of horse
race being held, and he says it brings him luck. Interesting
how old superstitions hang on, though it is disconcerting to
find them in one's own son." While traveling to London, the
Luckems planned to make a brief stop in Oxford to visit their
oldest boy.

With some pride Mrs. Luckem opened the coat. "Look at
this seam! There was a tear, but I took care of it." Along the
inside of the coat a ripped seam was held together with long
stitches in thread of the entirely wrong color. "I think it will
hold long enough for the race."

Jocelyn hid a smile. Her mother taught her to sew almost
as soon as she could speak, and she now kept the Luckems'
clothing presentable. Her aunt did like to feel as if she were

contributing her own housewife's skills, though they were somewhat less advanced than her archaeological knowledge.

After working in silence for a few moments, Arasta said, "Gaius and I have every confidence in you, Jocelyn. Please see about getting a new housekeeper for us. I am sure you can choose no worse that we have done in the past."

"Thank you, Aunt Arasta. I'll do my best."

When Jocelyn went to bed, she prayed that no serious crisis would occur while her aunt and uncle were away. She knew it was useless to pray against the minor disasters that were certain to happen the moment she took charge.

As she knelt on her rag rug, a picture of Hammond as she saw him last appeared to her. She added a prayer for him, asking that he would be well. Unbidden, a hope that they might soon meet again sprang into her mind. She did not ask for it aloud.

By morning everything was prepared for the trip. The sturdy horses that worked in the fields could be spared now the plowing was done, and young Daniel whose father rented the fields, sat upon the box, the reins in his hands. He could scarcely sit still, filled with excitement at the thought that he would soon see the Metropolis for the first time.

The barrels and the valises with their contents far more precious than clothing were stowed inside, leaving scarcely any room for the human occupants. Discomfort, however, was nothing to Mr. and Mrs Luckem as long as their treasures were safe. Their children and their niece waved goodbye, and even Mr. Fletcher and Mr. Quigg spared a moment to notice the departure.

CHAPTER THREE

JOCELYN STOPPED TO EXAMINE HER GARDEN BUT FOUND IT difficult to bend down over the beetroots. Her exercise of yesterday had left her sore, prey to strange twinges in her lower limbs. She walked slowly into the kitchen.

Sipping a cup of tea, she heard a knock at the door. "Come in, Mrs. Hodges!" she called. "Oh. Good morning, Martha. I hope your mother isn't ill."

The girl on the doorstep balanced two cans of milk in her broad hands. Her fresh face would have been pretty if not for the lines carved in her forehead, lines of care and worry that should not have been there for years yet. "Not to say ill, Miss Burnwell, but terrible worried in her mind. Dad didn't come back and didn't come back. He's never stayed out so long before." Crossing the kitchen, Martha poured the blue-white liquid into the pans in the pantry.

Martha Hodges's father, Matt, was a long subject of scandal in Libermore. He did no work, although his wife and daughter did, supplying milk and cheese to those households that did not have a working dairy. This concern should have brought them in a comfortable living except for his taking the money to gamble and drink away.

After Martha left, Jocelyn spent a moment shaking her head over Matt Hodges's iniquities. If it hadn't been for Martha bringing the milk, she would have known nothing about his latest misdeed. Mrs. Hodges never said a word of complaint against her husband, although she was marked by frequent, unexplained bruises and cuts.

While waiting for her cousins to come down, Jocelyn thought about the day ahead. Examining the pantry, she saw she needed many things to run the house efficiently while her aunt and uncle were away. She made up her mind to go briefly into town to purchase what she lacked. A brisk walk would limber up her stiff muscles, as well.

She knew in her heart that shopping was just an excuse. It would be easy to walk a few steps farther up the street to the inn and to visit Hammond. I'll do my shopping first, Jocelyn promised herself. And then if there's time . . .

She thought for a moment longer and then dipped a mug into the fresh milk in the pantry and took a new-baked bun from a covered plate. Upstairs, Jocelyn knocked on Arnold's door. "Arnold, dear," she called. "I've brought you some breakfast."

He did not answer. Before Jocelyn could wonder whether Arnold had disobeyed her by escaping from the house, the bedroom door slowly opened. With a sulky face Arnold sat on his low camp bed, kicking his heels and staring at the reptile in a small cage beside him. He refused to look at Jocelyn.

"You needn't stay in your room, you know. I don't think there'd be any harm even if you went into the garden."

"I'm not supposed to leave until I learn my declensions. Mr. Fletcher said so."

"Oh, that's right. You had no chance to study them yesterday." She set the food on the table, finding just room enough between a collection of small stones and a pile of leaves. She hoped there was nothing poisonous lurking among them. "Well," she said. "Good luck."

"Thank you," he replied glumly, reaching for the bun.

In her own room, while putting on her outerwear, Jocelyn hesitated between her tilted straw hat and her deeply scooped bonnet. The straw was far more becoming to her, but thinking of Constable Regin, she knew the bonnet would serve as a better disguise. Jocelyn took up her pattens from where they lay near the fireplace and tied them on firmly to keep her feet from the mud.

As she made out her shopping list in the kitchen, Granville came down the back stair and reminded her about advertising for a new housekeeper. He helped to compose the notice in elegant language. "Though it is a waste of time, Cousin Jocelyn. No one will answer it."

"Maybe," Jocelyn said. "But we need someone, and I don't know how else to get her."

"Have you tried prayer?" Granville wanted to know as he drifted from the kitchen.

She took along a few coins of her own to pay for the advertisement and for some small articles not worth adding onto Mr. Luckem's accounts. Arnold liked citron drops, and a few might lift his encabined spirits. Granville teased her last week for some lavender water to mix with his perfume, though he knew perfectly well the lavender was not blooming well. She would buy these things, plus a pennyworth of good tobacco for Mr. Quigg, a thing he rarely bought for himself.

With a private smile she admitted these things were bribes to keep the house quiet while the older members of the family were away. Five pence is a fair price for peace, she thought, jingling the money in her glove. Taking up a basket, she set out for town.

It had rained in the night, and she hoped her aunt and uncle were not caught in the storm as it passed over England. Not that they would mind the wet, having often braved worse weather while digging, but the specimens would be in constant danger of exposure. She did not find it difficult to imagine Mr. and Mrs. Luckem sleeping in their carriage rather than risk carrying their treasure-filled valises across a wet stableyard to their room.

Jocelyn stopped first at the dusty office of the *Libermore Weekly Proclamation*. She waited a few minutes for the clerk to attend her. Taking her advertisement over the counter, the young-old man read it through his half-glasses and said, "Looking for another housekeeper, Miss Burnwell? That's too bad. I hope you have better luck this time."

"So do I, Mr. Phelps. When will it appear?"

He promised her that their advertisement would be in the next issue. Jocelyn thanked him, although, like Granville, she felt that the effort was in vain. They gave their last housekeeper the position because she had been the only applicant.

After visiting the greengrocer's, where the fresh vegetables she craved were newly arrived from warmer climes, and the butcher's, where she used her nose constantly to guard against rottenness, Jocelyn walked along the street to Harry Yalter's shop. She paused on the step, knowing a few paces more would take her to the alley that led to the inn.

Jocelyn found it surprisingly difficult to make up her mind what to do. She stood on the wide steps, turning her head to look between the shop and the alley until she was dizzy. Finally Jocelyn decided it would be best to make her purchases before going to see if Hammond had regained his health. The few things she needed to buy would not long delay her. She pushed open the wooden door, setting the bell jangling.

Though everyone called it a tobacconist's shop, Harry Yalter sold many other goods. Jars of tea, coffee, and spice breathed out rich odors, as magicians in tales conjured sights of distant lands. Great bolts of cloth gleamed in the dim lamplight above the counters, unraveling like rainbows when a purchase was made. Racks of ribbons, to refurbish gowns if not to remake them, shone like pieces of the same rainbow shredded in beveled glass.

Several other people were in the store. A lady in shiny green twill considered a tray of two-penny embroidery thread while gossiping vigorously with the oldest clerk. A gentleman tested pomades with Mrs. Yalter, flirting innocently. Two clerks stood in the back taking an inventory of muslins. One was the proprietor's son, who, so Arnold liked to pretend, was in love with Jocelyn. He hastened forward upon seeing her enter.

In the darkness of the shop a small, elderly lady dressed in unrelieved black tried in vain to catch the eye of one of the clerks. When young Yalter came over, she brightened. He passed her by to attend Jocelyn, with a deep bow. The older lady looked so cast down that Jocelyn said, despite her impatience, "I believe you were before me, ma'am."

"Oh, thank you." The lady pulled from her reticule a list three pages long, closely covered, front and back, with minuscule writing. She groped for her spectacles. "Now, let me see. I shall want some red grosgrain ribbon for my great-niece Elviry. Red, mind you, not scarlet. She has a wish for scarlet, but I don't think it's respectable, do you? Even if no one's ever to see it. It's to trim her new night rail, you know."

The other clerk disappeared. Jocelyn waited a long while

as neither of the two clerks present in the store seemed in any hurry to finish with their customers. She took up a flyer for patent medicine on the counter and studied it, trying to create an interest in a miraculous cure for the stomach gout and noxious humors. Try as she might, however, she could not prevent her foot from tapping or impatient sighs from escaping her.

At last the elderly woman finished choosing and gave instructions for delivery. "It's the yellow stone house on the edge of the wood. Not the painted yellow house, mind. That's Mrs. Breagle, and I shouldn't trust her to pass *everything* on to me. Now, let me see. Did you remember the soap? And the cinnamon wafer? And Dr. Hexham's tincture? Thank you, then. Good day."

Finally Jocelyn could approach the dark oaken counter to make her own small purchases. Jocelyn gave the clerk her list, instead of trying to read it to him as the elderly lady had. "Yes, Miss Burnwell," he said, smiling and bowing. "I'll get these things for you at once."

Master Yalter went about collecting Miss Burnwell's desires in the most heedless fashion. He hung one-handed from the ladder that reached the top of the shelves to obtain the freshest tobacco. He searched among the bottles of scented water to find that with the deepest purple liquid. He opened the big glass jar and dug deep into the center of pale candies for those with the richest flavor. Bringing her purchases to her like a rajah laying rubies before a princess, he said eagerly, "May I do anything else for you, Miss Burnwell?"

Jocelyn felt that it was just as well that Arnold was confined to the house. He teased her unmercifully about her supposed admirer. She pretended not to notice that the young man held her hand a moment longer than necessary when returning her halfpenny's worth of change. He never left it on the counter like the other clerks.

"Thank you, Master Yalter," she said, putting her purchases in her basket. She couldn't help noticing how crushed he seemed by the boyish title. Perhaps Arnold is right, she thought as she turned to go, but that's hardly my fault. I haven't done anything to encourage him.

Master Yalter sprang to open the door for her and counted his acrobatic efforts worthwhile when she smiled her thanks.

Once more in the sunshine she turned to the left. A dozen yards away she could see the entrance to the alley that would lead her to Hammond. Surely it would do no harm to inquire for him at the inn. They would at the least tell her whether he was alive or dead. Jocelyn walked quickly along the pavement, wishing she could run as she had yesterday.

In a moment she would find out the answer to the mystery that plagued her. She asked herself if the mystery was Hammond himself or how Hammond would behave when he saw her. She ignored the question. There seemed no time for it now.

A dish-shaped barouche came to stop beside her, the harness jingling. "Jocelyn!" A beautiful young woman dressed in perfect accord with fashion stepped down from the open carriage. Miriam Swann seized Jocelyn by the arms, a square indispensable swinging from her elbow.

"My dear, let me see you," she cooed. "Out of the way, you booby!" she said sharply to the tall footman beside her.

Blocking the pavement, Mrs. Swann turned again to Jocelyn. "My dear, you should bless the heavens you're not overly burdened with servants. They are always exactly where you don't wish them to be. Let me look at you. . . ." From beneath her white hat she looked her friend over carefully. "You're blooming. Such a color in your cheeks."

Jocelyn said, "You're looking well, too, Mrs. Swann."

"Thank you, my dear. London agrees with me wonderfully. But never 'Mrs. Swann' between us. Come, call me Miriam as you used to."

A man pushed between the two young women, not even bothering to raise his hat. "And let us get out of the street," said Miriam. "Sit in my carriage." With a wave of her violet-gloved hand, she indicated her black and gray carriage, a gray horse standing patiently between the shafts and a smartly clad coachman holding the reins.

"Are you visiting the shops?" Jocelyn asked, stepping into the barouche, holding up her skirts to keep them from the gutter. She hoped it would not be long before she could get away.

"Yes, but I'm in no hurry. Only a trifle my mother-in-law took a fancy for."

Miriam Driscoll and Jocelyn had been jointly instructed at

a dame school in Libermore and retained a friendship from
it. Much admired for her vivacity and flirtatious blue eyes,
Miriam had been pursued by many beaux and finally caught.
Two years ago Jocelyn attended Miriam during her wedding
to the well-set-up and fashionable Bartlett Swann of London
and Libermore. Since then they had exchanged a rare letter
and visited whenever Miriam came down with Mrs. Alastair
Swann to her country house.

Seated across from Miriam and looking at her in the strong
light of day, Jocelyn saw new fine lines about her eyes and
noticed that her hair had lost a measure of its blond fluffiness.
London, for all its glories, was evidently more trying than
Miriam said.

Miriam coughed stagily to distract Jocelyn from too close
an inspection, crimping the bow on the ruffled neck of her
peppermint-striped silk gown. She ran her hand lingeringly
over the sleeve of her pink waist-length spencer as if reassuring herself of its fashionableness.

Jocelyn, accustomed to her friend's artifices, did not trouble to compare her self-sewn book muslin to a London
modiste's creations. She admired, however, the new narrow-
ness of the costume's skirt augmented by deep tucks all around
Miriam's ankles. Jocelyn wondered if it would be possible to
add these embellishments to her own clothes and looked
closely to see how they were achieved.

"Yes," Miriam drawled, pleased by this sort of attention.
"Never in my life have I had such a time as in this Season.
Last year was nothing to it. Dear Swann spoiled me dreadfully, though, naturally, I found myself left somewhat to my
own devices. Such routs and parties, all quite gay. I attended
the theater virtually every night. And, of course, His Highness's plans for this Peace Celebration have sent everyone's
hat over the windmill. Oh!" She placed her fingers over her
full lips, flicking a glance at the stiff back of her coachman.

She said in a more natural tone, "I didn't mean to say that;
it's so vulgar. They call it 'cant.' Isn't it dreadful? Mrs. Swann
says it's the worst thing a lady can do."

"It doesn't seem so bad."

"No, and everyone in London does it. It's so frightfully
wonderful there, Jocelyn. I can't begin to tell you. But then,

Libermore hasn't been exactly peaceful. I was never so surprised in my life as when I heard.''

"Well, trade has improved enormously with peace, and—''

Miriam looked at her friend with raised brows. "No, my gracious! I mean this awful business about the knife! Not to dissemble, that is why Mrs. Swann sent me to town. We only know the barest details and Harry Yalter's sure to have more information. He hears everything.''

"I'm afraid I know nothing. What knife?''

Miriam put her hands together and leaned closer to whisper, "The bloody knife! They found it, all stained bright crimson, in a cart under a load of fish. Nobody knows how it came there, and nobody knows whose blood it is.''

Jocelyn felt in her basket for her handkerchief and pressed it to her lips, looking into the water-swept gutter. The horror whispered so gleefully into her ear made her feel strange. That, coupled with the thought that she knew quite well whose blood it was, caused the small carriage to whirl about her.

"Oh,'' Miriam said, waving away Jocelyn's foolishness. "If you're going to be squeamish . . . isn't it thrilling? I wonder where they'll find the body?''

"Body?'' Jocelyn asked.

"Well, of course! Our butler said . . . and he got it from a gardener who is related to the man carrying the fish, and that's as good as I want. Anyway, Mincer said the wound must have been a mortal one because the bloodstain ran clear up the blade to the hilt. Which means there must be someone dead somewhere. It's just too thrilling!''

"Oh, yes,'' Jocelyn said faintly.

Mrs. Swann peered into her friend's face, noting her sadly drab bonnet. Why the girl didn't trouble to dress when one could do it so cheaply . . . There would be no possibility of a husband for Jocelyn. After two years in London Miriam Swann had become quite talented at recognizing the differences between those who would marry and the unfortunates that could not. Her friends were often left limp with laughter after Miriam described the Season's hopefuls.

Miriam had also learned how to conceal her thoughts and said only, "My dear, you look ghastly. Now, you won't walk all the way home. No, I refuse to let you, that's all. You'd faint in a minute even if it wasn't so very hot. You sit here until I've had my little chat, and we'll have you home in a trice.'' Mrs. Swann stood up and rapped the footman briskly on the shoulder with her parasol while making a comical face at Jocelyn.

Jocelyn did feel a sinking in the pit of her stomach. However, she did not know if this was the harbinger of a faint or the fear brought of knowledge. She knew Hammond had been stabbed, and yet she'd never stopped to think of who had done it. She hadn't even considered the possibility of a thief stabbing his prey and leaving him for dead.

The temptation to go and see Hammond again, if only to question him about his wound, grew ever stronger. She would sit for another moment until her knees, queerly shaking, steadied themselves. Then she would go ask him. She leaned her head against her hand.

With a gasp she remembered his dry lips moving and the words *Damn Frenchies*. The coldness she felt before was nothing to the chill that went over her now. She tried to dismiss the words as the wandering wits of a wounded man. The terrible Corsican was utterly defeated and safely en route to Elba. The talk had been of nothing else since Wellington's victory over Soult at Toulouse. Hammond must have been confused. After twenty years of war, a man could hardly be faulted for blaming all his misfortunes on England's erstwhile enemies.

Jocelyn pressed her hands against her cheeks. Sitting where she did, she could see Stone Alley plainly. She half-rose to her feet before it occurred to her that Miriam would think her behavior so odd. And everyone knew Miriam's tongue was hinged at both ends.

She sat down again and chanced to look up the road. Lumbering toward her was Constable Regin. Jocelyn became fascinated by the stitching of her glove.

''Good day, miss,'' the constable rumbled as he passed.

''Constable,'' she said in reply without lifting her head. The large, deep bonnet covered her face like a knight's vizard but felt very revealing. Surely Regin could see through her female styles to the raucous boy of the day before. The heavy footfalls continued past the barouche without a pause.

Jocelyn let out her breath in a great sigh. She couldn't go down Stone Alley now. How odd it would be for her to descend from the elegancy of this carriage to walk down a dirty and dingy alley to a disreputable hostelry. Miriam would talk about her. Constable Regin would certainly follow her, to protect her if not to interrogate her. No, it would be too dangerous to try to see Hammond now. Jocelyn fought down her disappointment.

Miriam came out of the shop. Unfortunately for the Swanns, Harry Yalter knew no more than they, except to say that the magistrate had sent for the knife and for the men who found it.

"That's good news, at any rate," Miriam said, once more seated across from Jocelyn. "We know Sir Edgar very well. I think he is fond of Mrs. Swann, although they're so old. I'll mention that he's looking into the matter, and I'm sure Mrs. Swann will invite him to take supper. Perhaps even tonight, although there's nothing fit in the house to offer him. Tomorrow night will more likely be convenient."

The carriage set off, rattling over the stony street, the footman clinging to the tiny seat dangling behind. As Jocelyn caught at her bonnet, she looked again at the entrance to the dark alley, the end of which contained so many mysteries. She felt an impulse, nearly impossible to resist, to stop the carriage and get down.

She half-turned in her seat to reach for the coachman. The memory of Miriam's lively curiosity stopped her once more. Jocelyn looked at her friend and thought her like a curious kitten, determined to explore all the mouseholes in her reach. She couldn't give Miriam any reason to explore Stone Alley. Hammond's secret, whatever it may be, should not be revealed by any action of hers. All the same, she wished Miriam had not decided to be kind.

Putting her thoughts into pleasant words, Jocelyn said, "It's very good of you to drive me home, Miriam."

"Nonsense." The blonde leaned closer again, her pagoda-shaped parasol waving over their heads. "To tell you truthfully, I am grateful to have the excuse to stay out. I can't tell you what a trial it has been trapped at home with that awful old woman. Just when everything is happening in London!"

For the journey home Miriam Swann talked animatedly about her present existence, so dull after the myriad delights of vast, ever-changing London, especially now as every day brought notables arriving for the great Peace Celebration. Miriam mentioned the Czar or his staff with every third breath and told quite a funny story about the Prince Regent calling on the Grand Duchess of Oldenburg at Pulteney's Hotel before she was even dressed, so eager was he to greet his guests.

Jocelyn nodded and smiled, trying to keep track of the names of people with whom she was unacquainted. "It sounds very exciting," she said, feeling quite content that Miriam should be the one to deal with London society.

"Oh, it is. And here am I, fastened onto Mrs. Swann because she's taken it into her head that she's dying at last. It doesn't seem to slow her up much, however. I expect to be long cold in my grave before she's done with *her* life."

The stylish barouche made the turn between the trees into the Luckems' short drive. "I must call on you soon, Jocelyn. I know you think it terribly remiss of me not to have done it before now. You would forgive me if only you knew how difficult my mother-in-law can be."

"I understand you have much on your mind. Is your husband visiting with you?"

"Dear Bartlett! He did come down for a time, but he found it necessary to go back to Town last week. I shouldn't be half so dull if he were here."

Nor so eager to see me, Jocelyn thought. "Please come," she said. "If Mrs. Swann is well enough, perhaps you both can take tea tomorrow after church."

"Oh, I am sure she will recover from her frets if something so pleasant is offered her. I, of course, should like it above all things. And . . ." Miriam whispered as Jocelyn took the footman's hand to step down. "And I'll be able to tell you all about the knife. I'm sure to know everything by then."

"Oh, yes," Jocelyn said thinly. "By all means."

She waved farewell as Miriam poked the coachman and he started the horse. Miriam waved her parasol gaily above her head as she passed by.

The inside of the house seemed very dark and cold after the brightness of the sun. Jocelyn sat slowly down upon the steps and, heedless of her hat brim, leaned her head against the ornate newel post. Fear hung inside her breast like a large stone, weighting down her heart. She seemed to hear Miriam saying, "The wound must have been a mortal one. . . ."

Perhaps Hammond was dead. She seemed to see his pale face and bit her lip.

The front door was hurled open, and Arnold raced in, catching the door behind him so it closed with a thunderous bang. He sprinted halfway down the hall before he realized what he'd seen. "What's wrong with you?" he demanded, clumping back. "Are you sick?"

"No, dear. I'm perfectly well."

"You've still got your hat on." If Arnold knew one thing about women, it was that they were always taking off hats and putting them on.

Eagerly he said, "Did you hear about the knife they found? Mr. Quigg said they did. All bloody. I wish I'd found it. Like Macbeth or somebody." Mr. Fletcher only recently ventured to expose Arnold to Shakespeare's darker plays, having found the romantic comedies stirred only loud disgust.

Jocelyn lifted her slow arms, untying the ribbons to take off her bonnet. She hung it on the newel post. "Yes, I've heard about it."

"Is this a dagger I see before me, the handle toward my hand?" Arnold declaimed, flinging his hands about in what he considered an appropriately theatrical style.

"Arnold!" Jocelyn snapped suddenly. "You've been out. Where did you go?"

"Just into the garden. You said I might. I was helping Mr. Quigg with planting. We were mixing manure and soil."

"I can believe it. Go and get ready for a bath. I'll bring up the water."

"What for?"

"You're filthy. You've got mud all over your feet, and you've tracked it up the hall. Why didn't you rinse them outside? Sometimes you're little better than a goose."

Arnold turned red with anger. "You've been nothing but prickles since last night! What's wrong with you?" His feet, not in the least muffled by their heavy coating of mud, thundered up the stairs.

"Arnold," Jocelyn called before he'd turned the corner on the landing.

"Oh . . . what?" he asked, most reluctantly.

Jocelyn rose and stepped up until her eyes were level with his knees. He was terribly dirty, but she had no reason to talk to him as if he were a bad boy. He couldn't know that the story of the mysterious knife made her feel as if it were twisting inside her.

She rummaged in her basket for the small bag of sweets she'd bought him and pitched it up to him. He reached out lazily and caught it, though she'd thrown it badly. Arnold stuffed his mouth at once and only belatedly mumbled his thanks.

"Not too many before dinner," Jocelyn said.

Swallowing, he said, "Jocelyn, I've been thinking about something. I've decided you are right about my staying in the covers for a while."

"Did something happen while I was out?" she asked in sudden anxiety.

"Oh, no. Nothing. You never know, though. Tomorrow I guess I'll just stay in my room, studying my classics."

Jocelyn smiled as she realized what this sweet reasonableness lead to. "That's very noble of you, Arnold. However, I'm afraid you will have to come to church."

"But—Constable Regin! He might see me then . . ." He pointed dramatically into the distance. "Off to gaol!"

"Constable Regin is a Dissenter, as you very well know. You'll be quite safe on Sundays until your parents come home to make all right. Now, go and get ready for your bath."

CHAPTER FOUR

SUNSHINE FILLED THE CHURCH FROM ABOVE, GLANCING OFF
the gold embroidery on the red plush altar cloth and burnishing the old wood panels. As fishermen and farmers, the cit-
izens of Libermore kept the clear glass of the Roundheads,
preferring to see how the weather did than colored bits of
glass. The children, though, found it difficult to sit still when
they could see the blue sky of a perfect spring day beyond
the church walls.

Arnold felt especially vexed. With incredible patience he
waited through the first day of restricted bounds. In the back
of his mind, however, lived a plan for escape. He hoped to
salvage some part of the day if Mr. Fain didn't make a long
sermon. He was disappointed. Not having a watch, he
couldn't say how long it went on. The vicar seemed to drone
on as long as during the Christmas service, when Arnold had
been eager to get home to open his gifts.

Swinging his feet, the hard pew numbing his hind end,
Arnold stared at Mr. Fain, silver-haired and kindly looking.
He thought hard, boyish thoughts while listening to the vicar
going on and on about a deaf adder or something. Arnold
knew perfectly well that snakes don't have ears.

Couldn't Mr. Fain feel all his parishioners willing him to
get it over with? Arnold always knew when people wanted
him to be quiet, though sometimes he ignored them. Was Mr.
Fain ignoring them? Looking up at the vicar in the pulpit,
Arnold toyed for half the sermon with a pleasing fantasy of
some civic-minded person sawing at the carved canopy's sup-

45

ports and the resulting sight of Mr. Fain crushed to a form-less mass.

Mr. Fain, unaware of his imminent peril, wound up his sermon at last. The gassy sound of the old organ, inade-quately pumped, breathed out, and the adults reached for their hymnals. Feeling his cousin's gaze, Arnold turned his head toward her. He could not see her face, for his view was obstructed by the deep well of her bonnet. For once he agreed with Granville. It was an ugly thing to put on one's head.

He peered at the hymnal she shared with him. Good. It was one of the louder hymns. Arnold enjoyed singing. He could make a lot of noise without anyone telling him to hush.

Most members of the congregation liked the Luckems, though they knew Arnold of old as a young limb of Satan. Their glances were fond. Jocelyn would have been comforted to know how many people kept a careful watch over her while her aunt and uncle were away. Most of their hearts held at least a measure of pity. They doubted that Libermore would ever see Jocelyn Burn-well stand in front of the church as a bride.

In the dimness at the rear of the old stone building, one person saw her as attractive, even if he shared Arnold's opin-ion of her hat. He watched her idly for a few minutes, ad-miring the delicacy of her body and her grace as she knelt and rose during the service. Soon though, as if he felt uneasy about noticing a young woman on holy ground, he took to studying the vicar with an intensity that suggested he was a man interested in his soul.

He, in turn, was observed by the females in the small church, marked down as an unaccompanied, and therefore unmarried, man. A heavy woman held possessively on to his arm, but they knew her. She'd been whispering at him for the last half hour. When the service let out, they'd have a chance at him. Disappointingly, he slipped away, full of the freshest gossip, before the hymnals were passed.

The gossips were concerned with two topics to the eclipse of all others. The first and most exciting subject was the story of the bloody knife and the magistrate's investigation. The other item began with pitying glances at Mrs. Hodges, pale and worried in the middle pew. Several of the kinder women approached her after the service to offer what comfort they could in good conscience give. The best that could be done was to reassure Mrs. Hodges that news of her husband, whether drunk or imprisoned, would soon reach her.

After church, when Arnold ran whooping away to meet with his friends, Jocelyn paused to speak to Mr. Fain and his half-sister, Helena. The vicar's face was all but unlined, in contrast to the thick silver hair that topped his long frame. His manner of bending low to catch every word spoken to him was very flattering, and the older ladies were much pleased by his distinguishing attentions. His sermons tended to be mild and unenthusiastic, although very learned.

Though other members of the congregation were competing for his attention, he smiled at Jocelyn. "Miss Burnwell, it pleases me much to see that you do not permit your cousins too much liberty. Boys should be hardly schooled to fit them for the difficulties that lie in every man's way." He took her hand and patted it. "If you require any aid with them in Mr. Luckem's absence, I trust you will come to me."

Jocelyn replied in some surprise, "Yes. Yes, I will."

The vicar said one word more. "What a charming, maidenly bonnet you are wearing. Just the sort of thing a young lady should wear." Mr. Fain smiled and then turned aside to greet Miriam's mother-in-law, Mrs. Alastair Swann, dressed in spotless, gleaming white, as was her unvarying habit.

Helena Fain took Jocelyn's arm and walked with her down the church steps onto the green sward. "My brother is in a good mood this morning," she said. "He praised my eggs and admired your bonnet. He must have had pleasant dreams."

"He must have been joking. How could anyone like this bonnet? Even I don't like it—I only wear it."

Plainly dressed and smoothly coiffed, Helena wore neither bonnet nor hat, living as she did directly behind the church and busy throughout the service playing the organ. The sun struck golden highlights from her chestnut hair and revealed the clarity of her skin. Her lavender dress with raised spots brought out the blue of her eyes so that they shone in their setting of thick dark lashes.

Helena Fain was Jocelyn's closest friend. Her half-brother had held the living at Libermore for nearly two years. She had arrived only six months before from a school for young ladies near Brighton. Born in France, she had been left destitute in neutral Switzerland at the death of her mother. Mr.

Fain paid for her passage to England and her education. At eighteen, almost two years younger than Jocelyn, she possessed so much more knowledge of the world that she sometimes made Jocelyn feel like the younger girl. Mr. Fain was forty-three.

Helena pulled Jocelyn farther away from the people coming down the church steps. "Speaking of your bonnet," she said rather loudly, "is that the new style of tying ribbons? You'll have to teach me."

In a whisper she said, "I must talk with you." Helena looked over Jocelyn's shoulder. The vicar, his hair shining like plate in the sunlight, still stood beside Mrs. Swann, surrounded by an admiring circle.

Jocelyn followed the direction of her friend's glance only to see Grim Cocker staring at the pair of them. He leaned against one of the gravestones by the church steps. Pointedly, she turned with Helena so that he could not see their faces.

"What is wrong?" Jocelyn asked. "You're all a-tremble."

Before Helena could speak again, Miriam Swann approached, beautifully and fashionably dressed in a pale yellow silk gown, elaborate frills emerging at her breast and wrists. She'd curled her hair into all-over ringlets, which were peeking out beneath the tied-down brim of her hat of smooth straw lined with light green. "Don't forget we're coming to tea, Jocelyn," she said in her high laughing voice.

Jocelyn smiled warmly. "I've not forgotten. Your mother-in-law is accompanying you, I hope."

Miriam looked disgustedly at the church's squat Norman tower at the mention of her husband's mother, but her voice held a pleasure that seemed sincere. "Oh, yes. She is so anxious to see you again. We'll be along after a quick prayer at the late Mr. Swann's graveside."

Miriam put up her parasol against the sun. "Are you coming too, Miss Fain?" Before she could answer, Miriam's mother-in-law called her. With a droll look and a wriggle of her shoulders, she walked away.

"Jocelyn," Helena said hurriedly, lowering her voice. "Do you have everything you need for your tea? I have some biscuits that are very fresh. . . ."

"Thank you," Jocelyn said, puzzled by her friend's secretive manner. She knew that Helena and her half-brother did not get on, though Helena felt grateful for his goodness to her. Yet, she had never behaved so strangely before, not even when she and Mr. Fain argued over the silly things people who are not used to each other quarrel over.

In hope of enlivening Helena's spirits, Jocelyn said, "I'd be even more grateful if you could come as well as the biscuits." She leaned closer to her friend's ear and whispered, "To condemn myself, I must confess I'd forgotten I invited them."

Helena giggled and then said, "Let me ask my brother if he needs me, then I shall follow you in a few minutes." Her lovely face sobered. "I need to talk to you privately, later. I . . . I don't know what's going on. I need to tell you . . . Matt Hodges was here Thursday and . . ." She looked up with a start when a shadow fell between them.

Mr. Fletcher, for once without a book in his hand, though one bulged in his pocket, said, "Pardon me, Miss Fain. Miss Burnwell, we'd best leave before Arnold gets into trouble." He pointed to where Arnold was trying to stand on his hands for the edification of some girls. Jocelyn darted off across the green grass, thinking furiously about what Helena had said. Matt Hodges at the church on Thursday! Mrs. Hodges found it impossible to get her husband there even on Sundays, so it was very odd that he should . . .

Watching her friend fly away, Helena said, with a return to her natural style, "I am glad to have no younger brothers when I see Arnold Luckem. How do you manage him, Mr. Fletcher?"

"Not very well, I'm afraid. Only long experience would help me with him, and I've no brothers, younger or older." He could not help flashing a swift look toward Mr. Fain, still talking to his parishioners. Mr. Fletcher stepped a trifle closer to the girl. The strong sun turned her eyes hazel. "Miss Fain," he said, becoming more intense, "I wonder if you are—"

"Helena?" the vicar called, coming down the steps. Mr. Fletcher saw her nervous start and the blank expression she turned upon her brother. Taking her arm, Mr. Fain said, "You must come and speak to Mrs. Gleason about the Organ Fund. Good day, Mr. Fletcher," he said pointedly, turning Helena about.

"Good day, Mr. Fletcher," she echoed. Her gaze rested on him briefly as she was pulled away.

The tutor stood looking after them for a moment before turning toward home, kicking a rock away from the neat border of the path.

At the priory Arnold dressed in a rough costume of old knee breeches and a wilted shirt. He then made his escape, scorning the easy, familiar routes. Out of range of any authority he rumpled his hatefully slicked hair and dug his toes deeply into the moist soil, enjoying the squish. For no reason he then ran as fast as he could down the garden path and leapt the low stone wall, landing squarely and joyfully in more mud, knee and toe.

Beyond the garden wall the grass grew lushly next to the sown fields. Flowers made a clandestine appearance among the sprouting crops, illicit gillyflowers and cornflowers and very small poppies, nodding on long stalks, like spies in the enemy camp.

Arnold traveled in the general direction of a young river where he spent all last summer. It came down through the Luckem property in a boyish way, turning all the way round itself once or twice as it sought the big river that ran purposefully through Libermore. The water flowed higher this year than last and faster, rushing along, but not too busy to play.

Arnold crouched by the root-tangled bank, looking on while the river showed off. The surface ran marvelously smooth except where mysterious dimples appeared. It did not disturb his pleasure in the least to know that he had lied to his cousin, telling her he would be in his room studying and that he could get his own tea later. This was the best place to be.

The water swirled down over rocks and lapped flippantly against roots thrust out from the narrow rows of weedy trees and sprawling bushes on either side. Arnold remembered that one year he built a dam, both for stepping across and for the fun of seeing the water come down, smooth, rounded, and full of color, like the Roman goblet his father found. Was this the same place? Perhaps not. Everything had changed since last summer.

Arnold liked wild things. They never repeated themselves or acted like fools because that's how they'd always acted. He didn't like grown-ups in the least, and every time he went where they came together, he confirmed his opinion. Think as he might, though, there didn't seem to be any way of getting rid of them.

"I could poison their hymnals." He entertained himself with the thought of them all falling down dead in church. Probably go right up to heaven. He'd like to see that. Arnold caught at his throat and gagged, swaying from side to side.

"That's a fairly disgusting idea," said a laughing voice.

Arnold turned around in a defensive crouch. His first idea was that Mr. Fletcher had come to drag him back to the house, replaced quickly by the fear that perhaps Constable Regin had crept up on him once more. Fortunately, it was neither of those two fearful authorities. Arnold instinctively liked this man. His clothes looked like his own, comfortable, though another might call them shabby.

As Arnold looked up (it seemed a very long way) into the stranger's lean face, he half-smiled. He felt a kinship as if the man remembered his own boyhood clearly. Seeing only an answering smile, Arnold straightened up, disdaining to brush at his breeches.

"Nice bit of river you've got here. Is it yours?"

"As much mine as anybody's. Nobody else ever comes here." Arnold dragged a dirty hand across his face. "Built a dam along here someplace last year."

"Are you going to build another?"

Arnold shrugged. "Maybe."

"If you did it right, you could keep fish in it. Save a lot of money, raising your own fish." The stranger picked up a stone and tried to skim it across a smooth place. The stone sank. He made a face. "I used to be able to do that quite well. Got out of the habit, I suppose."

Arnold shook his head. "Wrong kind of water. You need a lake. Bigger, calmer."

"You're right. I did use to do it at the Lakes." The man put out his hand. "I'm Hammond. How do you do?"

"Very well, sir. I'm Arnold Luckem." They shook hands.

"I know," Hammond said. "I've heard of you."

Arnold grinned. He knew what kind of stories were told about him. The stranger chuckled. "Yes, you're right. Very little of it was to your credit. So little, I was surprised to see you in church."

"My cousin makes me go. You must have walked fast to

get here so soon.'' His tone indicated he hadn't expected such a feat from an old man.

"Yes, I'm a fast walker. I'm tired now.'' Hammond sat down on a largish rock, without looking to see if it was clean. He put his black stick down beside him and stretched out his long legs with a sigh. The sunshine was pleasant on his up-turned face. He almost wished he had no business.

"You seem to be a leader of men and boys, Arnold. Do you know anyone named Joss or maybe Josh?''

Arnold grew wary. So far, they shared a pleasant conversation about important things, but now the man came up with a strange question. It didn't seem quite fair, as if he were asking for information he had no right to. Arnold looked sideways at the man on the rock. "Joss or Josh?'' he repeated slowly, his brain working fast.

After a moment he smiled and spread his hands. "No, sir. I don't know anyone by that name.'' He wondered gleefully what Jocelyn had been doing the other day in Libermore and of what use this secret could be to him.

Reaching down and plucking a piece of lank grass, Hammond changed the subject. "All right. No Joss. Do you know Matt Hodges?''

"Yes, of course. Everybody knows him.''

"What do you know about him?'' He noticed Arnold's sidelong look and said, "Nothing embarrassing, old fellow. Just who his friends are, where he goes, where he is now?'' Hammond knew they'd need a clergyman to tell them where Hodges was now.

"I'd like to talk to him.'' Hammond laid the blade of grass on his thumbs, lifted them to his lips, and blew gently, making the grass vibrate with a sharp whistle.

"Show me!'' Arnold demanded, coming closer.

Hammond obliged, showing him the right type and width of grass. "That's right. Easy, isn't it, when you know how?''

"Why'd you come to church?'' Arnold asked suddenly.

"I like church.''

Arnold groaned, clutching his stomach. The man ignored his theatrics and went on. "It's the best place to find out what is going to happen.''

"They don't know anything,'' the boy said scornfully. "Just mumble, mumble, Amen. Mr. Fain is dull as Cicero.

He even makes the good stories come out rotten, like Daniel in the lion's den. Now, Jocelyn can—'' Hurriedly, Arnold said, ''Well, you know, if you were there today. I didn't see you, though.''

''I stood at the back. You might try standing there. Good acoustics and it's quicker when you want to leave. You don't have to push past everybody. Do you know anything about Hodges or Joss?''

''No, I said I didn't.''

''You said you didn't know about Joss. What about Hodges? Do you know who his friends are?''

Arnold sat back on his haunches and looked up at the man. ''Matt Hodges doesn't like children. Says we make too much noise in the morning. He likes gin.''

Hammond nodded. ''I've heard.'' He was certain now that the boy lied about Joss and told the truth about Hodges. The difference in his voice would have been obvious to the deaf. Hammond changed the subject again. ''So, your vicar's name is Fain. I didn't know. The woman I talked to called him only 'the dear, dear vicar.' ''

Arnold rolled his eyes. ''Mrs. Gleason. I guess she thinks that bony old daughter of hers is going to marry him. She gooshes.''

'You mean gushes.''

''No, I don't. She 's just like jam on bread. When you bite into it, the jam gooshes out the other side.''

''I don't intend to bite Mrs. Gleason's daughter, so I wouldn't know.''

Arnold thought that was hilarious, but even while laughing, he wondered about the real reason Mr. Hammond went to church that morning. He didn't *look* religious. It was hard to tell. Arnold tended to doubt it, though. Most adult people who admitted going to church wouldn't have been able to resist lecturing him about worldly pursuits on the Sabbath. Hammond, though, never even mentioned improving literature or quiet walks as an alternative to an interesting afternoon's exploration. He wondered if Hammond would like to see the rocks he'd found last year that he had almost been sure were gold.

Gleefully he remembered Jocelyn. It must be her that Hammond asked about. At least, Arnold hoped so. That would be exciting. Arnold knew every boy for miles, and there were no Josses or Joshes. And she had been a boy not three days ago.

He snapped his fingers. "You know, I just remembered I've got a book I should be reading. It's very interesting . . . about a boy who gets eaten by tigers 'cause he doesn't know his psalms. I never know mine. I'd like to see some tigers someday, wouldn't you?" Arnold grinned. "Bye." The boy tore off through the trees, his bare feet flashing behind him as he ran.

Hammond's dark eyes narrowed as he tried to think boys' thoughts. He took up another stone and skimmed it across the water but felt no satisfaction when it skipped three times.

The two nights he spent on his back in that foul inn used up much of his precious reserve of time. He couldn't move efficiently before today. The pressure on him was building. Word that the letter had gone astray had undoubtedly come over from France by now. He must get it back before the body of the dead man was found. Once the corpse appeared, strangers were going to be much more closely scrutinized.

Mrs. Gleason had surprised him in church when she told him that only the knife had as yet appeared, somehow disengaged from the man he'd left it in. Perhaps the dead man's friend, the one who yelled, "Go to it, Matt!" while he himself ran away, had obliged Hammond by removing it and the body.

Now, God alone knew how long he'd have to follow Arnold Luckem before the boy led him to Joss. From the moment he saw Arnold in the churchyard with the other children, he knew him to be at the head of whatever young mischief brewed in Libermore. Such a boy knew or heard everything sooner or later. Arnold Luckem held the key to one mystery.

Hammond's discreet questioning of Mrs. Gleason had brought forth a spate of information, mostly censorious. Her opinion of the missing Hodges was that he was a loner, useless, and, expect for his downtrodden wife and daughter, friendless.

Hammond knew otherwise. One friend had stood by Hodges in the dark shed by the water's edge, though not the kind to wade in during the thick of the fight. In that regard, he'd been more a friend to Hammond than to the unfortunate Hodges. Hammond pressed his hand against his ribs as he remembered the knife thrust just a trifle outside. He'd known that if the second man hadn't run away, he would have been finished, unable to meet a new adversary with the necessary speed and violence.

Witty as she was upon Hodges, the full-bodied Mrs. Gleason became positively brilliant when Hammond expressed an interest in the "pretty girl in the Luckem pew." With an arch look at her daughter, who, sadly for her, Arnold described correctly, Mrs. Gleason said, "That poor child. It's always been given out, sir, that her mother was Mrs. Luckem's sister, and indeed, so she may have been. But who? I repeat, who was her father? A sea captain? And in the navy? And honorably dead?" She sniffed.

"And yet never a word from his people, not for . . ." She coughed. "I shall be candid, sir," she said as she prepared to lie. "Not in twenty-six years has a word been heard from her people. Burnwell, indeed. Ne'er-do-well is more like it," the woman added with a final snort of severity.

"Burnwell?" Hammond looked again at the ugly bonnet. Yet, neither Mrs. Gleason nor any of the others Hammond listened to mentioned a boy and his mother living with the Luckems. According to gossip, only Miss Burnwell, her two young cousins, and a tutor were presently at the house. The parents were off on some queer business concerning "dead bones and suchlike." Some tongues were wagging over the presence of the tutor, but by and large no one seemed to think the Burnwell girl could attract a fly in midsummer.

Sitting by the water's edge, he reflected on the manner in which an entire town could get the wrong idea about a woman, for good or for evil. Hammond had not looked into the well of Miss Burnwell's hat, but he noticed the delicacy of her bones and the graceful way she moved. Surely under her pelisse and that bonnet was a woman of attractions more subtle than those endowed by the mere possession of a lovely face.

Hammond shrugged. Whether she was as beautiful as temptation or as ugly as the devil made no difference. He would not allow himself to be distracted by a woman. Not when so much depended on him acting in a rational manner, and he'd learned long ago that indulgence in female attractions did not encourage cold rationality. He followed the muddy track of the boy.

CHAPTER FIVE

As soon as Jocelyn came in, she poked vigorously at the fire in the stove. She put the kettle on and brought out the good silver set before she removed her bonnet and pelisse. Mrs. Swann carried a reputation for accepting nothing but the best. Her house, Marlbridge, was famous in Libermore for the number of servants it employed and the splendor of its furnishings.

To feed this paragon, Jocelyn brought out fresh butter and newly made bread to be sliced very thin. She could also give them a seedcake, not yet marauded by Arnold. Because it was so early in the year, she had only black currant jam left over from last year's making. Jocelyn rinsed the teapot twice before setting the tea to steep in fresh hot water.

Helena came in, a covered basket over one arm. "The Swanns are still by the graveside. I doubt they will be very much longer. Mrs. Bartlett Swann seems to be impatient."

"It must be difficult for her. I have heard her mother-in-law is terribly particular. This is the first time she's ever been in the house. I don't quite know if I am pleased to be honored or not." Jocelyn brought out a round silver epergne, highly polished, and set the plates on it. In addition to her biscuits, Helena also contributed tiny jam tarts and a small pot of strawberry preserves.

"Thank you," Jocelyn said while she scooped it into a glass bowl the size of her palm. "I had only the one kind."

"Nicholas said I might bring it, when he heard who was coming. I thought it nice of him. He loves strawberry jam. I could scarcely credit that he was giving it up. But I could believe anything of him this morning. He is in such a good mood.''

Jocelyn picked up the silver stand by the elaborate finial on the top and carried it into a room at the rear of the house. Helena followed with the tea tray, although she did not heave her usual sigh of pleasure upon entering the salon. The green and white room with curved doorways and arched Gothic windows was the most easy and elegant room in the Luckems' house. The furnishings were old-fashioned and supremely comfortable. It had been decorated by Jocelyn's mother, and Jocelyn kept it scrupulously clean, both as a memorial and because she, too, thought it beautiful.

''I shall have to go down and listen for the Swanns. With no housekeeper again, they might knock half the day and I'd never know they were there.''

Helena did not seem to hear what Jocelyn said. She looked fixedly out the far window. Jocelyn said her name, and the girl looked at her. ''Oh, I am rude. . . . Don't go down just yet. I . . . I have a favor I wish to ask of you.''

''You know I will do whatever you ask.''

Helena held up one small hand with a half-smile. ''Don't be so quick. I might ask you for something you don't wish to do. I-I want to invite myself to stay with you. Just until your aunt and uncle return.''

''Of course. If you're brave enough.''

''Brave enough?'' Helena said, taken aback.

''I'm afraid the calm can't last. The boys, you know.''

''Oh, yes. I'm not worried about the boys. Mr. Fletcher seems to keep them well in hand,'' Helena said, tasting his name on her lips.

Jocelyn kept silent regarding her opinion of Mr. Fletcher's methods, saying only, ''Granville has the chance to attend Oxford next year. I hope he can; he wants it so.'' Cheerfully she added, ''Would you like to come tonight?''

''If I could, that would be wonderful!'' Helena straightened up and seemed to feel more gratitude than the size of the favor merited.

''Pardon me for asking, Helena . . . are you all right?''

''I? Yes, of course.'' Helena smoothed her lavender dress at her waist, looking only at that. Jocelyn waited, certain her friend could not keep the cause of her distress secret. "To be frank, Jocelyn, I am disturbed by my brother hiring that man."

"I wondered about him myself."

"It was so strange of Nicholas to take Cocker on," Helena said, turning toward Jocelyn. "Everyone knows his reputation. They say he half-killed Jem Stanton last year and . . . I have heard other stories. It surprised the congregation as well. They've mentioned him to me, not liking to disturb Nicholas. They always tell me about the things that disturb them, never approaching my brother directly."

"And did Mr. Fain explain?"

"I asked Nicholas his reasons. He only gave me one of his looks and said the more a man is hated, the more he needs the help of the righteous."

"I suppose a vicar might try only to see the good in people, but to inflict Cocker's company upon you is going a little too far. Has Cocker's behavior been . . . correct?"

A flush of color mounted into Helena's pale cheeks. "Yes, of course. That is . . . I try not to speak to him. It's ridiculous, I know, to avoid him the way I do. It isn't because I'm afraid, I wouldn't want you to think that, but he looks at me like . . . oh, I don't know."

Jocelyn knew very well the look Helena meant. The thought of it made her feel as if she had stepped on something squashily unmentionable. She patted her friend's hand. "Never mind. I think avoiding him is the wisest thing you can do. You shall stay with us as long as you like. Even after my aunt and uncle come home. Goodness knows, Uncle Gaius won't mind, if he ever notices. You know Aunt Arasta likes you." Jocelyn went toward the door, wondering if she'd eased Helena's mind.

"I hope Cocker goes away again soon," Helena murmured.

"Away?" Jocelyn asked, absently returning. "When did he go away?"

"Let me see." Helena wrinkled her forehead as she concentrated. "Not last night, or the night before. Thursday. That's right. I remember because he slept all day Friday, and I wanted him to repair the chimney pot. Nicholas told me not to disturb him."

A flash of impatience sparkled in her eyes. "It's the third time in two weeks he spent the night away. Nicholas seems always to consider Cocker's convenience before mine. It's very vexing. And all the worse because when Martha Hodges came to do the washing, she complained that his clothes reeked of fish. I can't speak to the man about the condition of his clothes, can I?'

"Fish?'" Before Jocelyn could explore that oddity, they were interrupted.

Behind them Granville opened the salon door, saying in his clearest and roundest tones, "I am certain my cousin wishes to meet you in here." He stood aside, with a graceful gesture, to allow both Mrs. Swanns to pass in before him. The two unmarried girls rose to their feet. To their amazement, Nicholas Fain followed the ladies into the room. Granville shut the door behind him.

The elder lady touched hands with Jocelyn. She smelled faintly of powder and, unexpectedly, of raw potato, carried to prevent rheumatism. The vicar steadied a white armchair that matched Mrs. Swann's attire as the lady sank slowly into it. Her grenadine shawl draped across the chair arms as elegantly as if she'd spent an hour arranging it.

The silver-haired vicar asked, "I hope I am not *de trop*, Miss Burnwell? Mrs. Swann pressed me so earnestly to come to your delightful tea, I could not resist."

Jocelyn wasn't quite certain what *de trop* meant, but she said, "I am always glad to see you, sir," as she took her place behind the teapot. After exchanging one wondering glance with Helena, Jocelyn made an effort to be pleasant to all her guests, although a curious feeling of oppression, as before a thunderstorm, seemed to have entered the genteel salon.

Miriam and Helena sat on opposite ends of the settee, looking like a pair of unhappy caryatids. All Miriam's bright chatter vanished, and her round blue eyes showed white around the edges. Helena's color had drained away, and she never took her eyes from her half-brother.

Mrs. Alastair Swann listened intently to Jocelyn and the vicar's rather desultory conversation about their hopes for this year's roses. Jocelyn thought of a cat watching a bird and felt Mr. Fain was about to be snatched up.

Granville alone seemed at ease, lounging by the cold fire-place, toying with the small, rather blurry portrait of Joce-lyn's father, her mother's lone memento of her husband.

"What is it you have there, young man?" Mrs. Swann called. Granville came and put it into her hand. "Such a stern expression . . . it quite puts me in mind of someone. I wonder who it could be? Miriam, my dear, look at this and tell me of whom I am thinking." Granville spared either lady the effort of passing the portrait.

"What nice manners young Mr. Luckem has," Mrs. Swann confided to Jocelyn across the vicar. "Not quite as polished as they will be after he journeys to London. Your aunt and uncle are in London now, are they not?" Before Jocelyn could answer, Mrs. Swann demanded, "Who is it, Miriam?"

"I cannot say, Mrs. Swann," Miriam answered, holding the portrait out to Granville, only to have it taken by the vicar.

"Well, you do not yet move in quite the circles I have attained. Perhaps after your next Season you may be able to tell me." Jocelyn passed Miriam a cup and saw she blushed angrily, feeling the sting in her mother-in-law's words. "Ah, Mr. Fain, do you know of whom it is I am thinking?"

Mr. Fain shook his head, his perfect teeth flashing for a moment in his brown face. "No, I am afraid I do not myself move in very exalted circles. Perhaps it is the uniform, Mrs. Swann, that deceives you. All young men in the navy look alike."

He held out the portrait, and Granville collected it. Mr. Fain looked at Jocelyn for a long moment, his white teeth still showing. It was certainly only her imagination that made her believe that if Mrs. Swann was a hungry cat, Mr. Fain was a well-fed wolf.

Mr. Fain turned to the older woman and said, "How soon do you return to London, ma'am?"

"I cannot say, my health being what it is. Ah, me! I must not drone on about my own affairs when all the world is agog at the events now taking place in the Capital. The fetes and the fireworks! The Princes from around the globe! Miriam, you recently received a letter from London. Tell us all the news."

In a slow, careful manner, quite unlike her usual effervescent confidences, Miriam outlined the Czar's itinerary, fin ishing by saying, "And the Regent has invited His Imperial Majesty down to Oxford to dine." She smiled openly. "Isn't that too amusing! He did not ask him to address the students or the teachers, nor to the services there, but to dine!"

As soon as Miriam began to show an interest in what she said, Mrs. Swann interrupted. "Tell me, Miss Burnwell, did you by any chance see Mrs. Hodges this morning?"

"Her daughter delivered the milk today, Mrs. Swann. I did not notice whether Mrs. Hodges was in church."

"Yes, she was there. Unusually subdued, I thought. I have heard that that husband of hers is missing again." Mrs. Swann nodded her white-swathed head portentously.

"I saw Martha when she came to do the washing," Helena volunteered. "As I told Jocelyn—"

Mrs. Swann interrupted once more by exclaiming, "It's quite beyond me how these Hodges are always about when there's a penny to be turned."

"I quite admire them," Jocelyn said. "Matthew Hodges is a scoundrel without a doubt; however, his wife and daughter never speak slightingly of him."

"They do their duty," Mr. Fain added.

Miriam said, her voice hard, "They work hard enough to keep him in drink."

Her mother-in-law looked at her for a moment. "Drink is sometimes a man's only refuge from the wrong wife." An uncomfortable silence fell. Mrs. Alastair Swann seemed to realize she spoke too harshly. To recover, she asked, "Might I take another of those little tarts, Miss Burnwell? They are quite delicious, nearly the same as those served at Austrian House. Did you make them?"

When Jocelyn indicated that they owed the treat to Helena, Mrs. Swann inclined her head toward Miss Fain, the small egret plumes in her turban nodding limply. "Quite delectable, my dear. I trust they do not require too much sugar. Nothing is more injurious to household economy than too much sugar. Why . . ." She went on with a tale about some miserable housewives she knew.

"I used no sugar except that of the preserves and the pastry," Helena said with mock seriousness.

Jocelyn studied the teapot with great attention, hoping the twitching muscles of her cheeks were not noticeable.

Mrs. Swann seemed uncertain whether the vicar's sister was making sport of her. "Ah, yes." She coughed a little "ahem" that seemed to restore her equilibrium. "What preserves will you make this year?" she asked.

Helena said, "The strawberries look as if they'll . . ." Her voice died away, and her blue eyes grew rounder. A flush came into her skin, and a long moment passed before she continued speaking. Mr. Fletcher had opened the salon door.

He came completely into the room before he seemed to realize anyone was there. Jocelyn, however, noticed his eyes went instantly to Helena, and only long after he saw her did he pay attention to the rest of them.

Jocelyn said, "Good afternoon, Mr. Fletcher. Won't you join us? I shall just go and refill the pot and get more cups."

"Permit me, Cousin Jocelyn," Granville said quickly, eager to show off before members of the best family in the county. He smiled charmingly at Mrs. Swann. "Even my cousin must admit I do know how to make tea passably. Pray excuse me." He picked up the tea tray, without so much as a rattle from the spoon in the sugar bowl, and left through the opened door.

"What?" Mrs. Swann said with an air of confusion. "Have you no one to help you, Miss Burnwell?"

"Yes, ma'am, I have my cousins, and Mr. Fletcher is always to be relied upon."

"I must wonder greatly at your aunt's leaving you alone in a household where there are no other females."

"Fortunately," Jocelyn said smoothly, "Miss Fain has accepted my invitation to stay." She saw the tutor's serious eyes fasten on her friend.

"I am surprised you did not see fit to inform me of this, Helena," the vicar said, his strangely dark eyebrows lifting.

Helena stammered, "I . . . we only just arranged it between ourselves, Nicholas. I was going to tell you this evening."

"I see."

Mrs. Swann spoke up. "I would not permit it, myself, Mr. Fain. Better to keep your sister safe at home. Two young ladies, even with the protection of . . . Mr. Fletcher, is it? Two young ladies are exposed to all sorts of dangers." Her eyes rolled toward the tutor, as if to say that he was one of the dangers. "I do not feel Libermore to be safe at the moment. Why, the magistrate tells me they still have no clue as to the ownership of that knife. You know about this unpleasant matter, Miss Burnwell?''

Though Jocelyn realized the finding of the knife was a subject for common discussion, she still jumped when anyone mentioned it. Unnerved, she began, ''Yes, your daughter-in-law . . .'' recollecting too late that Mrs. Swann mightn't be pleased by Miriam revealing gossip before she had the chance.

Mrs. Swann said, ''Yes, Miriam does so enjoy hearing all the news. Nevertheless, she perhaps did not know that Sir Edgar tells me he is instituting a thorough search for any miscreants who may be lurking in the vicinity. He assures me that they'll be locked up at once and questioned about this mysterious knife. It's too strange that a large knife should be found in a wagonload of pike.''

Jocelyn said, ''Indeed, very strange. Has Sir Edgar considered that the knife may not be connected to Libermore at all?''

''Why, how do you mean, Jocelyn?'' Miriam asked.

Everyone was listening. Jocelyn sipped from her cup, hoping her color had not changed, and said, ''I believe odd things are often found in catches pulled in from the river. Weren't twelve American silver dollars found in a fish three years ago? Mr. Quigg knew the man who found them. All the boys were tremendously interested in fishing after that.''

''But a knife, Miss Burnwell?'' Mrs. Alastair Swann exclaimed.

Mr. Fletcher's deep voice cut through the women's surprise. ''I believe a whale taken off the Norfolk coast contained two cannonballs, Mrs. Swann. I doubt a pike would boggle at a knife.''

Helena spoke up as well with the story of a bear she'd heard of while living in Switzerland who ate with great delight boots offered him by his master. Then Mrs. Bartlett Swann, ignoring her mother-in-law's dark looks, told about a man in London famous for eating pounds of pickled cucumbers and who made his living challenging people to eating duels. Mr. Fain alone said nothing, gazing absently into his cup. The tea party began at last to take on some liveliness, contributed to in no small way by the sudden appearance of Arnold, filthy and munching on a scone.

His attitude was so lighthearted that Jocelyn braced herself for trouble. "Hello," he said, more loudly even than was his wont. "Mrs. Swann, Mrs. Swann, Mr. Fletcher. How-de-do, Miss Fain, Mr. Fain. Cousin Joss." He nodded his head respectfully to each of them while his grin grew wider.

Around a mouthful of crumbs he said, "Well, this is quite a party, Joss, old thing. I'm sorry I was out, or I would have come earlier."

"Arnold," Mr. Fletcher said sharply, recalling his duty and making a fierce face in the boy's direction. "Don't tease your cousin. Call her by her proper name."

"Oh," Arnold said with an expression of such innocence even Jocelyn was fooled for an instant. "She likes it. Don't you, Joss?"

Murdering her cousin immediately was out of the question. There were too many witnesses. Mrs. Alastair Swann stared at Arnold with the same horror she would have shown the boot-eating bear.

"Don't eat there. You'll bring the mice. Come down to the kitchen, and I'll give you some milk." Jocelyn stood up, saying, "Excuse me for one moment," and went out. Arnold followed her, brushing crumbs off himself onto the carpet. Jocelyn looked back, smiled, and shut the salon door.

Helena glanced at Mr. Fletcher, her raised eyebrows and his sending the same message. "Well," she said brightly, rising to cross to Jocelyn's now vacated position. "I hope she hurries Granville along with more tea."

Silence met this essay. Helena felt the eyes of the vicar upon her, and her head emptied of new topics. Then Miriam Swann, with real inspiration, began to chatter of how the new fashions were to be made. The older woman found it impossible to keep aloof while her daughter-in-law made so many errors. Eventually even Helena forgot her brother's dampening presence long enough to take an active part in the conversation.

Mr. Fletcher was torn between his duty to discover Arnold's latest malfeasance and remaining in a room where he could hear Miss Fain's voice, even if none of her words were addressed to him. He nodded at each of the ladies in turn, though he understood nothing of what they said.

Mr. Fain sat perfectly still and perfectly silent.

CHAPTER SIX

THE PRICKLE OF EXCITEMENT BENEATH THE SKIN WAS THE same whether infiltrating into the heart of a foreign government or burglarizing a house. Hammond waited for the good-looking boy to leave the kitchen. The old man stooping over in the garden never looked up while Hammond stood in the shadows at the corner of the house peeking inside through the shutter. At last the blond boy, older than Arnold, put a teapot on a tray and carried it out of sight.

Hammond went in. He looked under the cloth lying on a basket, but found it empty. He began to look behind the narrow door beside the fireplace when he knew he was no longer alone.

A girl stood on the top step, one hand against the wall. After a moment he realized she was the girl he'd noticed in the church, the one Mrs. Gleason has spoken of so disparagingly. He could see why. Her beauty was such that no other woman could create it or copy it, for it had nothing to do with her clothes or hair. She met his eyes boldly but with no hint of the coquette. Her smile was friendly and welcoming.

She stepped down into the kitchen. The light from the open door behind him fell on her rounded contours and glowing skin. He knew he stared. He hadn't expected a girl. His manner and voice were gruff. "I want to see Joss," he demanded. "The other boy said he'd send him down. I'm not going to hurt him. I just want to ask him a question." She was smiling at him as though she'd received a gift she'd always wanted. "Who are you—Joss's sister?"

As if he were looking through a distorting glass, he saw the face of the boy he remembered. He blinked again to shift the illusion. But the eyes were the same as his and so was the curling hair, despite the scarf twisted through it. What a damnable complication!

"Oh, hell," he said tiredly and sat down on the edge of the table. "Please tell me you have a twin brother."

"No, sir. I'm sorry."

And her voice was the same. Hammond sighed like a defeated man. "I must have been more ill than I realized."

Looking at her, the gentle light burnishing her clear skin, he decided he suffered not from illness but madness. How could he have mistaken this female for anything but what she was? Was this what years of training and hard work came to?

Hammond's face hardened and he stood up. "Give me the coat you were wearing when I saw you last."

Jocelyn was taken aback. This was not what she had hoped to hear when meeting Hammond again. She knew now that she had been waiting for the moment when he saw her as a woman. Her heart had hammered painfully as she crossed the threshold into the kitchen, and it had not been from running down the corridor. Nor did its beat steady noticeably when she saw with what interest he first looked at her and knew her to be a woman. That interest soon faded, replaced by this expression of utter implacability.

She stuttered, "I—I fear you are not well yet, sir."

"Dammit, girl. Your coat, and quickly."

"I've not got it." Fire blazed up suddenly in his dark eyes, and she bit her lip but stood still.

"What! Who'd you sell it to?" He caught her by her wrist. "Tell me, or I'll break your neck!"

"Sold it? Truly, I . . ."

Her combination of bewilderment and concern would have been impossible for all but the most accomplished actress to feign. He reserved opinion as to whether she was such an actress.

"Tell me, please," he said, releasing his grip. "Tell me where the coat is. It's important."

"The blue coat . . ."

"Yes."

As though reciting a lesson, Jocelyn said, "It belongs to

my cousin Tom. My aunt and uncle took it with them to return it to him.''

"Where?''

"Oxford.''

"Oxford! Are you certain?''

"Of course. Let me get you some water, Mr. Hammond. I truly think you are not well yet.''

"Never mind that.''

Nevertheless, Jocelyn went to the bucket beside the sink, dipped in a mug, and brought it to him. "Drink this.''

Hammond meant only to feign to drink from the water, but he drained the cup. "Thank you,'' he said reluctantly. "I didn't mean to frighten you. You are frightened, aren't you?''

"Yes, sir. I am.'' She lifted her chin as she said it.

He wondered if he'd bruised her arm and felt a sudden shame. He said gruffly, "I'm sorry I frightened you. How long ago did your aunt and uncle leave for Oxford?''

"They left yesterday.''

"What was yesterday? Only Saturday? Then I may yet be in time.''

"In time?''

He waved his hand, as though his words were of no importance. Through the windows, the glow of the westering sun surrounded him, yet his smile seemed brighter to Jocelyn than the light in her eyes. "You know, I owe you a great debt. If you knew how important—''

"There is no debt, sir. You helped me first. If anything, we are even.'' She did not feel warmed now, even though his smile was friendly and held all the charm she'd hoped it might.

"Your name is Burnwell?''

"Yes, sir. Jocelyn Burnwell.''

He studied her face with renewed interest. "Are you related to Feldon Burnwell?'' There were many unusual stories connected with the Burnwell he'd known ten years ago in London. He seemed to recall hearing some gossip about the man's family, but the details were not clear.

"He is my grandfather, sir, but I am not known to him.'' Hammond still stared at her. She blushed and looked away.

Suddenly she thought of Mr. Fain and his wolf's look. Her face grew hot, and she said bluntly, "I don't know if you are aware of it, but I believe the authorities want to speak with you. They found a knife, bloodied, and they are looking for the owner.''

"Ah, yes." Hammond put his hand to his side and grimaced. "We never actually met, but I remember him very well."

"Does your wound still pain you?" His nod could have meant either yes or no. Firmly Jocelyn said, "I will make you a comfrey poultice. It will draw off any inflammation."

Hammond was about to offer a refusal with thanks, pleading a need for haste, when he heard a light step and a girl's voice calling, "Jocelyn?"

In an undertone Jocelyn said, "That's my friend, Miss Fain. She shouldn't see you. You can hide in there." She pointed to the door of the stair beside the fireplace.

The light through the shutters was full in Helena's face when she entered, and her eyes took a moment to adjust. She did not see the masculine figure slip out of sight nor the small door left slightly open. "Jocelyn, where have you been? They're getting ready to leave!"

"Oh, dear," Jocelyn said in some confusion. "I forgot!" She saw that her friend looked at her as if she had suddenly gone quite mad. "I hope they are not angry?"

"No, they don't seem insulted. Nicholas is exercising his charm, and Granville has been keeping us all beautifully amused. I didn't realize he knew so many things about London society."

"That has been his chief study for many years, which is why he has so much trouble with his education." She knew Helena still regarded her with alarm, and she said, "I had better light the fire, if we are to have any dinner tonight."

"I'll help you make it. But you're forgetting the Swanns, again."

"Oh, dear." Bundling wood into the stove, Jocelyn caught Hammond's eye. Her back blocking Helena's view, she lifted one finger toward the ceiling. He nodded briefly and faded into the shadows in the stairwell. She lit the fire from the kitchen lamp and left, followed by Helena, to return to her guests.

The elder Mrs. Swann seemed in no way put out by her hostess's long absence. She complimented Jocelyn once more on Granville's manners, refraining from bringing up Arnold's name. She drew on her white gloves and accepted the strength of the vicar's arm for the journey to her carriage.

Miriam walked down with Jocelyn, saying softly, "I shall try next time to come alone. We have had no chance for a good coze, and I am so longing to talk with you."

The young Mrs. Swann looked pointedly over her shoulder at Mr. Fletcher walking in silence beside Miss Fain. In a whisper she said, "You are very wise to invite Miss Fain to stay. If you only knew how people gossip about even the most innocent people. Miss Fain will lend an air of propriety to your house. I have made an effort to persuade Mr. Fain to agree with me."

"I cannot resist the blandishments of a beautiful woman, Mrs. Swann." It was not clear which Mrs. Swann he referred to, but Mrs. Alastair Swann simpered. Mr. Fain helped her into her carriage.

The vicar turned back toward his sister and said, "I shall not see you for the evening meal, then, Helena. If it is not too much trouble, please lay out my breakfast for tomorrow. I do not wish Mrs. Penhurst to have the key to the larder."

Helena said, "Of course, Nicholas. I will be prompt. Your supper is all but ready; it only needs to be warmed."

"I see I shall have to get used once more to a bachelor household. Good afternoon, Miss Burnwell." The vicar bowed to Jocelyn, clapped his black hat over his silver hair, and set off toward the church.

It seemed odd to Jocelyn that Mr. Fain, who did not seem to like the tutor, would make no greater objection to Helena's staying under the same roof with him. Jocelyn decided that tonight, after she'd blown out the candle, would be the right time to delve into her friend's confidence. Jocelyn further resolved that she would find a way to help Helena achieve her tutor, if he was what she wanted.

Mr. Fletcher had vanished. Jocelyn hoped he'd gone for one of his walks, with book and pipe. What would her position be if he came across Hammond somewhere in the house? With Mrs. Swann's hints about the dangers to young women alone still in her ears, Jocelyn was certain she would be suspected of harboring an admirer. Thinking of Hammond, Jocelyn tried a few hints of her own. "Aren't you

tired, Helena? The spare room is made up, and I know how
early you rise to help your brother on Sundays."

The two girls entered the kitchen. "No, I'm not tired in
the least," Helena answered, reaching for an apron. "And I
promised to help you with supper."

"You needn't do that!" Jocelyn's tone was sharper than
she intended, but how was she to slip away to see Hammond
if Helena cooked with her? "We're only having boiled beef.
Again."

"Oh? Don't you get tired of that? I do, by now." Helena
looked in the pantry. "I have a better idea. I will make a
quiche. You have everything I need."

"What is that?" Jocelyn wanted to know, having never
before heard the term.

"Very like the delicious salmon pie you made last week.
It doesn't take as long, though. If I must say so myself, I
make it very well."

She shushed Jocelyn's protest. "I insist. My brother does
praise my meals. I shall not mind going over to tend to him.
I myself do not trust Mrs. Penhurst to cook."

Helena sighed and Jocelyn understood. All Libermore
knew that Mrs. Penhurst liked to take a drop or two of liquor
now and then. "I wonder what she'll burn this week. You
know about the parlor curtains. Poof!" Helena threw up her
hands in a typically French gesture. "It was painful to lose
them when we worked so hard."

Turning aside from that subject, Helena took out the ingredients she needed, ignoring Jocelyn, from whom protests
still escaped like little puffs of steam from a teakettle. "I'm
not going to be an extra burden on you. Now, agree."

Jocelyn had forgotten how pleasant it was to have compe-
tent cheerful help in the kitchen. With a last glance toward
the ceiling, she said, "I wouldn't dream of arguing. What
can I do?"

After dinner, while Helena threw away the dirty water from
the dishes, Jocelyn filled a clean plate with Helena's carefully
cooked meal. The pie resembled her own but was much tast-
ier, to Jocelyn's mind, than the food she herself made. The
boys seemed to think so, too, judging from the way their
initial suspicions turned to blissful chewing.

Jocelyn set the plate down in her room and carried her

candle to look for Hammond along the hall. Not knowing where he was, she stopped to look in each chamber.

He was on his knees in Arnold's room, his head under the bed. Jocelyn said in astonishment, "Whatever are you doing?"

The look he turned on her was nearly savage. "I'm looking for that coat."

"Why? I told you it isn't here."

"Did you think I wouldn't check?" From under the bed Hammond dragged out a blue coat so furred and dusty, it looked as if it had been hidden there since Charles I sat the throne. The coat bore decorations of dried mud. Hammond shook it in his fist. Several moths, disturbed from their dinner, flew up toward Jocelyn's candle.

"That's not the right one," Jocelyn said. Hammond snorted in disbelief. "That's Arnold's Sunday coat which he'd said he misplaced. He was probably afraid of getting into trouble if he brought it in so mired. Give it to me. I'll prove it."

Jocelyn set the candle on Arnold's desk. She took the coat from Hammond. Tossing it around her shoulders, she wriggled into the sleeves. They were much too short, and the coat came nowhere near to closing across her front. Then she sneezed from the accumulated dust.

"God bless you," Hammond said grudgingly.

She tried to take it off and became stuck, one arm akimbo and the other pulled in tight to her body. Jocelyn looked at Hammond and laughed at her predicament. Unsmiling, Hammond helped her out of the binding coat, his fingers brushing down her arm. He held the coat at arm's length, frowning at it.

Ridiculously happy, for she felt his hand pause for an instant when he touched her, Jocelyn said, "Boot it under the bed again. I'll pretend to discover it the next time I clean up here. He's supposed to keep his room tidied himself, but what boy would?"

Hammond, his face tight, said, "I cannot take your unsupported word for what has happened to that coat."

"Then search all you like, Mr. Hammond. But carefully. Goodness knows what other horrors you'll find under Arnold's bed.'' When she took up the candle, however, he followed her from the room.

She could imagine what Mrs. Swann, so chary of reputations, would say about Jocelyn entertaining a man alone in a bedroom. However, not even the sternest critic could find fault when the young lady stood looking out the window while the man hungrily devoured a meal. Jocelyn looked down into the sunset-streaked evening, thinking.

"Thank you,'' Hammond said at last. "The food at the inn was poor, and I can't think when I last tasted good French cooking.''

"You've just come from France?'' Jocelyn said, taking the plate from his hands.

Hammond's eyes hardened. "How did you know that?''

She quoted, with a blush, "Damn Frenchies never do clean their knives. . . .''

"I must have been far gone to let out so much,'' he murmured. He gave her a sidelong glance, his dark eyes narrow as he studied her. She was reminded of those tense moments beside the shed in the dark alley. Almost to himself he said, "I'm in a position where I don't know who is trustworthy. Knowing what I do of you . . . your quickness of mind, your resourcefulness . . . I'd like to believe that you are, but how can I be sure?''

"You can trust me,'' she said, her heart in her words.

"Can I? Can I? I wonder.''

"Well,'' she said, retreating. "I trust you.''

For a moment Hammond said nothing. Then he sighed. Jocelyn knew he'd made up his mind against her. "Besides, it's too messy a business,'' he said. "I can't in good conscience . . . Do you have a horse?''

"I beg your pardon?'' She wondered whether, if in addition to the scrape along the ribs, he'd struck his head.

"More than anything, I need a horse.''

"My aunt and uncle took the only horses we have.''

Hammond frowned. Then his expression lightened. "I supposed Fain might have some sort of an animal?'' He grinned and then chuckled. Jocelyn had never imagined him laughing. Her own lips could not resist curling up in response to this unexpected merriment.

"Yes, he keeps a mare, but—''

"Then I shall 'borrow' it. That's poetic justice, if only you knew it."

"But if you'd only explain . . ." Jocelyn began. "What's so important about a boy's blue coat?"

"I hid something in the lining. A letter. It means my whole future. I can't tell you any more." Hammond stepped close to her once more. "It's vital that no one else know about me."

"Who would believe me? But you can't borrow the vicar's horse—"

"But I can," he said, with an echo of his smile.

"Because it's lame. It bruised a foot when he went to Barwith."

"Barwith? That's by the sea."

"Yes, he went there last week. He missed the service last Sunday because he couldn't get back without taking the post."

"I don't for a moment believe his horse is lame. He more than likely had business in Barwith. Dirty business."

"What do you mean by these references about the vicar? Helena Fain is my dearest friend, and you can't go about saying disparaging things about her brother without even telling me why!"

"I can't tell you," he said. "I'd rather like to, but it's not safe. I can tell you . . . I can tell you I am working for our government."

"The government?" About the only men she could think of who could make that claim were Constable Regin and the magistrate, Sir Edgar Baintree. They each went about their appointed duties with such a stolidity and attention to the rules that she could not for an instant imagine that Hammond had anything in common with government. "In what capacity?" she demanded.

Once again Hammond smiled, a slow half-hidden expression as though he were sourly amused at something she would not understand. "I'm a spy," he said.

"A what!" The plain earthenware plate dropped from Jocelyn's hands and broke into pieces on the floor. They both stooped to pick them up. Jocelyn gathered them into a fold in her apron as she stood up. Her head was whirling with half-remembered history lessons about intrigues at the court of Queen Elizabeth and Charles II hiding in oak trees.

"I'm a spy," he said again in an undertone. "Not the most honorable profession, but I've done my best and will do it still. Will you help me? Will you trust me?"

"I . . ." She could not help but recall how she'd helped before. Then, too, she'd had her doubts, but she'd put them aside. That had been a private matter. Now he suggested the importance of his work. Whether she believed him or not, she could do no less than she'd done already. She did not have to like it.

"I will help you," she said. The flickering candlelight made her eyes huge, sparkling with tiny flames. There were small curls clinging to her forehead and cheeks.

For reasons which he did not himself understand, Hammond said, "I hope I didn't hurt your arm when I was angry before."

"No," Jocelyn said shortly. "If you'll trust me a little, you'll have no more need to roam the house. I don't know how you've avoided the boys this long. You'll be safe enough here until you want to go. I'm always the last to retire."

"What about the servants?"

"There aren't any. Only Mr. Quigg, the gardener, and he doesn't sleep in the house."

"You care for this house, your cousins, all by yourself?" He looked at her hands, a little red and swollen with the shiny mark of an old burn on the right thumb. The apron about her slender body was stained, not by uncleanliness but by old stains that would never come out.

Jocelyn said, "Sometimes we have a housekeeper."

"But surely you must have a maid or . . ." It had been a long time since he thought about the finer details of managing an estate. For a moment he felt as if he really had come home, as if this were indeed England, and not merely another square on Napoleon's map of future conquests.

From below they heard a shout and a slamming door. Quickly Jocelyn said, "You'd better close the door. It won't be long before you can slip away. I'll just go down now."

In the hall Jocelyn leaned against the wall to catch her breath. Thinking of the look in Hammond's eyes when he'd praised her, Jocelyn felt more alive than she had ever felt before. Not even Harry Yalter's son ever looked at her so.

She wondered if this was how it felt to be kissed—breathless, warm, and thoroughly confused.

No man had ever paid much attention to her, except for a friend of Tom's who had visited the Luckems' two summers ago for one month. His attentions to her had not been marked though he expressed a warm admiration for her. But an admirable wife would not help a man with his way to make in the world half so well as a rich or well-connected one. Unacknowledged by her father's family and with no fortune, she was not surprised, nor even hurt, when Tom's friend left without declaring himself.

Though it was never discussed, she always assumed she'd take care of her aunt and uncle's house and sons until . . . surely there'd always be a place for her with her cousins' families. An old-maid aunt, accustomed to household tasks, could hardly be an unwelcome addition to a household, especially after the children started coming. Jocelyn thought of a succession of little Arnolds and shuddered.

Perhaps this bleak picture of her future accounted for her strong feelings toward Hammond. He gave off an air of adventure missing from any foreseeable life she would ever know. Perhaps it was merely that he was so different from the other men in her life, sober fellows, with well-defined places in society.

Jocelyn dismissed that idea.

When she was with Hammond, she felt as her garden must feel in spring. Everything in her bloomed.

Happier than she'd ever been before, Jocelyn went downstairs, only to hesitate at seeing Helena there. What had Hammond meant about Mr. Fain? He'd seemed worried about the vicar being in the house.

Helena raised her eyebrows at her friend's bringing down broken crockery from upstairs. "I wouldn't think you'd let the boys eat in their rooms," she said.

As Jocelyn dumped the broken pieces into a sack, trying to think of something in answer, Mr. Quigg opened the door, pitchfork in hand, and said, "Miss, miss! That there Cocker's comin' here again, miss!"

Helena gasped and said in disbelief, "Coming here?"

Mr. Quigg said, "Do you want me t'run him off, then?"

Jocelyn inhaled deeply. "No, Mr. Quigg. I'll speak to

him.'' The gardener went out, weapon at the ready. Jocelyn put her hand on her friend's arm. "What is it?"

Helena shook her head and licked her lips. "I hoped I shouldn't see him after I came to you. I . . . I lied to you earlier. He does say things . . . terrible things to me. He gives me nightmares.''

"Then he has spoken to you as he has spoken to me."

"To you? Did he dare to pass comments on . . . your physical . . . endowments?'' Helena colored deeply.

To hearten her friend, Jocelyn said smilingly, "I'm afraid I haven't many 'endowments' to be commented upon.'' An answering curve came into Helena's lips, only to be wiped away by Jocelyn continuing gravely, "But yes, Cocker has made suggestions to me both disgusting and impossible to consider seriously.''

"I was afraid I'd done something to encourage him," Helena said with rising anger.

"I believe he'd make such comments to any unprotected female. We, however, needn't take any notice of him. Try to put it out of your mind, Helena, as I have." Jocelyn went to the kitchen door.

"Oh, be careful," Helena warned. "I am so afraid of him. His reputation for violence—''

"You stay here. I'll manage *Mister* Cocker.''

"No, I'll help you." Her face hardened with resolution, Helena followed Jocelyn outside.

Hammond crept down the small stair beside the fireplace and walked across the stone floor, not allowing his bootheels to make the slightest noise. He pushed out the shutter an inch past the kitchen window to observe if it was safe to go out. The tiny streak of light, he knew, would not be noticeable, and his shadow stood beside him.

In the yard the evening light lingered, like a girl reluctant to leave her lover. Clouds ran across the sky, and Hammond wondered where he could take shelter against the night. His ribs still ached, and he felt somehow that sleeping in the damp wasn't going to help. He left the inn as soon as he was able to walk without falling down. Soon he'd leave here as well and be once again on his way to Oxford to obtain, by fair means or foul, the jacket that held the key to his future.

He did not want to remain trapped upstairs. This house

was not a suitable blind. It was too isolated and had too few inhabitants. A town house in a crowded city, an old inn with many back doors, an office beside a bustling dock were the places a hunted spy felt safest. However, he could feel the desire to stay the night, and he knew the longing for rest was just as much his enemy as the people who wanted him dead. If they knew where he was. He'd thought he'd shaken them off. Maybe this feeling of impending evil was the result of his exhaustion and his wound. But he could not rest. Not yet.

Three figures stood, tense and silent, in the yard. He recognized both the girls and saw that the man was the old codger who worked the garden. Hammond wondered what was wrong. At the sound of a horse clopping along the road, he saw them look up. He heard a gruff male voice. The prickles of raised nerves along his back and arms told him this new man was thoroughly bad.

CHAPTER SEVEN

"GOOD EVEN TO YOU, MISS BURNWELL." COCKER LEANED down to open the gate, as no one did it for him, and urged the horse through into the garden.

Jocelyn knew Cocker was a bad man. His suggestive words to her echoed whenever she saw him, poisoning the air. Now that she knew he also plagued Helena, she felt angry instead of ashamed. "You've been told before to stay away from this house." Her uncle had made that plain two weeks ago.

"Friendly, ain't you, girl? Well, I got a right to be here now. My mistress is here." His tone made it seem as if he meant "mistress" in a sense other than employer. He leaned down in his saddle, and his slits of eyes rested on Helena. Jocelyn heard the girl's quick in-drawing of breath.

"Well, there she is. Tell her what you've come for."

Cocker grinned and rubbed one hand along his thigh in a manner that made Jocelyn feel ill. She felt Helena's hand tremble on her arm and Helena half-opened her lips as if to speak.

"State yer busyness and get outta my garden," Mr. Quigg said sharply, stepping in front of the girls, his pitchfork pointing, business end up, at Cocker.

"Be good t'me, old duffer."

"Or what, you dog?" Mr. Quigg spat.

"Or you'd wished you had, that's all. I don't make no promises. . . ."

"What do you want, Mr. Cocker?" Jocelyn said tiredly.

"The vicar wants me to tell his darlin' sister how he's changed his mind an' she should be comin' home t'night."

Helena said, "What? But he promised . . ." She remembered Cocker was only a servant. "Did my brother say you could take the horse?"

"Why, sure he did. Got a little somethin' t'do in town later, an' he says I should take it. Ain't it right, I should take it?" Cocker's voice rose as his hands clenched into fists. Mr. Quigg shifted the pitchfork. Cocker's manner grew servile once more. "You hurry yerself along, missus. The vicar's in a rare takin'."

Helena stared at Cocker in fascinated horror. She shrank behind Jocelyn, leaving her to answer. "Remind Mr. Fain that Miss Fain will be staying with me over the next several nights. Thank you. You may go."

"Stayin' wid you? Nay, the master won't like it. Better she should go along home."

"Don't argue, please. Take my message to the vicar."

"Perhaps I should go home," Helena whispered.

"It's wrong of your brother to chop and change like this. He said you can stay. I think you should." Under no circumstances was Jocelyn going to allow Helena to go home to be leered at by Cocker. She felt like taking Mr. Fain severely to task for not restraining his servant's insolence. The vicar could not be so blinded by his love of humanity to miss Cocker's evil ways. Was that what Hammond had meant?

"Stayin' wid you, is she? Won't that be cozy?" Cocker said, one lid closing over a reptilian eye and his bright red tongue coming out between cracked lips. He looked at Jocelyn and said, "All alone in the house but for this old duffer an' her? How'd you like some company? Protect you real good, I will."

"Alone? My good man, what do you mean?" Hammond stepped out into the yard, his hat on the back of his head and his black and silver cane balanced on the back of his hand. His stomach seemed to have grown, to have become the proud property of a man built with the hard labor of knife and fork. "My dear niece, won't you introduce me? I'd like to know who I'm going to be put to the trouble of horsewhipping."

"Uncle, this is Mr. Cocker, the vicar's servant," Jocelyn said, nearly laughing at Hammond's pompous tones and the

expression of utter surprise on Cocker's dirty face. Her only
fear was for Helena's good opinion.

"No worries, mister. I just come to tell—"

"You've told her; now leave." Hammond tossed his cane
in the air and caught it in his fist. It instantly became a for-
midable weapon. "Go on. Get out."

Cocker gurgled like a clearing drain, the sound that in him
passed for laughter, and turned the large bay horse around,
riding slowly away in the red sunset with many a backward
glance. Only Jocelyn noticed the way Hammond's eyes followed the horse, disappointment drawing his brows together.
He looked at her, as if to say "Lame, indeed?" She tried to
communicate that she'd told him the truth as she'd known it,
but he looked, still frowning, at Helena instead. Jocelyn wondered if another heart was about to be lost to her friend's
beauty.

Mr. Quigg seized a bristle broom and swept away all trace
of the man's presence. Jocelyn patted him on the shoulder
and went into the kitchen, followed by Hammond and
Helena. She opened the stove and thrust the wood into the
fire.

Helena looked at Hammond with some of the dazed fascination she'd shown Cocker. Jocelyn tried to make the situation more comfortable for her friend. "Helena. This is . . .
Hammond. He is not my uncle. He is a friend."

"Of yours?" Helena observed Hammond's face, neither
attractive nor unattractive, and colored under the glint in his
eyes. Helena did not blame Jocelyn for keeping him a secret.
She wondered how long they had known each other and if
they were in love. It did not surprise her that Jocelyn con-
cealed his existence from the Swanns. Those two women
would consider it the gossip opportunity of the century if
Jocelyn found an admirer.

Helena smiled slowly and said, "I don't usually approve
of lying, Mr. Hammond, and as the vicar's sister, I can hardly
condone it, but I must thank you for telling Cocker you are
Jocelyn's uncle. I think you frightened him away."

"Some men should always be lied to. And some women."

Jocelyn decided to change the subject. She did not like
Hammond smiling in that way at Helena. "Well, if you are

going to stay with me, Helena, shall I loan you some things for the night?''

Helena did not have the opportunity to answer. She was interrupted by Arnold shouting, ''I didn't . . . Stop saying I did when I didn't!'' There was the solid smack of a head being hit.

Jocelyn ran out the back door. Helena followed. Arnold and Granville scuffled frantically. As the girls ran out, Arnold broke from his brother's restraining grasp and, arms flailing, returned to the attack. Granville pushed his brother away every time he got close enough to land a blow, not hurting him but frustrating him terribly.

Helena tried to go forward to intervene, but Jocelyn stopped her. Jocelyn knew better, having been knocked down accidentally a time or two before. ''Mr. Quigg!'' she called.

The old man came out, his pitchfork once more in his hands. He held out the long handle behind Granville, tripping him, then, when Arnold laughed to see his brother fall, pushed Arnold down by poking him behind the knee. ''Thank you, Mr. Quigg,'' Jocelyn said with a laugh.

The old man touched his cap and said, ''D'you want me t'be ready t'give a good hidin', Miss?''

''No, thank you. I'll manage.''

Mr. Quigg walked away, shaking his head. ''Too late t'send 'em up widout supper. Just one damn thing after another 'round here.''

''Boys, apologize to Miss Fain. Behaving so when I told her how good you'd been.'' The boys got up, with sour faces and mumbled apologies.

''Tell him to stay out of my room, Jocelyn. Everything's at rag's end.'' Granville seemed to realize he had not upheld his ideal of elegant indifference and straightened his jacket, tossing back his head. ''I won't have dirty little boys stealing my things. Trying to give himself airs to impress his silly girlfriends.''

At this accusation Arnold lunged at Granville again, but Jocelyn locked her arm lovingly about his neck and kept him against her without too much trouble. ''Yah,'' he said, thrusting out his tongue. ''Girlfriends? I wouldn't have that fat cow Isabelle Franklin for a hundred million pounds. All la-di-da and crooked teeth.''

Behind Jocelyn, Helena laughed, stifling it too late. Outraged, Granville tugged his cuffs into place and wheeled away. Jocelyn didn't try to make peace between the brothers. She knew they'd be friends again as soon as a common enemy—such as their tutor—appeared.

She was relieved the question of who rumpled Granville's shirts had been shelved. Letting go of Arnold with an exhortation to be good, she realized that she had not seen Mr. Fletcher. Usually, when Granville and Arnold began to brangle, he would admonish them, though nothing he ever did was as effective as Mr. Quigg and his pitchfork handle.

Hammond had also taken the opportunity to disappear. Helena said, ''We need to talk, Jocelyn. We have been keeping secrets from each other.''

''I don't know what you mean. Hammond is someone I met by chance a few days ago. He happened to be visiting here just now.''

''Visiting? Why, then, did he take supper privately, upstairs?'' Jocelyn said nothing. ''Oh, very well. I shan't pry,'' Helena said. ''But he isn't staying, is he? I couldn't . . . you heard Mrs. Swann's innuendos. She isn't the only one who will talk. Some of the congregation has wondered at your aunt and uncle leaving you alone with . . . an eligible man.''

''They must mean Mr. Quigg,'' Jocelyn said. ''For I can think of no other man here whose affections are not already engaged.'' Neither the fading daylight nor rising moonlight was bright enough to reveal Helena's blushes, but the appearance of her white teeth in a happy smile was plain.

''Go put on your hat,'' Jocelyn said. ''We'd better go for your clothes.''

''Oh, yes.'' Helena's blue eyes widened in alarm. ''You don't think . . . Cocker . . . I mean . . .''

''He said he was going into town. If we hurry, we can go and return before him. It may be cowardly of me, but I think we'd best avoid your brother until the morning.''

Noises from down the hall told her that Arnold and Granville were loudly and obviously ignoring each other. It would be impossible to look for Hammond without their noticing her behavior. Speaking more loudly than she usually did in the hope that Hammond would hear, Jocelyn told her cousins that she and Miss Fain were walking to the vicarage and would only be gone a short time. "Arnold, it's time you were in bed," she added, knowing she wasted her breath.

By the time the girls left, the moon had risen, its brightness undimmed by the ancient scars on its surface. It shed its beams along their path but did not illuminate it. The shadow of even the smallest stone was black and deep. The lantern Jocelyn carried did little good on the path turned strange. They did not see, but they heard the brush of wings over their heads as an owl flew by in search of prey. A funny damp smell filled the air. They heard a sound like stone beads pulled through bony fingers.

Helena stopped, clutched Jocelyn's arm and said, with a half-giggle of nervousness, "Maybe I *should* borrow some clothes for the night. We can come for my things in the morning."

Jocelyn said heartily, her voice unnaturally loud, "Oh, it isn't much farther."

"I know, but . . ." Helena looked over her shoulder. "I feel as if someone's watching us," she whispered.

Involuntarily Jocelyn looked back. She saw nothing, but it occurred to her that if Helena was right, the person behind them might be Hammond. It was pleasant to think he was near, even if her pleasure was somewhat spoiled by the idea he followed only because he still didn't trust her.

"Come along, Helena." She forced a smile. "It's a beautiful spring evening. You're acting as though it were All Saint's."

"I suppose it is just nerves," Helena said, responding to Jocelyn's tone. But as they walked on, they couldn't help looking back from time to time, though they saw no one. They paused a long time on the edge of the cemetery before they mustered enough nerve to walk among the crumbling headstones.

The vicarage was a small stone building set back from the edge of the road just to the side of the church. Most vicars, cursed with large families, found the tiny rooms a nuisance. Not so Mr. Fain. He was used to scholarly pursuits, no one ever came to stay, and his half-sister hardly saw him from week to week, except at meals, for he was always prompt in that regard.

Helena opened the front door and listened for her brother.

She heard nothing. To be certain he was not in, she called, "Nicholas? Nicholas?" There was no answer. "He may be at the church. Let's hurry."

The girls went up to her narrow room under the eaves. Jocelyn set their lamp on the floor. Helena said, "My second-best valise is in the attic. I'll climb up for it. Will you hold the ladder?"

No sooner had Helena climbed down than they heard a definite thump from the floor below. Helena squeaked with fright and clutched at her friend. "Oh, what is it?"

"I don't know. I hope it's your brother. I want to talk with him."

"No, Jocelyn. Let it wait till morning. You don't know how cutting he can be."

The girls went back into Helena's room. The sound they heard made Jocelyn nervous, and she constantly stopped to listen. Finally, to relieve Helena's mind and to make the packing go faster, Jocelyn volunteered to go down and see if anyone was there. Helena did not want her to go, but Jocelyn insisted. She still hoped to have a chance to tell Mr. Fain what she thought of his unreasonable behavior.

The house was very quiet when Jocelyn walked through it. She could hear nothing, except a dripping sound as though water were falling into water. Investigating, she walked through to the vicarage's kitchen, tiny compared to that at the priory.

It would be difficult to say why, but she felt as if someone had left the room only the moment before. There was no trace of anyone, but still she had the feeling. Water from dishes, neatly stacked on the drainboard, dripped into the dark greasiness of used wash water. She smelled a thick odor of oil and tobacco. Knowing that Helena had not left the kitchen so, Jocelyn said disgustedly, "Men!" She shook her head and went back up the front stairs. The house was utterly silent, except for a bumping noise over her head.

Helena jumped and let out a little shriek when Jocelyn walked in. "Did you see anyone? I can't imagine why I am so nervous. It's silly." She straightened her shoulders and grimaced, as though ordering herself to be brave.

"Do you want to take this picture of your mother?"

Jocelyn gave Helena a miniature painted on ivory that she had taken from the chest of drawers.

"Of course, I couldn't leave her behind. I was forced to abandon many things in Switzerland, but never this. Like your picture of your father, it is all I have."

Jocelyn removed several pairs of stockings from Helena's bureau drawer while Helena brought out two round gowns from the wardrobe. Jocelyn asked, "Was your brother fond of his stepmother?"

"I can't say. Whenever he speaks of her, which isn't often, he speaks respectfully. I don't think Nicholas has ever been fond of anyone. Some people are like that."

"You and he deal together well enough. Except for when he is unreasonable, like tonight."

"Oh, he usually doesn't fuss. As long as I don't trouble him with trivialities, and serve his meals on time." She closed her valise and opened her hatbox. "I will still come over to fix them, I think. I am sure he will be more reasonable in the morning, and Mrs. Penhurst cannot be trusted with food. She can't keep from burning things, and not just the parlor curtains."

Perhaps it was only because Helena mentioned fire, but Jocelyn could have sworn she smelled something burning now. She looked quickly at the lamp. It gave a gentle light with little smoke. She said, "I think one hat will be enough, Helena."

"I shall take this little cap . . ." Helena stopped and sniffed the air like a rabbit on a misty morning. "Do you smell something . . . strange?"

"I think so," Jocelyn answered. "Mrs. Penhurst isn't here this evening?"

"No, she never comes at night. Also, her sister, the one in town, is about to have her baby, and Mrs. Penhurst went to be with her this morning."

Helena took up the lamp and opened her bedroom door. Tendrils of smoke curled and writhed in the wavering lamplight. She gasped. Jocelyn looked past her. A curious roaring came from downstairs, as though a wind struggled indoors. They were both gasping now, for the air was oppressively hot.

A shattering crash came from below, and they felt the floor

lurch beneath their feet. Startled into sudden life, Jocelyn drew her friend back into the bedroom, closing the door.

Helena stood in the center of the room, saying, "What? What is it?" Jocelyn looked out the small window under the eaves. Fire illuminated the lawn below, not the homelike glow of a hearth seen through a window, but savage flames crackling with glee as they overleapt themselves. The noise increased. She found it difficult to think.

Helena coughed as the air filled with smoke. Pushing a low table out of her way, Jocelyn fought the window sash, panic rising in her throat as she strove to open it. Finding the trick of it after what seemed hours, she flung open the window, gulping in a mouthful of fresh air. It steadied her.

She caught Helena by the arm. "Come along; we're going out the window."

"What?"

"Come on, we'll have to jump."

"Jump? But we'll kill ourselves!"

Jocelyn placed a firm hand on her friend's head, pressing down so it wouldn't strike the sash. "The lower level is on fire. Look." She pointed at the light on the grass. "We can't get out that way. So jump."

Half-in and half-out the window, her foot braced against the small table, Helena hesitated. "I can't," she said in a tone of the greatest conviction and began to back toward Jocelyn. The lamp on the floor burst with a tinkle of glass and the oil spilled in a widening river.

Jocelyn saw Helena's white face and rolling eyes. Soon she would refuse to do anything but cower in the corner while the flames came for her. Struggling with her own fear, Jocelyn knew that in another moment she'd be hammering at Helena, forcing her out. Jocelyn gathered all her self-control and said reasonably, "If you don't jump, how am I to get out?"

Helena bit her lip, nodded once, and crawled the rest of the way out. There was a tiny sill under the window. She brought her legs under her and rested on the ledge, looking down. An unbelievable fact from an old class ran in her head. "The earth is twenty-six thousand miles in circumference." The entire planet seemed to be below her.

Helena felt frozen to the little piece of stone. If she let go, she would fall crushingly down upon the earth and in the same instant float up to heaven. She heard Jocelyn choking behind her. Helena shut her eyes tightly and pushed off into space.

There wasn't a long way to fall. The earth seemed to reach out strong arms to her. Helena knew she found her eternal resting place.

Mr. Fletcher, blissfully holding the woman he adored in his arms, was shaken from his happiness by a valise falling to the ground quite close to his beloved one's head. "Oy!" he shouted, looking up.

He saw Jocelyn half-in, half-out the window. Mr. Fletcher put on duty once more like a cloak around his shoulders. He tenderly lay Helena Fain in a safe spot behind a headstone for protection against falling sparks. Boldly ignoring the danger, he returned and held out his arms for Miss Burnwell.

The instant Helena jumped, Jocelyn had put her head out of the window to see if she was all right. She was surprised and grateful to see her cousins' tutor falling to his knees, his arms filled with Helena's fainting form. She had expected him to look up, if only to give thanks for Helena's deliverance, but he didn't. Jocelyn had called and hallooed, but the sound of the fire swallowed up all lesser noises.

In desperation, Jocelyn had sought some way of attracting his attention. A vase, two books, and a set of hairbrushes that Helena had not packed had sailed out the window, but Mr. Fletcher paid no heed. Finally Jocelyn had thrown out the valise.

If Mr. Fletcher had not been there, she would have hurled herself into space as Helena did, risking the consequences of broken limbs or even death, but as long as the tutor was there, he should make himself useful.

Jocelyn scrambled the rest of the way onto the narrow ledge and looked over her shoulder. The paint on Helena's bedroom door bubbled. The heat was of such intensity that the oil-soaked sisal mat on the bedroom floor was beginning to smoke in sympathy with the rest of the house. She could feel the heat on her face and back. Commending her soul to God, Jocelyn jumped. She knocked Mr. Fletcher to the ground.

Jocelyn got up. Her bones ached and she tasted blood from her bitten cheek, but she was otherwise unharmed. Mr.

Fletcher had the wind knocked out of him and lay gasping on the grass. Jocelyn helped him to his feet, then turned to watch the fire. The glass in the windows burst like an artillery barrage, showering them with splinters.

"We'd best get away," Mr. Fletcher murmured breathlessly.

They huddled beside Helena bulwarked by the stout granite grave markers of early Libermorians. "I do hope the church won't catch," Jocelyn said, brushing mud from the skirt of her plain blue pelisse. She seemed to have lost her bonnet.

Having regained his breath, Mr. Fletcher said, "I can hear the bells ringing. Help will soon come." Jocelyn listened but heard nothing.

Sternly the tutor looked at Jocelyn and said, "It was very foolish of you to waste time over Miss Fain's valise, Miss Burnwell. You should have been saving yourself."

"Yes," Jocelyn said dryly. She began to say something more when the windows upstairs shattered. She decided to let the matter rest. They were all safe now.

While waiting, Jocelyn considered an idea. "Mr. Fletcher," she asked, "why were you following us?"

"I . . . I wasn't," the tutor stammered.

"No?"

"I was—"

"Please don't tell me you were reading Gray's *Elegy* in an actual churchyard."

A slow smile spread across Mr. Fletcher's attractive face. "No, Miss Burnwell. I wouldn't tell you that."

"Well, then?"

"I was watching over Miss Fain."

"Watching over her? What do you mean?" She'd realized some time ago that Mr. Fletcher was probably fond of her friend, but this seemed to be carrying things to an extreme.

"I suppose now that Fain is dead, I can tell you something of my mission. On the other hand, perhaps, it would be wiser—"

"If you don't wish for me to lose my mind, Mr. Fletcher, you will tell me exactly what you are talking about."

Mr. Fletcher had often heard her take that tone with the boys. Every time it had taken him back to his nursery, and he knew from long experience that the voice of an angry woman was unanswerable save by the truth. "I'm talking about Fain."

"Mr. Fain!"

Mr. Fletcher knelt beside Helena. His expression was all tender devotion, but his words were filled with stern adherence to duty. "I suppose now that he's dead . . . for some time now, my superiors have suspected Mr. Fain of being implicated in activities of a treasonous nature. More than that—"

"*Your* superiors?" Jocelyn exclaimed, interrupting.

"Yes." Mr. Fletcher turned up the lapel of his coat and removed from the inner facing a thin strip of dull metal. Jocelyn took it. Holding it to the light of the fire, she saw incised upon it in tiny figures a five-digit number and the words *Engaged upon the King's Service*.

Fletcher a spy, too? How many of them were dodging about Libermore tonight? "Then you have been under my uncle's roof under false pretenses?"

"Well," he said with a wry smile, "I would not have otherwise stayed on as tutor to your cousins. Flesh and blood could hardly stand it without orders."

Jocelyn acknowledged the truth of this with a brief smile. More seriously, she asked, "What exactly is it you suspect of Mr. Fain?"

Mr. Fletcher gently removed his identification from Jocelyn's fingers and replaced it in its secret pocket. "I can't divulge that information, Miss Burnwell."

"What information can you divulge, sir?"

"None, except that I was happy to have been of service to you and to Miss Fain." He looked at his love.

Jocelyn wanted to ask what his superiors thought about their men conceiving a tendre for the sisters of criminals, but another idea was in her mind. "Tell me," she asked. "Does everyone . . . that is, do all your colleagues carry . . ." She gestured toward his chest.

"Yes, Miss Burnwell. From the highest to the lowest of us, we all carry the mark of the king's favor."

Jocelyn was afraid that must be his answer. She pressed her fingers to her forehead. Perhaps Hammond simply had not wished to volunteer . . . but Jocelyn saw again the air of

simple pride with which Mr. Fletcher tendered his strip of
metal. She realized she was shaking uncontrollably.

Mr. Fletcher said, "I fear you must have injured yourself
when you fell. Lie down on the grass until the doctor
can . . ."

She shook her head. The temptation was very strong to
take Mr. Fletcher into her confidence, but it battled uselessly
a stronger desire to see Hammond and force an explanation
from him. He had drawn her into a mystery and thus far
refused to answer her questions. The little information he'd
given her in her bedroom only led to the creation of more
questions in her mind.

Instead of telling Mr. Fletcher all, she asked, "I wonder
where Mr. Fain is now?"

"I believe he is in there," Mr. Fletcher said gravely, pointing toward the burning building.

Helena, emerging from her faint in time to hear the question and its grisly answer, gave a little scream and grasped at
Mr. Fletcher's sleeve. Jocelyn took the girl's hand and patted
it. "No, Helena, please don't faint again. We need to have
you awake."

Helena struggled upright and leaned against the young
man. "Oh," she whispered. *"Mon pauvre frère."*

In a convulsive movement Mr. Fletcher put his arms around
the girl's waist and pressed his lips to her white face. Helena
turned to him, misery filling her throat like a great stone. She
clung to him desperately. "Never mind, Helena," he murmured as he rocked her in his arms. "You have me, you
know. I'm here. Never mind, darling."

"I know," Helena said softly in answer, her tears hidden
against his chest.

Embarrassed, for these intimacies were not for her ears,
Jocelyn got to her feet. "I'll see if anyone's come to help
yet." The two people huddled on the grass paid no attention.

Flames leapt out the shattered upstairs windows to catch
on the roof. It would not be long before all but the original
stone walls would be destroyed, and they would be so black-
ened and charred as to prevent anyone's rebuilding. Shaking
her head at the frightful waste, Jocelyn made her way to the
road, shards of glass tinkling under her wooden pattens.

Already, a small group of men formed a line between St.

Agnes's Well and the church, passing two or three buckets between them. Wisely they ignored the hopeless task of saving the vicarage and wetted down the trees and grass between the doomed building and the church. More people ran up to help every moment. Bill Gallagher grabbed her arm and excitedly told her the new fire exhaustion engine was coming from Libermore. Soon there would be enough people to start actively trying to prevent the church itself from catching.

Mr. Quigg sprinted over to talk to her, his voice creaking with excitement. He helped her remove the larger pieces of glass from her curls. She asked about the boys, certain Arnold had again broken bounds. Under the present, exciting circumstances she could hardly have expected him to remember prudence. Her only hope was that he would not run into Constable Regin.

"They're 'bout the place sommers," Quigg said. "Look fer where's the most mischief to be done." He dropped his voice and said harshly, "Haven't seen t'other one about."

Jocelyn nodded and parted from him, walking about for some time, looking for one particular person among all those milling around waiting for someone to tell them what to do. But Hammond did not seem to be there. She supposed he lay low for reasons of his own.

Tired, she sat on the wall rimming the churchyard, her feet drawn up on a projecting stone. While Mr. Quigg formed her neighbors into orderly brigades, she wondered if Mr. Fletcher and Helena had come to some arrangement or if they still huddled together behind the grave marker discovering the freshness of one another's affection.

Jocelyn wished that someone's arm were about her in the midst of this chaos and destruction. She recalled Hammond's arm about her body in the alleyway and seemed to feel again its strength. She sniffled, a single tear coursing through the smoke and grime on her cheek. "Here," she said out loud, "this will never do."

Jocelyn stood up and headed back toward the cemetery. She found Mr. Fletcher and Helena still together. Helena was on Mr. Fletcher's knee, her hands in his, and her head on his shoulder, dark hair flowing freely. She lifted her head, her face made lovelier by great happiness, when Jocelyn stood over them. Mr. Fletcher looked as if the wind had been knocked out of him again.

Helena sprang up and embraced Jocelyn while Mr. Fletcher climbed slowly to his feet. "Wish me joy!" she demanded. "Mr. Fletcher and I . . ." Shyly she looked at her love. "I don't know your first name."

"It's Mark, darling."

"Mark Darling," Helena said, her lashes meekly down.

Mr. Fletcher looked as if he'd liked to kiss her, but refrained saving Jocelyn's presence.

Helena turned toward the burning building and said, "I feel so guilty. Thinking of my future when my brother may be . . ." She caught the words back on a little sob. In another moment she'd cry again.

Jocelyn said sharply, "People are bound to start tiring soon, and some of them will have burns. I'm going home to brew some tea and gather bandages and salve."

"Oh, yes. I'll help you. It's our duty." Helena said to Mr. Fletcher, looking at him as if he were a young god, "Will you help fight the fire, dearest?"

"No, I'm going to stay with you."

She was puzzled. "But . . . the fire!"

Jocelyn intervened, saying, "Enough people have come to put it out, Helena. I should be glad of Mr. Fletcher's company."

"If you think so, Jocelyn." Helena brightened. "You will take my hand, Mark . . . darling?"

Mr. Fain entered the mail coach at Libermore. He knew every other occupant, personally or by sight, yet he climbed in without hesitation. Disguised as a large and coarse woman, he noticed that no one, after one glance, wished to look at him again. Biting on a smile, he made a great noise about his comfort in the corner of the stuffy coach, bullyragging the guard over his luggage. He completed his characterization by using foul language when anyone tried to put down the window.

In the last communication he had received from France, he had been warned that to attack Czar Alexander in London was not wise. Security had been stepped up in the Capital for the visits of the foreign heads of government. Failure would not be tolerated as once the Czar left England, it would be impossible to strike against him.

Fain had some time ago written for permission to attack the Czar during his wide-ranging visits to the English countryside. Though permission had not yet come, Mr. Fain had decided to act without orders before the Czar grew disgusted with England and her foolish Regent and returned to his northern empire.

For three years, Mr. Fain had played the part of a man of peace. Returning to violence was to him as relaxing as putting his feet into an old pair of slippers after a long day in boots. As the coach started forward, Mr. Fain pictured the change of history he prepared, thinking of the joy of the multitudes when his Emperor, Napoleon the Great, returned in triumph to Paris. Mr. Fain smiled widely now and the other occupants of the coach stirred uneasily at the quality of that smile.

CHAPTER EIGHT

HAMMOND'S EARS RANG AND TEARS FILLED HIS SMOKE-FILLED eyes as he ran, leaping over obstacles and ignoring whiplike branches, after Cocker.

In a copse behind the church he tripped over something that cried out. Hammond fell down, sliding across sodden leaves. Cocker leapt up from his hiding place and ran. But Hammond held on to his stick even as he fell. He flung it out, sending Cocker flying. Somehow, the gross servant didn't fall, saving himself with a twist like a fish on the end of the line.

In the leaping firelight the two men stared at each other for a moment. Then, with a whimper of fear as he recognized the man who had seen him set the fire, the uncle of a girl he'd just, as far as he knew, murdered, Cocker threw himself at Hammond.

Though Cocker was bigger and undoubtedly stronger, he'd never realized these things could be disadvantages in a fight with a man who knew his business. Hammond blocked the most vicious blows easily, using his forearms, and the more obvious dirty tricks he returned with greater cunning. Only once did Cocker land a blow, and that, by design or accident, landed just above the slice along Hammond's ribs. He gasped, and for a moment knew nothing but a wave of pain. Cocker waded in to try and follow up on his enemy's weakness, but Hammond recovered his presence of mind just in time. After a scientific strike, a right to the jaw, Cocker fell.

After a pause to press his hand to his throbbing wound,

Hammond removed his two-foot-long cravat and secured Cocker's hands before him, leaving the ends trailing. He delayed one moment more to search for his stick. The leaping firelight winked on the silver head, leading him directly to it.

Looking out from the trees, he noticed that, although there were men between the burning vicarage and the church, they were all on one side and milling about to no purpose. No one saw him drag Cocker by his arms inside the church.

Once there, Hammond rolled him over and retied Cocker's hands behind him, lashing them to his feet with a length of bell rope, in a method he had learned, long ago and to his discomfiture, in Italy. Retrieving his cravat, he soaked one end in the font. He wrung it over the unconscious man's head, then slapped him sharply. Cocker moaned and rubbed his face against the cold stone of the church floor.

Squatting down before him, Hammond prodded Cocker with his stick. "Hallo there," he said, smiling as Cocker lifted his head off the pavement, peering about him dazedly. "Suppose you tell me all about it? Please don't leave out any of the details. I am, believe me, fascinated by every word you utter."

"You ain't no cause to treat me this way," Cocker said.

"No? Your memory is faulty. I saw what you did."

"T'was a n'accident. Didn't mean no harm t'yer niece."

"Niece? Oh, yes. We'll have to have a long chat about that before we're through. But you should know, old man, I wasn't referring to the fire." Hammond studied the profile of the man beside him and saw Cocker's eyes narrow as he reviewed his past crimes.

In a voice as kind as if he were talking to a dear but troubled friend, Hammond said, "I thought before that your voice was familiar. Perhaps we met by the sea not so many days ago. I'm still carrying the gift your friend—I think you called him Matt—gave me. Tell me, what did you do with his body?"

Cocker struggled with his bonds. "Rot you, rot you! You had no business t'kill him."

Hammond held up his hand. "My, my, your memory is dreadful. He tried to kill me first. I seem to remember your insisting he do it while I lay there as helpless as . . . as

helpless as you are. Was it you, by the way, who hit me over
the head when I got off the boat from France? How did you
know who I was?''

For answer, he received a brief critique of his immediate
ancestry, delivered with muffled vehemence. Hammond admired Cocker's vocabulary even while he deplored the choice
of subject.

''I'm sorry you feel that way about it. Perhaps I should
mention that the building we are in is a church, just next door
to the vicarage.'' Alarm mixed with Cocker's anger. ''Fur-
thermore, if you are hoping your vicar will arrive to release
you, I think, upon reflection, you will discover he has already
left.''

''I know that, curse you.'' Cocker wriggled on the floor,
attempting fruitlessly to free himself.

''That will do you no more good that it does the chicken
about to go into the pot, old lad. You, unlike the chicken,
however, have some choice. You can give me all the details
of your vicar's plans, not forgetting to mention where you'll
be meeting—did I tell you I know all about Oxford? I bring
it up just in case you were thinking about fobbing me off with
some story about London or Plymouth.''

Cocker once more displayed his wide-ranging collection of
epithets.

Hammond's smile was charming as he continued. ''As I
say, you can tell me all or I can walk away and leave you
here. You might prefer that. There is always the chance that
the church will not burn. Tell me, in all the time you've
worked for the vicar, did you ever notice that this church has
the remains of a very fine Tudor roof?''

Cocker was silent.

Appearing entirely at ease, Hammond continued. ''Quite
nice, I think, only the slate has so much of the natural oil in
it that it will burn nearly as well as the vicarage, once you'd
oiled it. Pity you're not in a position to look and admire it.
It may not be there much longer. Of course, it is some con-
solation to know that if it goes, you will. Strange to think
that Becket also died in a church. If you meet him on what
the Puritans described as the farther shore, you can compare
experiences.'' Hammond's smile was now beatific. ''Oh, I

shouldn't have mentioned that. Tactless of me. You will hardly reside with the saints.''

It seemed to Cocker, lying painfully on the cold stone, that the crackle and flare of the burning vicarage were growing louder and brighter with every moment that passed. All along one side of the church, he could see the brilliance of the fire blazing in the clear glass windows of the clerestory. Perhaps because the floor was so cold, he began to feel an uncomfortable warmth growing on his back.

It cannot be said in his defense that he felt any remorse about consigning two young women to a fiery death, but he felt considerable horror at the thought of dying in a burning church. He seemed to see so clearly the fall of the slates, each bearing a load of fire, as they piled around his helpless body. Cocker began to talk.

"He said I'd be the important man in these parts, once he got his way. They'd all play kiss me hand then, they would, those dirty—''

Hammond prodded him once more with his stick. "Now, now. I've heard enough of that kind of thing from you. . . .''

"It was them, those women, all of 'em. Makin' faces and lookin' at me sideways. I'm good as they. Mr. Fain, he says, all men are just as good as all other men is.''

Cocker rambled on, repeating half-grasped slogans of Revolutionary philosophy and mouthing the twisted catchwords of freedom fostered by Napoleon and those who followed him. While in France, Hammond had been forced to listen to weary hours of such pointless discourse, and he'd hoped that with peace he would be freed from the necessity of ever having to listen to it again. But he sat patiently enough by Cocker, discovering many things he wanted to know.

He was aware of how messages were sent from Paris to England, for he intercepted many. Most he sent on their way after a careful noting of content. Only the letter he himself brought into England was abstracted from the courier, left dead on a French beach. However, Cocker gave him the details of how the system worked from the English side.

Cocker hinted that he knew so much due to his absolute devotion to Mr. Fain. He repeated this idea several times. Hammond, however, was certain that Fain kept Cocker near

because he saw in his servant the depths of mindless violence
that were so useful to a man in his position.

Hammond took careful mental note of the names that
Cocker mentioned in his bragging, thinking it was high time
these men were exposed to the War Office. Further, Cocker
mentioned several inns where the English sympathizers to the
Bonapartist cause were apt to make their rendezvous. Among
these was the Marigold, an inn in Oxford. Hammond did not
let on that this information was of value.

After half an hour of this weary listening, Hammond again
asked for the location of Cocker's meeting with Fain. But
Cocker had talked himself into once more believing his superiority and would not tell, not realizing that he had already
said too much.

"Now, I have only one more question. Oh, it's an easy
one," Hammond said in answer to Cocker's defiance. "What
did you do with your horse? The horse you were supposed to
ride into town on?"

The question was so unexpected that Cocker gulped and
spoke the truth. "I left it with them Hodges women. They
don't ask nothin' 'cause they know what will come t'em."

Hammond stood up. "You've been very helpful, Cocker.
Thank you." He walked past the servant's trussed body.

"Let me go! You said—" Hammond cut off Cocker's voice
with a kick in the side.

"I'm certain it will break your heart, Cocker. Miss Burnwell escaped the doom you set her. And if she escaped, surely
Miss Fain did as well. But it wasn't your fault they are not
dead. So I think I'll leave you here, for a bit, so you can
think about them and the roof. I shall just go out and see if
it is burning yet." Hammond left, ignoring the man's curses
and pleas.

By a stone wall some half-dozen men, begrimed and black-
ened, rested after their relief by new fire fighters from the
town. One saw Hammond and called to him, "Hey, mister?"

To ignore the summons would lead to questions and possibly pursuit. He came over to them. "Quite a mess, isn't
it?"

"Aye, indeed." The one that called to him was a thin man
of forty or fifty years. His sharp eyes looked out beneath his

thick brows. "I'm John Arlen, churchwarden. You're a stranger, I take it."

"Yes, Mr. Arlen. My name is Hammond." The men shifted on their feet, looking at one another as if to see if their suspicions were seconded. To relieve their minds, Hammond said, "I am known to Mr. Fletcher, the Luckem boys' tutor, and to Miss Burnwell."

"Ah. You've known Mr. Fletcher a long time, then."

"We attended the same school."

The men nodded to one another, their postures relaxing. Mr. Arlen said, "Don't think hardly on us. This here fire, we come to think, didn't start without a bit of help."

"No!" said Hammond, looking skyward. The smoke rose in shadowy columns, rising like a temple lit by flame and moonlight. It would have been beautiful if the air had not been so full of stinging ashes.

Mr. Arlen said, "You mayn't think there's so much villainy in the world as to burn down a house with a vicar in it. But as I was saying just a moment ago, I don't see how a fire could start so fast and burn so hot—"

Another man broke in. "That's as I said. I been in the vicar's house not two hours before it all started. They weren't no paper, nor wax, nor nothing, barring a firkin o' oil, and that was safe sealed or my name ain't Josiah Hale."

"What's happening now?" Hammond asked.

"Well, the fire'll be out in an hour or so. Then, when the ashes cool enough, we mean to look for Mr. Fain's body, that and his sister's," the churchwarden answered. "There's those that say I didn't have much use for him, and maybe it's true enough, but whatever's left of him deserves a proper burial." He leaned a little closer to confide, "Miss Fain, of course, was good right through."

"Ah, Miss Fain," Hammond said. "You know, I believe she may be with Miss Burnwell."

"That's good news!" the churchwarden said, repeating it to his comrades. He pumped Hammond's hand. "Are you sure of it?"

"I know they were together before the fire started. I just strolled over this way when I saw the fire go up."

"You were hereabouts?" one of the other men asked, suspicion returning.

"Yes, I was just passing. I like to walk in the evenings."

"Did you see anybody as might be loiterin'?" the church-warden asked. "I tell you plain, mister, nothing's been seen of that rascally Cocker about, and folks know he's got a bit of a grudge against Miss Fain, if he seemed fond enough o' the vicar."

Seeing his opening, Hammond said, "I didn't want to mention it, as you might be friends of his, but I saw this Cocker man running away from the fire. I overpowered him and put him in the church. Whether he was leaving the scene of a crime or simply running for aid, I didn't stop to inquire. I've not heard much to his credit since I came to Libermore."

"In the church?" Mr. Arlen said, looking toward that building. A small area of the roof burned, and a group of figures rushed back and forth below it. A spry, elderly man, whom Hammond recognized as the one who worked in Jocelyn's garden, came running toward the group by the wall.

"Mr. Arlen! Do you go and get the bell tower door open, man. Young Arnold thinks he can get out on to the roof wid a bucket o'watter. I reckon he can. And ye know the devil takes care of his own." The group by the wall divided, the churchwarden running as fast as possible toward the church.

Mr. Quigg took a moment to say, "Fine to see you, mister. Miss Jocelyn'll be wanting to see you, I fancy. Least that's the feelin' I took when I saw her last."

"Thank you. I'd like to see her, too." Hammond felt there wasn't much point in trying to hide anything from the singularly quick eye of the old sailor.

Mr. Quigg cackled and wiped his brow with a handkerchief that could pass for a mourning band. "Spends too much of her time lookin' arter other people children," he said cryptically. "Wants t'be lookin' arter her own. Well, get on wid it, sonny, can't spend all night talkin' to the likes o'you."

CHAPTER NINE

To HELENA AND MARK, THE IDEA OF A WALK THROUGH THE moonlight would never hold the charm it had for other couples. It would always be marred by the remembrance of Jocelyn urging them to hurry and by the foul odor of smoke that blighted the cool air. Mark had a small, painful burn on his right hand where a spark had extinguished itself. Helena was disturbed by the idea that Mark would rather go to a kitchen with women than distinguish himself fighting for her home.

But once at the Luckem house, they were both distracted by the behavior of their friend. Jocelyn opened the small door by the stove and called, "Hammond! Hammond, are you there? Come down at once!"

Helena tried to coax her friend to sit in a chair while Mark stood by the pantry, his forehead creased as if he were trying to remember something. When Jocelyn refused to sit, Helena lit a candle and began to feed the fire in the stove to heat water for tea. Her friend, she decided, needed it far more than those fighting the fire. She turned around when her new love said in a tone of enlightenment, "That's it!" He stared at Hammond as he entered.

Jocelyn said, "Hammond, this is Mr. Mark Fletcher, also of the King's Service. He possesses a form of identification. I would like to see yours." She willed him to produce the little strip of metal, prayed for him to produce it.

The fire in the stove leapt up to illuminate Hammond's expression, alarmed, obviously measuring Fletcher's strength. Leaves hung on Hammond's coat. His cravat was badly tied, and one end of it seemed to be wet. One long-fingered hand was pressed against his side. Helena shut the stove door with a harsh clang like the last stroke of a funeral toll. The single candle shed too little light to let Jocelyn read Hammond's face.

Ice forming in her blood, Jocelyn walked across the room and pushed Hammond out into the moonlight. He allowed her to move him along, though he could easily have avoided any such effort.

"I haven't any identification," he said.

"Of course he hasn't," said Mr. Fletcher loudly, following Hammond and Jocelyn outside. "He sent it back. We all admired you very much for it, Captain, though everyone thought it quite unnecessary. Mistakes do happen."

"Mistakes!" said Hammond, turning from the girl's accusatory glance to the boy's open admiration. "My 'mistake' cost a thousand lives and more. My 'mistake' may have kept this . . . bloody war going another year."

"Yes, sir, but to resign your commission over some Judas?" Fletcher remembered there was another party present to this conversation and looked over his shoulder. In the doorway Helena watched him with an expression of wounded bewilderment. Mr. Fletcher went to her and took her hand in his. She let it stay there, limply, not returning his ardent pressure.

Hammond laughed mirthlessly. "Aren't you in rather the same boat, Mr. Who-ever-you-are? That is Fain's sister?"

"Half-sister," Mark corrected. He regarded Hammond with professional interest. "You've heard about Fain?"

"That is why I am in England once more." His bitter glance took in the visible countryside and the people around him. He seemed to reach some decision. "There is to be an attempt to assassinate the Czar."

"What! But Miriam said . . ." Jocelyn began, but nobody paid any attention to her.

"We're up to all of that, sir," said Mr. Fletcher with a confident nod.

"You know?"

"Yes, of course. The fellows at the War Office aren't as thick as all that. We've kept an eye on Fain for some time now. Regular correspondent with the Tuileries. One of Napoleon's favorite sons.''

"You're . . . you're talking about my brother, aren't you?'' Helena said.

Jocelyn jumped. She'd almost forgotten her friend stood behind her. As tenderly as her anger would permit, she said, "I'm afraid they are, Helena. Mr. Fain . . . your brother . . . it seems he hasn't been terribly wise.'' She poked Mr. Fletcher in the waistcoat. "You tell her.''

Mr. Fletcher, looking down into his love's confused eyes, would have far rather committed treason than explain to Helena her brother's perfidy. Being afraid, he was brutal. "So far as anyone can tell, your brother has always worked for France. He got involved with some dirty characters when your father, who, if you'll pardon me, may have been on the queer side, too, went to France and married your mother.''

"What has that to do with Nicholas?'' Helena asked. Her hand slipped out of Fletcher's to hang by her side like a dead thing.

Duty Mr. Fletcher's lodestar, he said, "Fain wasn't very old, just seventeen, but he was a known friend and supporter of the Jacobins during the Terror. Like the rest of that lot, those that survived, he threw in with Bonaparte. He's apparently been waiting for these orders for a long time.''

Helena closed her eyes and shook her head as if to clear her mind of some mirage. "I can't believe it of him. Nicholas has always been so good to me. When Maman died and I found myself destitute in Switzerland . . .'' She paused for a long, queer moment. Then she went on. "He sent money. He found someone to bring me here. He takes no interest in political matters. He lives so quietly. You might as well suspect me!''

Jocelyn saw the quick lift of Hammond's eyebrows answered by an infinitesimal shake of Fletcher's head. She realized that Helena had been, and could still be, suspected of complicity in her brother's actions. She wondered if Fletcher held proof of Helena's innocence or if he assumed it based on his feelings. While admiring Helena for her loyalty to her half-brother, Jocelyn's own opinion was that though Helena did not lack the spirit to be of use in an enterprise of daring, she perhaps lacked the necessary quickness of decision. Jocelyn did not now wish to think of those moments in the burning vicarage when it seemed as if Helena would never jump.

Fletcher said, "I'm afraid your brother's true nature has been very well hidden. You must believe that we are not speculating idly. We have proof, copies of letters written to France and copies of those he received in return. Also, well, we can place him at the scene of certain crimes against our efforts in the late war."

Jocelyn asked, perhaps irrelevantly, "Is Mr. Fain truly an ordained minister?" She thought of all the people she knew who had been christened, married, or buried under his auspices.

"Yes, he's ordained," Hammond answered with a bitter bark of laughter. "He went to Oxford, all right and tight, ten years ago. Not, however, under the compulsion of religion, but by the orders of Charles Varmont, sous-chief of Napoleon's own secret police. Varmont retains a Revolutionary sense of humor and thought an English assassin who's an Anglican priest would be a fine joke."

Suddenly Helena stamped her foot and said, "I won't believe it! Why haven't you arrested him, if he is so . . . so dangerous?" Helena's accent grew more and more foreign as her passion overrode her English training.

"That's an excellent question," Jocelyn said. "Why haven't you acted if you've all this evidence?"

"Policy reasons," Mr. Fletcher answered and then shut his mouth tight. But his worried eyes strayed to Helena, who looked at him as if she did not recognize him. A beggar in the streets would have received more compassion than she showed Fletcher.

"You'll have to do better than that," Jocelyn said.

Hammond said, "From what I remember of the War Office, I can make a fair guess as to why Fain isn't in gaol at this moment."

"He's not in gaol, sir, because he's dead!" When Fletcher tried to comfort her, Helena pushed him away with all her strength and buried her face into her hands.

"Dead!" Hammond exclaimed.

Mr. Fletcher explained about the fire. Hammond said nothing, pulling at his chin and thinking deeply. "The girl's suffering from shock," he said at last. "All this, on top of jumping out of a window, has been too much for her. Fletcher, isn't it?"

"Yes, sir?"

"Take her up to Miss Burnwell's room and let her rest."

"Alone, sir?" Mr. Fletcher said, scandalized.

Hammond's face indicated what he thought of such scruples during a crisis. "Miss Burnwell will go with you as chaperon."

"You'll come, too," Jocelyn demanded, fed up with his ordering people around when he was not only a stranger but a liar. She'd lost count of the lies he'd told and the truths he'd suppressed. Why couldn't he have told her all this earlier? Didn't he know she'd do everything she could to help in a cause such as this?

The wry smile touched Hammond's face yet again. "Now who lacks faith? If I'd known what a difference that little snip of tin was to make, I never should have surrendered it. Please remember, Miss Burnwell, the circumstances under which we met. You trusted me well enough then."

Jocelyn's new opinion of Hammond solidified. How contemptible to remind her of the debt between them. She felt like a fool for having wasted any dreams on his account. But he was right. She trusted when she knew nothing, and it would be wrong to hold back aid now. The fate of the country, of the world, might depend on him, and the faster he went to save it, the better she would like it.

"Oh, pick her up," Jocelyn said to Mr. Fletcher.

"No!" Helena backed away from the former tutor. "I am perfectly well."

"They're right, Helena. You are overwrought."

"No, I'm not. Listen to me!" she ordered, silencing their babble. "The horrible thing is that I believe you. Completely. I have no doubt that every word you say is true. I've known for a long time that my brother . . . that Nicholas is not what he seems. So many things were wrong, like a picture with demonic faces hidden in it. That's what's so terrible. I believe you."

Jocelyn slipped her arm about the other girl's waist. She could feel her trembling. "I think you should go up to rest, dear. A nice wash to rid ourselves of the smoke"—Helena

gave a convulsive shudder at that—"then a lovely long sleep."
The tension drained out of Helena's body as she nodded.

In quite a different tone Jocelyn said to the men, "Now,
keep a guard on each other, will you? I swear I don't know
who's who anymore." She realized she spoke to them in the
same tone of voice she used with Granville and Arnold. It
worked as well with men as with the boys.

Thinking of the boys, for the first time that night she
blessed the vicarage fire. With such an excitement in the
neighborhood the boys would never come back in time to find
the strange goings-on in their own house. It was bad enough
that Arnold knew Hammond had come looking for her.

While Jocelyn prepared Helena for bed, the men sat in the
kitchen and talked. "You needn't tell me if I've guessed correctly," Hammond said. He paused for a moment, combin-
ing in his thoughts the memory of his former superiors'
manner of conducting business and the information contained
in the letter he'd carried from the Continent, the letter for
which two men died at his hands, the French courier and Matt
Hodges.

He put the thought of those men from his mind and said,
"The way I see it, the government thinks that the Czar won't
be too impressed with us if we only *say* there's a plot against
his life and that those responsible have been removed. There's
been too much of that kind of plotting in Russia, considering
how many of their czars have died in bed. However, if we let
the assassin get close enough to His Imperial Majesty to give
him a good fright, the Russians look fondly on us and we get
an edge in their policies."

"Well," Fletcher said with a cautious glance round, "let's
just say, shall we, that it is a good thing we didn't help the
Finns when the Russians decided they'd like to have a water-
ing place on the Baltic."

"When was Fain going to try it?"

"Soon." Fletcher decided to take the plunge. Though
Hammond had been melodramatic about sending in his res-
ignation, the prevailing opinion at the War Office was that he
could still be relied upon. Peace put paid to Fletcher's traveling abroad, but he remembered Hammond had been one of
the men in France an agent should find if he wound up in
serious trouble.

"Rather clever, I thought. He was planning to dress as a woman and attack at the Worshipful Fishmongers' dinner on the twenty-third of June. We foxed him, though. There won't be any women allowed. We were going to get him at the door, pistol or knife or whatever in hand, and be able to show him to Alexander." He chuckled. "Rumor is that His Highness is glad the order's gone out, interdicting women. He's supposed to be getting tired of 'em, although I think the heavens'll fall before Prinny gives up his bits o' bounce."

Hammond curved his lips and then said, "You know all about me, or seem to. What's your antecedents? Had much experience?"

"Some," Fletcher laconically admitted. "Spent a bit of time on the Peninsula and not with Wellington, if you understand me?"

"I've never been to Spain." Hammond thought for a moment and then said, "Well, since there's nothing new about my information, I suppose I must just go and kick my heels at the War Office. They'll likely have me guarding Princess Charlotte's pup until they decide I'm reliable."

He looked down at his hands and shook his head. "I'll tell you plain, Fletcher. I want back in. I'm damned tired of charging around like a loose cannon, playing a lone game. Tell me, do you think I'm in good odor with the Old Man?"

Fletcher, ten years younger than Hammond, felt flattered to be asked advice by a man whose exploits on the Continent were legendary. "Yes, Captain. I think he'd be delighted—more than delighted—to have you back again."

"Thank you." Hammond looked up at the ceiling with a considering air. Slowly he said, "Is Miss Burnwell any relation to Feldon Burnwell?"

"To confess my own cowardice," Fletcher said with a wry smile, "I was afraid to ask him."

Hammond smiled in sympathy. "Somehow I don't much blame you. I shouldn't care to ask *him* a personal question when the kettle's boiling." He stood up. "I'll leave for London in the morning. Do you have a horse stabled somewhere that I can take?"

"There's a gray mare waiting at the Brass Ring just beyond Libermore."

"Thank you. If you'd care to send your dispatches by me,

you can explain about Fain and his fire. I'll add my hapworth
of tar for all the good it may do. It's not your fault the fool
got caught in his own trap.''

"Trap, sir?"

"Yes, hadn't you realized?"

"I don't understand."

"A common enough trick. Burn down the place you've
made your base. Destroy any evidence you might have forgotten or misplaced and clear out. Poor old Fain. So clever
and so careless."

Hammond had seen the love between Fletcher and Fain's
sister. If he asked for Fletcher's help, help he could dearly
use, he'd be involving the younger man in exactly the same
kind of moral trap he himself had floundered in for years. He
couldn't do it.

He tapped Fletcher on the chest. "I shouldn't worry about
Miss Fain. I've seen this kind of thing before. You start talking to her, taking good care of her, and in two weeks she'll
forget she ever possessed a brother. Especially such a ras-
cal." As if it were an afterthought, he added, "You're
entirely confident that she's not part of this plot?"

"As certain as you are of Miss Burnwell!" Fletcher answered at once, his head thrown defiantly back.

"Ah. As sure as that." For a moment Hammond stood
looking down at the clean kitchen floor. "I'll stop by at first
light for those dispatches. Good night."

As he started for the door, Jocelyn came down the back
stair, each footstep loud and heavy. Hammond paused. "Helena would like to see you, Mr. Fletcher," Jocelyn said. "I
believe she wants to break off your understanding with her."

"What?" Mr. Fletcher said, standing up, horrified.

"Take a firm line with her, old man," Hammond said with
a wink and a nod. "Remember what I said."

Mr. Fletcher left so fast that Hammond said, "They're
teaching them to run better these days."

"Mr. Hammond," Jocelyn began.

With his charming, sad smile, Hammond said, "Please
remember, I'm just Hammond."

"I believe Mr. Fletcher called you Captain?" Jocelyn said
sweetly. "Whoever you may be, would you be so good as to
step outside?"

Hammond's eyes went to the small door beside the stove, hanging open from Mr. Fletcher's flight. Very quietly, he said, "Yes, I remember that little stair. Remarkable acoustics, I could hear every word you and Miss Fain said before. How much easier life would be if every house had one. Outside is better."

Once there he took control of the conversation by saying, "What is it, Miss Burnwell?"

"How did you know Helena Fain jumped out a window tonight?"

"I saw you jump."

"And you did nothing to help us," she demanded, "although we were in there?" Her dark gray eyes, previously shy when with him, stared into his, revealing plainly the depth of the blow he'd inflicted.

It was one of the risks of his profession, this wounding of the innocents. He'd accepted it a long time ago, but just at that moment it seemed too much to ask of him and of her. He explained, "I knew you were there. However, I didn't know Fain's servant soaked the place with oil until I saw him throw in the lantern. The house went up at once. I could do nothing to save you. I went after him. I lost him in the dark. He knows the country. I don't."

He did not tell her about holding Cocker in the church. He'd been cruel to the man, justifiably he thought, but Hammond could not be sure that Jocelyn would see it that way. Besides, he did not want her to believe in him again because he'd captured Cocker. It would be pleasant, for once, he thought, if someone would care for me despite the things I've had to do.

"Cocker burned the house?"

"On his master's orders."

"No," Jocelyn said, overwhelmed by the callousness of the action he spoke of so calmly. "Mr. Fain never would have condemned his sister to such a dreadful death. I have never noticed any particular fondness he held for her, but surely no one could kill so mercilessly."

"You understand very little of the world, Miss Burnwell. The history of man is full of such incidents as might have taken place tonight were it not for your bravery."

He saw she did not soften at the compliment and continued. "I don't believe that Fain intended to murder you or Miss Fain. But tell me, does Cocker wish you harm?"

"No, of course not. I don't like the man. He is impossible to like. Not because he is a servant. His manner is . . . he is nasty. You saw him."

"I doubt you troubled to conceal your revulsion."

"Both Helena and I . . . oh, I see." Jocelyn felt sickened. She seemed to hear again Cocker's whisperings and brushed her curls away from her ears. To hear Hammond continue to speak, calmly and rationally, was like taking another bath.

"He is the kind of man who demands slavish politeness from those he considers his inferiors. Such as women. I've met a few like him before. They become violent when treated with less than deference. He decided to combine his master's plan for the destruction of his house with his own revenge."

"He must be mad!"

"No," Hammond said. "Not mad. Just a little too certain of his own superiority. I imagine, however, should Fain ever find out about tonight, Cocker will be very surprised when Fain kills him for it."

"You don't think that Fain is dead, either, do you, Hammond?" When he shook his head, surprised by her matter-of-fact tone, she said, "I never cared much for him as a vicar, but I never thought he was a fool."

"No, he's not."

Jocelyn looked down and thought of Mr. Fain standing in the pulpit on Sunday mornings, preaching of the abiding love and peace of God. "Do you think Fain capable of killing?"

He was startled by the directness of her question. It was not the one he'd expected. Nor was the tone that of the simple country-raised girl he'd taken her to be, despite the times she'd proved herself more than that. He answered her just as directly, perhaps with some notion of discovering how much she could take. "Yes. I can think of five men at least that he has murdered. He never, however, sends another to do his work. I imagine Cocker did not tell Fain of the attempt he bungled on my life."

Once again her reaction surprised him. "Did Cocker attack you? He saw you tonight? Could he have recognized you?"

"No, it was dark when we met before. I remembered his voice and recognized him. He had no such advantage."

Hammond took a turn up and down the yard, looking at everything save her. Then he took her hands in his. "I can't thank you for all the good you've done me, Miss Burnwell. I realize I'm not appearing in the best light at the moment. Do try to think of me kindly. Nothing's important but the job at hand, you know."

"Yes, I understand that." How she wished he could forget it. Anger still bubbled inside her that he would rather care to capture Cocker than save her and Helena. To show she saw through his lies, she asked, "Can you find your way to Oxford from here?"

Hammond dropped her hands. "What!"

"The French must be very stupid, Mr. Hammond. The letter you want is in Oxford. You're going to get it. Then I imagine you will go to London and try to stop the assassination, yourself."

He shook his head, not to deny her assumption, but to clear it. Even knowing what he did of her background, Hammond was startled and amazed by her astuteness. With such a woman only the truth would suffice. Intently he said, "I must. You don't realize how far I've fallen. If I'm ever to recoup, to be again an honorable soldier in my country's cause, I have to do something as great in its way as the crime that caused my fall."

"What precisely did you do?"

In a low voice Hammond said, "I had a friend—who was no friend. He betrayed me. It was my fault to have trusted—"

"Mr. Fletcher said—"

"He's a boy! What does he know about honor?"

Her anger disappeared. If he felt like that, then everything he'd done from their meeting had a reason behind it. A reason she could understand and respect. Jocelyn touched Hammond's shoulder gently. "I see. I can tell him you are sleeping in the barn."

"I do owe you a great debt, Miss Burnwell. I promise to repay . . ." He thought excitedly about the job ahead. First, a long ride on whatever animal he could find, pushing it and himself onward, first to Oxford and then to London. Once

there, he'd think about what direction his life might take.
There were errors of the past to be rectified, and if he failed,
then he'd think again. The moonlight fell on Jocelyn's
face, silvering her tumbled hair. He noticed and smiled. "I
don't see her."

"Who?" Light badinage was all she could have expected,
though she'd hoped for more.

"The plain girl they say lives with the Luckems; I've never
seen her." The light was bright enough to show a dimple,
unsuspected until now, come and go beside her mouth. Prey
to a sudden impulse, Hammond stopped and kissed her cheek
as he would a sister's. He felt her start, and straightened at
once. Setting his hat at an angle, he half-laughed and said,
"Good night, Jocelyn."

Springing over the garden wall, he waved his hand. She
heard him whistle as his footsteps faded.

Overwrought, Jocelyn sank down on the garden steps. A
sigh escaped her. Her fingers pressed to the spot where Hammond's lips had brushed her cheek; she wondered if all the
kisses she'd receive in her life would be only brotherly. For
an instant, as he came near, she had thought . . . Tears cooled
her cheeks. Sternly she told herself what a relief it was not
to be involved any more in mysteries and confusions. And
yet, hearing his whistle fading on the still air, she felt as
though some part of her went with Hammond and would
always be his, though he thought of her as no more than a
pleasant, helpful girl. Jocelyn cried, but not for very long.
Her family needed her. She had much to do.

CHAPTER TEN

MANY WEARY HOURS LATER JOCELYN WENT TO BED. Between lugging tubs of tea and hills of rolls to the fire fighters, wrapping minor burns and looking in every now and then to see if Helena still slept, Jocelyn used up all of her energies. Although three hours of rest was insufficient, she felt refreshed enough to get Arnold and Granville's breakfast when they finally returned early in the morning, after the fire had been totally extinguished.

"Three times the church roof seemed sure to catch. Once I climbed up to dump a bucket of water on it. I was the only one of the boys not too scared to climb up." Arnold yawned as though about to swallow the table. "They couldn't use a man 'cause the branch wouldn't support much weight."

Both the boys were smoke-blackened and sweat-streaked. Granville, all pretension stripped away in a night's valiant effort, sat drowsing in his chair. Mr. Quigg refused any food, pleading a great desire to drink away the smoke with something stronger than tea. He retired at once to his small house.

Languidly Jocelyn said, "Please wash under the pump in the backyard before you go. . . . Please, Arnold. I don't want to have to wash all the sheets tomorrow."

To her surprise, Granville also protested the bath. The boys were interrupted by a knocking at the back door. Jocelyn felt as if she could not face visitors after her exhausting night, but politeness drew her to her feet as the door opened.

"Jocelyn, my dear! We've only just heard!" Miriam Swann poked her pretty face around the jamb. Seeing Jocelyn, she swung the door open and walked in, followed by the white-clad figure of her mother-in-law. The ladies entered, good-naturedly not letting on how rare it was for them to enter any kitchen, even their own.

Granville sat upright, his reddened eyes blinking in amazement and horror. Only in his worse nightmares was he ever placed in such a position. He looked dazedly down at his burn-spotted, smoky clothes and winced. What would His Highness do? he thought. Instantly the answer came.

He stood. He bowed. "Mrs. Swann. An honor, ma'am." From the cupboard he removed a white tablecloth and spread it elegantly over his chair. The black marks left by his hands hung over the back where they could not mar the purity of Mrs. Swann's pristine gown. He said, "Won't you take this chair, ma'am?"

Arnold sniggered. Jocelyn gave him a sharp look. He stood and bowed with as much grace as his brother.

Mrs. Swann, with regal appreciation of a grand gesture, seated herself on the draped chair. "Thank you, Mr. Luckem."

She turned her eyes on Jocelyn, genuine anxiety in their depths. "Miss Burnwell, we have only just this hour heard of the catastrophe at the vicarage. The wildest rumors are flying, as you may well imagine. Pray, can you tell me what has become of dear Mr. Fain and his poor dear sister?"

Jocelyn said, "Miss Fain is upstairs . . ."

The Swanns exclaimed with joy, raising their hands. The older lady said, "This *is* news. We'd heard that both Mr. and Miss Fain were at home when the fire began. At least, that is what Lydia Danforth said when she called on us early this morning with the news. I should have known she'd get it wrong. A more ditty-headed female never lived."

"Mother Swann!" Miriam said, pleased and scandalized. "That's . . . vernacular," she whispered.

Mrs. Swann sniffed. "Do I not know it? You should be aware that there is a difference, Miriam, when a mature lady chooses to lapse into more common speech and when a young girl like you throws her reputation away with her words. But this is not the time to teach you."

With a return to civility, she said to Jocelyn, "I am so pleased dear Miss Helena survived. How did she manage it?"

Gathering her wits, Jocelyn said, "Don't you recall my asking Miss Fain to stay? Her brother gave permission." She offered no details. Whatever she told the Swanns would be repeated in every household before the day was out. It must be a tale she and Helena could support. Surely, half the truth would be enough to satisfy curiosity.

Jocelyn continued. "As for Mr. Fain, I cannot say where he is." She recalled Hammond speculating on that very question, and her brows drew together in a frown.

Mrs. Alastair Swann misread Jocelyn's expression. She touched a lace-lavished handkerchief delicately to each eye. "Well," she said with a sigh. "It is at least a comfort to know that vicars and such are assured a place at their Master's hand. Were it true for all of us here below." She drooped her head like a dying plant. A short, somewhat respectful silence fell.

Feeling that the atmosphere was becoming a touch maudlin, she coughed and raised her head. "On to other matters. Dear Miss Burnwell, you and I are in a position to exchange favors."

"Ma'am?" Jocelyn said, her sleepy wits startled by the change of subject.

"Come in, Hargreaves," Mrs. Swann called.

A sturdily built woman of approximately forty years of age, dressed from feather to boots in unrelieved black as though in intentional opposition to Mrs. Swann, entered through the back door. She spared no glance for the grimy family at the table but looked up at the ceiling, hung with the remains of the winter store, then down at the floor, sniffed, and at last deigned to cast her amber eye upon Jocelyn.

"This," Mrs. Swann said while the inspection went on, "is Miss Hargreaves, sister to my own cook. She recently came on a visit, and finding the neighborhood of Libermore to be so agreeable, has decided to stop in the vicinity. If no employment is offered her, she is resolved to open a school for young females to teach them the fundamentals of good housekeeping. Though I am firmly in favor of such enterprises, my cook wishes to join this school so as to be closer to her sister. That, as you may well understand, is impossible."

Seeing that Jocelyn did not yet grasp her part in this, Mrs. Swann elaborated. "Miss Burnwell, I should be greatly in your debt if you could employ Miss Hargreaves as your housekeeper. By finding her an employment, I shall retain my cook, who is the most splendid hand.''

Jocelyn licked her dry lips. Though so tired she felt befogged, she realized that this was an opportunity too good to miss. She said, ''Miss Hargreaves, as you have heard, I require a housekeeper immediately. Will you take the position, if only until I can find a more permanent employee?''

Miss Hargreaves unclosed her lips. ''You and you!'' she said, pointing to the boys. ''There is a pump in the yard. Out to it, instantly. I won't have your dirty personages mucking up clean sheets. Then to bed with both of you.''

To Granville, she said, ''If you'll give me your cravats, sir, I'll starch them. And I'll have currant duff ready to follow your supper,'' she said, with a tolerant glance at Arnold.

As though enchanted, the boys walked past the table, made their best bows on the doorstep, and went out, where Granville actually helped Arnold with the pump and where Arnold did not throw mud on his brother when clean, as had been his unvarying custom.

Miss Hargreaves crossed to the pantry, jerked open the door, threw an inscrutable look over her shoulder at the ladies, and vanished in the depths. Every now and then a snort or grunt would be heard, depending on what she discovered.

The two ladies saw how difficult Jocelyn found it to listen to their chatter and being, after all, kind-hearted, began to take their leave. Suddenly a further knock sounded on the kitchen door. Miriam looked out the window. ''It's Sir Edgar,'' she said excitedly. ''With Constable Regin.''

''Who?'' Jocelyn gasped, suddenly not at all tired. She stood up. Her face tingled as if encased in ice that cracked when she smiled and bade the two men outside to enter. If she faced arrest and scandal, at least she could try to meet it with grace and what humor she could muster.

Squire and magistrate Sir Edgar Baintree's round face, reddened by years of hunting, was grave enough for a funeral. He removed his tall hat upon entering and bowed to the ladies, his eyes lightening as they fell upon Mrs. Alastair Swann. ''Ma'am,'' he said, his voice rumbling inside his wide chest, clad in a green poacher's coat. ''It is like your ready heart to come at once to offer your help and support to Miss Burnwell, friend to the late Miss Helena.''

Mrs. Swann, her cheeks flooded with a sallow blush, told the magistrate of their joy at discovering Helena Fain did not die in the fire as assumed.

His somberness gone on the instant, Sir Edgar gathered Jocelyn's hands into his. ''Yet another debt we of Libermore owe to Miss Burnwell! I have heard already of your selfless efforts last night in supporting those who came to fight the fire.''

Mrs. Swann said, ''I'm certain Miss Burnwell did no less than her duty. How I regret Marlbridge's remoteness from town. I did not even hear of the disaster until this morning.''

Though she'd given most of her attention to Sir Edgar, Jocelyn was aware every moment of Constable Regin's presence. Cautiously she looked around. The constable edged himself into a corner between the door and the cupboard. It was a poor fit. He seemed ill at ease, staring at her with a puzzled frown as he turned his hat around and around in his hands.

''I only wish,'' said Sir Edgar, ''that my thanks to Miss Burnwell could be my only reason for visiting you now. How it grieves me to execute the office of my duty at such a time.''

Lent speed by a guilty conscience, Jocelyn's thoughts flew once to Arnold and the escape from Constable Regin she had abetted. ''Please, Sir Edgar, what do you mean?''

The magistrate and Regin exchanged glances. Sir Edgar tugged his waistcoat more securely over his large stomach. ''Miss Burnwell, the churchwarden has told me a man named Hammond has been staying here in your uncle's absence. May I speak to him?''

Skirts rustled as the two Swann women leaned forward, their eyes round with speculation. Mild little Jocelyn accused of harboring a *man*! Impossible. Unthinkable. What would she say?

''Yes, Mr. Hammond stayed here but as Mr. Fletcher's guest, not as mine. Would you care to speak with Mr. Fletcher?'' She heard plainly the whistling as the Swanns drew breaths in horror. How she wished the magistrate would summon Mr. Fletcher and question him rather than her. He was a liar by profession and should be able to answer questions without this uncomfortable sensation of wrongdoing.

"This Hammond fellow is gone, then?"

"Yes, he left last night, feeling we had enough to do without him here. I was alone . . . I mean, I had then no housekeeper . . . that is . . . Miss Fain was with me." She saw she was only getting in further trouble and retained wit enough to close her mouth.

Sir Edgar, aware his interview had witnesses, suddenly realized that he'd not been tactful. Mrs. Alastair Swann might well resent imputations laid against Miss Burnwell, a childhood friend of her daughter-in-law. Sir Edgar did not want Mrs. Swann to be in any way prejudiced against him. He had long cherished a desire to be the lady's second husband but believed he understood it might take years of dedicated wooing to win her away from the pleasures of independent widowhood.

Regin stepped up to whisper urgently to Sir Edgar. Jocelyn stood by, avoiding the eyes of Mesdames Swann while straining to hear what the constable said. She was nevertheless vividly aware of their scrutiny. She could almost hear their thoughts, spinning along like wheels.

They at first assumed that Sir Edgar erred. Then they considered the idea that Jocelyn had, indeed, fallen. Within an instant it was fact.

Jocelyn knew if she looked at them now, she would see them goggling at her as if she were some new species brought in from the Caribbean Islands. Her lips twitched as she thought, Once the Swanns leave the house, I might as well move there as I won't be able to stay here.

Mrs. Alastair Swann now accepted that she had been grievously deceived in Miss Burnwell's character; at the same instant, however, she thought about her plan to marry Sir Edgar. Mrs. Swann would cheerfully consign widowhood to the devil the moment Sir Edgar expressed his intentions. To encourage him overtly would be a shock to the conventional man. She hoped in time, however, to abbreviate his years of wooing to one or two and would, in the meantime, spare no effort to hurry the slow workings of his mind.

She walked around the kitchen table and put her arm about Jocelyn's waist, surprising her as well as Miriam. "Sir Edgar

Baintree, if you are imputing any shame to Miss Burnwell, I shall never speak to you again.''

"No, er, I . . ." Sir Edgar winced under Mrs. Alastair Swann's stony gaze and chose a scapegoat, fortunately not present. "That is to say . . . John Arlen tells a queer story about this Hammond fellow . . . and then with Cocker found trussed like a chicken in the chancery . . ."

"Explain yourself clearly, Sir Edgar," Mrs. Swann demanded, implying she had no hope of his ever managing it.

Ignoring caution, Sir Edgar said, "Well, then, last night during the fire . . ." He quickly described the story he'd heard of the stranger. "They found Cocker there, right enough," the magistrate said. "I've heard his story. Cocker said he saw the fire lit by this Hammond fellow . . . the man in black, he called him, and he was dressed like that when Arlen saw him . . . and that Hammond attacked and immobilized him, leaving him to burn with the church."

"But the church didn't burn," Miriam Swann said.

"No, thank the Lord! It has been too wet the last several weeks. Perhaps Providence took a hand, though t'was a near thing, once or twice." This wandering into philosophy plainly unnerved the magistrate. He tugged down his rising waistcoat once more, a quick nervous gesture. It seemed to restore his attention to the dignity of his office. "Therefore, Miss Burnwell, it's a pity this Hammond fellow . . ."

"Would you kindly not refer to him as 'this Hammond fellow'?" Jocelyn said, impatiently and unwisely. Mrs. Swann stepped away from her. Jocelyn saw two pairs of Swann eyebrows go up.

"Er, yes," Sir Edgar said. "As I said, it's a pity he has gone away just as we'd want to have a word with him to clear this matter away. Mind you"—he chuckled—"nobody in his senses would believe a word Cocker says. A rotter through and through and so I've always said. If it weren't for the vicar . . ." He blushed, his weather-reddened face flooded with a bloodlike tinge. He had nearly spoken ill of the dead, and he glanced sheepishly at Mrs. Alastair Swann to see if she noticed.

"Then why," Jocelyn asked, her tone defensive, "if that is what you think of Cocker, do you want to talk to Mr. Hammond?''

The Swanns' censorious eyebrows were waggling like semaphore flags.

Sir Edgar spread his large hands in what a Frenchman would have called a shrug. "Because, my dear young lady, he's a witness. I think. And we can't hold Cocker on the charge of burning down the vicarage without his witnessing!"

"Oh," said Jocelyn lamely. "Of course." Why had she thought for one moment that Hammond might be in some danger from this large and bumbling representative of England's king and England's law? She had known Sir Edgar from her childhood and knew she need fear nothing from his cheerful visage or uncomplicated mind.

"It is only your roundabout way of asking questions that made me nervous, Sir Edgar. I'm sorry if I was impertinent."

"Never you mind, my dear Miss Burnwell," the magistrate said, patting her shoulder. He winked over her head at the constable, not realizing or perhaps not caring that Jocelyn could see him. After all, she was only a female and a young one at that. His duty was to protect her from the silly ideas she'd get if she knew this Hammond fellow was wanted by the law for the murder of Matt Hodges.

Cocker's testimony, supported by his producing the body from where he'd hidden it, was damaging in the extreme. The wound in Hodges's body, a frightful thing, was matched to the knife found several days earlier in a cartload of fish. Cocker could not be proved to have ever purchased or possessed such a knife. That fact, together with his tale of being attacked in the dark on Friday night by a man matching John Arlen's description of Hammond, compounded by the same man committing mayhem on Cocker's person a second time, gave Sir Edgar enough cause to attempt to find and question the mysterious Mr. Hammond.

Jocelyn saw the wink and wondered at it. She contrived to keep her tone light. "If Mr. Hammond returns," she said, "I shall tell him to call on you at once, Sir Edgar."

"You do expect him to come back, then?"

"No, I do not. Though I hope that he will." The Swanns were taken aback once more by her boldness. But Jocelyn watched the men and judged by their faces that neither thought it likely that Hammond would ever come to Libermore again.

Jocelyn wondered why they were finding it so easy to believe badly of the stranger. Her desire to see Hammond again was entirely true and yet her expression of it gave the magistrate the impression she was trustworthy, if only a female. How interesting to learn that truth could be misleading.

"If he does return, some day, I hope you will tell me at once, Miss Jocelyn. As a friend of your uncle, I think I have some small right to oversee your gentlemen admirers." The magistrate laughed, and Jocelyn could almost believe the feeling of menace she was experiencing resulted from her exhaustion.

Jocelyn simpered convincingly at the magistrate's sally. "Should he come back, I will certainly tell you, without saying a word to him. I should not wish him to think admiration of me is a crime."

"That's a good gel." Now confident that Jocelyn could be relied upon, Sir Edgar gazed upon Mrs. Alastair Swann and said, "If you can forgive my lack of tact, my dear Mrs. Swann, might I call upon you this evening?"

Mrs. Swann drew herself up, and the magistrate quailed beneath her flashing eye. His goddess's anger seemed to relent in reaction to Sir Edgar's servility. "Why not come with us now? Your horse can follow our carriage."

She vowed never to show herself in London again, if she did not have the entire story of this Hammond fellow by the time Sir Edgar saw the bottom of his teacup. And if he did not ask her advice before his second biscuit, she swore to be forever sweet to her daughter-in-law. A more hideous forfeit for lack of cunning she could not devise.

Mrs. Alastair Swann took a strained departure from Jocelyn. She obviously did not know how much slander she was to believe, though Jocelyn had no fear her doubt would make her less ready to spread gossip. Mrs. Swann was not dismayed enough, however, to order Hargreaves to leave with them.

Miriam, on the other hand, leaned near to say, "I shall call on you when you are rested, dear. I have so much to tell. I've just received a letter from my bosom-beau, and there is nothing save about His Imperial Majesty. Just think . . . Coming, ma'am! Must flutter away. Good-bye."

Like a leaf caught up in the draft behind a passing carriage,

Jocelyn followed the magistrate, the constable, and the ladies outside. Slowly Jocelyn rolled her eyes to the left and the right. Arnold and Granville were nowhere to be seen. She prayed they'd gone to bed. Regin seemed not to recognize her, but he certainly could identify Arnold.

As the ladies entered their carriage, the magistrate turned once more to Jocelyn. "Has Master Arnold returned yet?"

Jocelyn jumped, for it was as if Sir Edgar read her mind. "Yes. He was at breakfast. Why?"

"Merely a question I—or rather the constable here—wished to ask of him. Nothing to be troubled over, Miss Burnwell. Good day. Convey my condolences to Miss Fain when she awakens." Mrs. Swann added her exhortations to this parting word, for she had overheard everything. It was as well, then, that Jocelyn had not lied about Arnold, for Mrs. Alastair Swann would surely have contradicted her.

The Swann carriage creaked in alarm as Sir Edgar heaved himself up into it. He leaned out the door to say, "Remember to let me know when Mr. Hammond returns." The driver had to give the command to start twice, before the horses would consent to pull the increased weight.

The constable walked away. The crown of his hat could still be seen over the garden wall when Mr. Quigg hissed, "Miss Jocelyn!" She turned around, startled, to find the gardener thrusting two cabbages at her. "He's back again."

"Who is? Oh!" Incautiously she looked over her shoulder. Regin stood on a hillock beyond the wall, craning his head to look once more at her. Rather loudly Jocelyn said, "Fine cabbages, Mr. Quigg. What shall we do with them?" Under her breath, she murmured, "What happened?"

"Found him this mornin'. Damp wid dew and shiverin' and shakin'. Couldn't get a word of sense from him. He blethered about you and lame horses and stars, I think it were."

"Why did he come back, I wonder?"

"Seems the horse he were supposed to take wasn't there or sommat of that. The dew dizzied him some, like it do. He come back here to friendly folk. I gave him whiskey t'prevent inflagramation. He's a nastly old cut along one side o'his ribs, miss."

"I know." Slowly Jocelyn began to drift toward the small whitewashed building at the bottom of the garden. It had long ago been the monk's stillroom, now converted into a simple gardener's cottage, one room up and one down. She felt a great temptation to look back to see if the constable was still there but thought it would seem suspicious, so she refrained. How terribly hard not to look, though.

Loudly again, just in case, Jocelyn said, "I'll look into it, Mr. Quigg. Why not take those in to the new housekeeper?" In surprise she said, "You don't know about her! Mrs. Swann recommends her highly. Miss Hargreaves is her name."

"Hmph! If that pair sent her, she'll likely be a spy on our doin's."

Shuddering to a stop at the word *spy*, Jocelyn looked blankly at the gardener. Then she heard from behind her, "Psst! Jocelyn!" She twitched, startled, hoping her reaction was not noticed by unfriendly eyes.

Arnold, standing close to the house, peered out at her. "Is he gone?"

Pretending to be absorbed by the sprouting herbs near her feet, she asked, "Who?"

"You know. The constable. I saw him come into the garden. He's looking for me again."

"Why? What have you done?" From the corner of her eye she could still see the constable's black hat, just above the wall.

"Nothing! He saw me last night." Arnold edged forward to look around the corner.

"Get back," Jocelyn ordered. "He's watching. When did he see you last night?"

"After I climbed down from the church roof, he started after me, but I dodged around until I lost him. It was easy," he said with naive pride. "There were so many people, and it was dark except near to the fire."

"I see. Stay right there." Performing strenuously for the benefit of their single onlooker, Jocelyn looked for Mr. Quigg. The gardener dropped to his old knees and weeded carrots vigorously. She went to him. "I'm afraid Arnold's gotten into another scrape. Take him into the house, will you, and keep him there if you have to sit on him." She pointed at the asparagus bed, hoping it appeared as if she were giving instructions.

"Young Regin got it in fer him? Ah, me. Knew that lad were gettin' too big fer his britches. If ye want me to, I'll take care of the lad and him over there, too."

"With luck, you won't have to." She spoke a wish aloud: "If only Uncle Gaius were here."

"He'd sort young Regin out straight enough. Widout havin' t'pound him, much. When's he comin' home, then?"

"Not for a week, maybe not for two. We can't keep Arnold hidden until then. I couldn't keep him home for two days."

"Aye, is a proper old puzzle. I'll take him up to his room. Tell him my old sea stories, like he pesters me to. Go by the back way, we will." Mr. Quigg coughed. "You're not forgettin' t'other one, are you, miss?"

"No, of course not. I'll go right now." An idea sprang into Jocelyn's head. Since her uncle and aunt would not return for a week, perhaps it would be better to go to them. Oxford was only two days' journey, with a good carriage and frequent changes. She could hand Arnold over to his parents and let them deal with him. It would be a relief to have him off her hands. However, she could not possibly travel alone with her cousin. She would require the protection of a man. Mr. Quigg could not go because of his rheumatism. Mr. Fletcher would rather stay with Helena. It would be as bad to travel with Granville as with Arnold alone.

Jocelyn paused on the dark threshold of Mr. Quigg's little house. In her heart she knew these were only the most facile excuses. She knew only one man she'd feel safe traveling with, and it just so happened he had a pressing need to go to Oxford himself. He, of course, would probably not see the matter her way. But she felt fairly confident that she could persuade him.

CHAPTER ELEVEN

MR. QUIGG'S SMALL COTTAGE SMELLED OVERWHELMINGLY of tobacco, undercut with a sharp scent of liquor. Only a little of the bright morning light filtered through the shutters. Jocelyn paused until her eyes adjusted. It was quiet enough inside the small room for her to hear plainly the rattling breaths of a man asleep upstairs. She decided to go up to see if Mr. Quigg's assessment of Hammond's health was correct.

Her slippered feet were silent on the rickety stair as she ascended through a roughly cut hole in the ceiling. The light was better up there, for two windows had been knocked in the walls, and one set of shutters hung open. A coat, waistcoat, and shirt she recognized huddled on the floor, with a silver-headed cane and an old hat on top of them.

Hammond slept on Mr. Quigg's narrow cot. She peered at him from a distance. Though he'd been ill in the night, he looked healthier than the last time she'd seen him asleep, the shadows beneath his eyes lighter and his cheeks less hollow. He needed to shave. One brown arm with a pale old scar across the top was flung out. He lay beneath a blanket she herself had knitted, dragged up to cover his shoulders and revealing his feet. Creeping closer, she straightened it, hoping to make him more comfortable without disturbing him.

He grabbed her hand and forcefully pulled her across his naked chest. His face twisted with anger. As his fist rose, his eyes flew open. "My God, Jocelyn," he said, flinching away and letting go. Off-balance, Jocelyn fell to the floor.

Though jolted, as much by his sudden violence as by the

fall, she could not help laughing. His expression was much what hers would have been if surprised in her bed by a man.

He looked down at her, the blanket clutched to his chin like any maiden lady. "I'm sorry; I didn't realize . . ."

"Never mind," she said, rising and shaking out her blue gown. "I'm not hurt. I think." She wiggled experimentally. "No, I'm not hurt. Do you always wake up like that? You almost hit me."

He apologized again. "I had a dream," he added. "You were in it."

"Is that any reason to strike an unarmed woman?" Jocelyn asked, suddenly quite happy for no reason at all.

"Ah, but I didn't. What are you doing up here, anyway?" He leaned back on his elbows, the blanket falling to his waist. The red, puckered mark of his latest wound rose just above the edge.

Jocelyn turned her eyes away, aware they had stayed too long on the rest of Hammond's torso. "I shall wait for you downstairs."

"Something's troubling you. What is it?"

"I need to ask a favor, once you are dressed."

"Oh." He put out a breeched leg from under the blanket but drew it quickly in again. "Yes, I'll be with you in a moment."

When he came down, his hat and coat were on, though his shirt still gaped open. Sighing, Hammond sat in Mr. Quigg's rockable chair and put his head in his hand.

"Are you . . . is your wound . . ."

"No. I drank something from a stone jug last night . . ."

"Mr. Quigg's whiskey. He claims to purchase it, but I suspect he makes it himself."

"Yes, I remember now. A blaze down the throat like a comet and the feeling of a rocket going up in the back of my head. I think it cured my side, however."

"If you'd care for more, I know where he keeps it."

"No, another drink would kill, not cure. After my busy evening, I mean." He smiled a small, bitter grin and then went on in a sudden outburst, "Of all the towns that ever spawned spavined, thrush-ridden, swaybacked, glandered beasts, Libermore is the worst. Cocker's horse was limping like the walking wounded. The only animal for hire at the inn was touched in the wind. I tried to steal one from that big house in the park and was chased off by the groom and three dogs, or a dog and three grooms. It gets a trifle blurry about then. It was raining, I think. And I couldn't even find the inn where Fletcher keeps his horse. And if I had, I would have had the staggers and the bots, I'm sure. In the end I tried to walk to Oxford, but I wound up back here." He rested his hands between his knees and raised his dark eyes to her face. Only now was he beginning to wonder why his feet had instinctively turned toward the priory. "What is the favor, Jocelyn? If I can help you, I will."

"Thank you." Hammond behaved so differently when at ease like this, she felt as if she were talking to a stranger. She found it surprisingly awkward to ask his aid. Perhaps he would misunderstand what she required of him. Nervously she said, "We're in rather a difficulty. I'm happy you came back because I believe you're the only person to help us."

"Us?"

Briefly she described Sir Edgar's visit and the hidden threat she suspected behind his smiling face. "And now Constable Regin is outside. It's likely I'm being stoopid and imagining things, but—"

"I have faith in your intuition." He smiled at her as he crossed the room to spy outside. Pleasure rushed through her. Hammond trusted her!

"Yes, your constable is still there. If you can call lying on one's back in the grass while smoking a pipe watching a house, then I suppose he is watching you. He's quite large, isn't he? All the same, I shan't have any trouble getting away, even in this broadest of all broad daylights."

"*We* shan't have trouble, you mean."

"Jocelyn, my dear, don't be a fool. I can't—"

"If Constable Regin captures Arnold, I shall have no choice but to confess that I rendered him unconscious with an unripened gourd."

The smile she loved crossed his usually austere face. "You did what? You didn't tell me that. Is there nothing you can't do?"

Softly she answered, "I'll do anything if someone I love needs me."

Hammond cleared his throat and looked at the ground. "Please, my dear girl . . ."

Jocelyn went on, more normally. "Arnold needs to be gotten away from here. His parents are in Oxford, as you know. I can give this responsibility to them. I hope they can arrange to reconcile Lord Netherham."

"Who?"

"His is the big house in the park. Arnold poached on his land."

Hammond laughed. "Did he, indeed! I'll tell you; I like that boy. I wouldn't want one precisely the same, as I prefer to sleep at night, but there's something admirable about the scamp all the same."

Jocelyn frowned as she studied him. Since coming down, he'd behaved oddly, almost as if . . . Jocelyn cried out, "Stop it! You're playing a part with me. Just like at the inn! And yesterday, with Cocker in the garden! Treating me like the . . . like the enemy! How dare you?"

She ran at him, her heart twisting in her bosom. Nothing at all had changed between them, though she'd fooled herself in thinking it had. She slapped him with all her might and would have run out if he had not caught her.

"Yes! I admit it! Stop, stop now." His face red with her fingermarks, Hammond tried to draw Jocelyn toward him, his hands on her upper arms. He fought to meet her eyes, but she looked away. Hers were wet. He had no doubt they were tears of fury. Still they affected him.

He said against his will, his voice a husky whisper, "You're more dangerous to me than Fain or the French. You know you are. You're so . . . I suppose *gallant* is the word I'd choose. That's why I chose you to help me, that's why I ask you to help me now. Help me, Jocelyn. Help me to do my duty."

Though his words touched her, and would serve to warm her later, she could only say, "Are you going to take Arnold and me with you to Oxford?"

"No, I'm not." Not letting her speak, he entreated, "Listen to me! Do you think I want to leave you here? Go away from you? You know what's at stake. Fain got away last night. Thanks to my weakness, he's got a day's start on me. If I take you two along, I'll go that much more slowly. If I can get the letter and Fain, I'll come back. I promise you."

"Thank you," Jocelyn said shortly. "Most likely, Arnold and I will be in Australia by then."

"Then, by God, I'll come to Australia!"

Demonstrating more restraint than he'd known he possessed, he ran his hands down her back as though smoothing down raised hackles. Jocelyn meant to hurl herself out of his embrace but found her hands instead entwined in his lapel. Still angry, she raised her chin defiantly. She felt a whispered chuckle against her cheek as he kissed first it, then her mouth. His whiskers tickled her, as lightly as the pressure of his lips.

Greatly daring, she touched the back of his neck where his hair grew low and curling. He crushed her against him, kissing her powerfully. Jocelyn kissed him back with shy enthusiasm.

After a moment Hammond raised his head, keeping her close against him. He sighed, his chest expanding between her arms. Gazing deeply into her eyes, he held his hand against her cheek for a long moment and then murmured, "I'm going to try again for Fletcher's horse. Is there a rear way out of here?"

Taken aback—she should have known!—she said, "Only the window upstairs." Her empty arms fell to her sides. It was impossible to hold him against his will, so she let him go.

"I will see you soon."

"Yes." In a few moments she heard his boots scrape on the wall outside. Mr. Quigg raised trellised roses at the back of the cottage, and their still-gray stems would see Hammond safely down, if at the cost of a scratch or two.

After Hammond had gone, Jocelyn remained in the dreamy world of the now imaginable future. She looked around the odoriferous cottage, smiling as if she found it a lily-scented paradise. Sitting in the rockable chair, still warm from him, she indulged in womanly phantasy for some time. She ignored the fact that she knew nothing of Hammond except that he had lost his employment with the government. For all she knew, he could be the criminal she'd once thought him or, for that matter, king of the Canary Islands. She could only hope he'd keep his promise to come back. But with Hammond, one never knew.

The ringing of the church bell, a beacon still in spite of fire and war, reminded Jocelyn that she should see about the noon meal. She wondered when she'd have the opportunity to show Hammond what a fine cook she was. So far, the only meal he'd eaten at her hands had been prepared by Helena.

As she drifted across the garden, the smell of Constable Regin's pipe smoke recalled her to her senses. He was still there, recumbent on the other side of the path. Jocelyn waved at him gaily and went into the house. Though her heart was light because Hammond would return, he had done nothing to help her. He was gone, leaving behind him one bereft female and a large and gaudy problem.

The kitchen table was empty of dishes. In sudden panic Jocelyn called out, "Miss Hargreaves!!" Had the housekeeper left already? What had Arnold done to her?

The sturdily built housekeeper came down the steps from the dining room. "There you are, miss," she said. "I wondered if you'd gone out. I couldn't hold the chicken mousse back another instant, or it would go flat, so I served without you. Hope you're not displeased, miss."

"Not in the least," Jocelyn said, following the broad back of the housekeeper into the dining room. When she cooked, she served every meal except dinner in the kitchen because, though informal, it was easiest for her. Miss Hargreaves, however, apparently did not serve in the kitchen.

One look at Mr. Fletcher's face in the dining room and Jocelyn knew that Helena had not forgiven him during their last interview. He paid no attention to Mr. Quigg's story of near-piracy in African waters.

"Got the glooms, doesn't he?" Hargreaves whispered as she set a filled plate in front of the girl.

Jocelyn tasted the meal. "How wonderful! Even better than Helena's quiche because I hadn't anything to do with it."

Hargreaves said, "Thank you, miss," and returned to the kitchen.

Rapping the table with her knuckles, Jocelyn looked sternly down at Granville and Arnold. "I want the two of you to pay strict attention to me. Pardon my interruption, Mr. Quigg. Arnold! Listen! If either of you say anything or do anything to frighten away Miss Hargreaves, you can get your own meals, for I won't cook for you. Do you hear me?"

If the boys had not been truly fond of their cousin, they might not have taken her seriously. They knew her well, so hurriedly grunted their assents through mouthfuls of the new housekeeper's excellent bread pudding.

Jocelyn could do no more than send a sympathetic glance

Mr. Fletcher's way while the boys sat there. Any other signs of interest would pique their curiosity too much. Already they noticed that Mr. Fletcher read no book at table and exchanged many glances and whispers over this unusual lack.

After they ate, Miss Hargreaves insisted on a proper bath for each of the boys, quelling Arnold's attempted escape. "You may have removed the top layer of the dirt under the pump, young sirs, but if I know boys, and I do, there is depth after depth of dirt lingering behind. Why, I could start seedlings behind your ears, Master Arnold! Into a hot tub and I'll be along to scrub your backs."

Granville protested at this. "I can scrub my own."

"Not half so well as I'll do it." Hargreaves rolled up the sleeve on her right arm. It was a strong arm, yet undeniably feminine in contour. "When you've beaten so many cakes as I have, you develop a tone." Arnold gaped in amazement, and Jocelyn could almost swear he was willing to beat cakes to acquire such muscles.

Once alone with Mr. Fletcher, Jocelyn found him grasping her hand. "Miss Burnwell, I . . . I don't know what to do. Please, help me." His large eyes were full of anguish.

"What is it? Is there something the matter with Helena?"

"I don't know," he said, clutching at his wavy brown hair. "I've knocked twice this morning, and she never answered. Please go up and beg her to talk to me."

"The poor girl was sound asleep when I last looked in on her, Mr. Fletcher. But I will go see if she would like something to eat. I don't think she's eaten any breakfast." Jocelyn went down into the kitchen. Over the sound of vigorous splashing, she said, "Miss Hargreaves, did Miss Fain take breakfast?"

His hair shining against his scalp, Arnold spluttered in the large copper tub before the stove, his exposed shoulders pinker than Jocelyn had seen them since he was born. "Help!" he cried when he saw his cousin. "She's drowning me."

Rather heartlessly, Jocelyn laughed. "A drowning every now and then is good for you, Arnold."

With a strong hand Miss Hargreaves sent the boy beneath the waves again. "Miss Who did you say, miss?"

"She's probably still sleeping. Like the rest of us, she was up half the night. I'll wake her now, and then take her a morsel to eat, if she wants it."

Miss Hargreaves nodded as she continued to scrub at Arnold, ignoring his heartrending cries for mercy. "Be still, boy, or I'll get the brush out. This is nothing but a cloth."

Jocelyn rapped lightly on the door of the chamber next to her own. After waiting a moment, she knocked harder and called, "Helena? Wake up, dear."

Pressing her ear against the solid wood, she listened for any sound. The door was thick, but surely she would hear a groan or sob, even if Helena did not wish to open the door. "Helena?"

Jocelyn ran down the stairway and into her uncle's library. In one of the desk drawers lay a jumbled assortment of keys, supposedly one for every door in the house. She took down from a shelf a precious bowl, too fragile to stand the trip to London but the nearest container to hand. Jocelyn dumped the keys in the bowl and ran back up the steps, catching her foot in her hem and nearly tripping. Kneeling, she began trying the keys in the lock of Helena's room. Mr. Fletcher found her at it a few minutes later.

"I'm a fool!" she said bitterly when he inquired into what she was doing. Up on her feet as though propelled by a spring, Jocelyn dashed to her room, removed the key from her door and fitted it into the lock. A moment later she stood inside the empty bedroom. The bedclothes sprawled on the floor, as if pushed away in a hurry. Helena's valise, dropped on Mr. Fletcher last night, was no longer in the corner. A much-blotted note lay on the pillow.

Jocelyn,
You have been kindness itself, but blood is thicker than water. I realize that Nicholas is not dead. I know where he has gone. Please tell Mark I'm sorry. He should not come after me.

Affectionately,
Helena

"I don't understand," Mr. Fletcher said, frowning like Arnold when he wished to keep from crying.

"She wrote this in great distress of mind," Jocelyn said, more to herself than to him. "Look at the water blotch by your name. A tear, I think."

"How can she say Fain isn't dead?"

"What evidence is there that he perished in the fire? None. Hammond didn't believe it, either."

"Hammond!" Mr. Fletcher clutched again at his hair.

"Mr. Fletcher, have you a horse?"

"Yes, as I told Captain Hammond last night—"

"No," Jocelyn interrupted. "He's taken that one. Another horse." When Fletcher still looked blank, Jocelyn fought down the desire to shake him and said, slowly and clearly, "We must follow Helena. We must go to Oxford. You and Arnold and I."

"Oxford? What makes you think Helena has gone there?"

"Because her brother is there, Hammond is going there, and . . . and the Czar will soon be there!" Fletcher's jaw fell three inches. The War Office trained its soldiers well. Within a few moments Mr. Fletcher forced down his panic at the thought of Helena alone on the roads and took an active interest in the organization of the party.

"I don't see why Arnold must accompany us," he said.

Past all concern over her reputation, Jocelyn gave a brief description of Arnold's latest trouble and her own part in his rescue. Like Hammond, Mr. Fletcher boggled at the thought of Jocelyn dotting a constable on the head.

"That's not important now," she said impatiently. "We must hurry away. I only hope we catch up to Helena quickly. I don't know when she left, of course, but if she's on foot, she can't have gone far."

After a few moments thought Jocelyn told Miss Hargreaves she had received a communication from Mr. and Mrs. Luckem, inviting her and Arnold to come to see Cousin Tom win his race. Her conscience blushed at this bold-faced lie. She ignored it. The truth would not serve nearly so well.

Arnold was beside himself at the thought of going on a journey, and Jocelyn almost despaired of making him understand that he was in serious trouble. Stern and sharp by turns, she packed their two small bags, keeping him running back and forth to his room to collect the things he'd need in the probably vain hope of wearing him down. Taking for herself only a change of chemise, underclothing, and a shawl, Jocelyn filled the rest of the space with Arnold's clothing. He'd be making a protracted stay with his parents, she hoped, while she would be returning to Libermore at once. She must return to Libermore before Hammond, or, she thought with a smile, he might go off to Australia to find her.

Surprisingly, Granville helped her the most. Once the danger to Arnold was clear to him, he supported Jocelyn's story with many a groan at having to miss the trip. "My duty is here," he proclaimed with theatrical fervor. Miss Hargreaves looked at him suspiciously.

Further, Granville pledged to keep Constable Regin occupied long enough to give them a chance to get clear. Granville also promised to misdirect any inquiries that reached him, whether from the constable, the magistrate, or Mesdames Swann, the most dangerous of the group. He practiced a studied vapidity, which, unfortunately, he never got to use.

While in the kitchen putting on her heavy duffel coat, a thought occurred to Jocelyn, and she said, "Miss Hargreaves! I hope you don't think it is always like this. We are usually a very quiet household. You will stay, at least until I return?"

The new housekeeper drew herself up, and Mr. Quigg looked at her sturdy figure with admiration. "I have passed my word that I'll take the position, Miss Jocelyn. I never go back on my promises."

Hearing this reassurance, Jocelyn felt less guilty about leaving her responsibilities behind her. After all, she owed Helena her best efforts in trying to recover her, whether or not Helena wished to be saved. Jocelyn could not let Helena go off in all innocence to a brother allegedly both a traitor and a murderer.

By the time they'd gone twenty miles, Jocelyn's tailbone ached, as did her back, her neck, and her head. The wagon's wheels were egg-shaped, the boards rattled unceasingly, and the seat was as hard and comfortless as a Puritan conscience. The hired horse, however, shone in the sunlight and pulled the wagon as though it were Miriam Swann's own light barouche. Mr. Fletcher drove extremely well, but in his desire for speed he drove right through the ruts and holes in the road, instead of attempting to smooth the ride by going around them.

With an imperturbability Jocelyn envied, Arnold went directly to sleep on some musty horse blankets before they'd traveled three miles. *He* was not disturbed by thoughts of the trouble he faced, both from the law and his parents.

To take her mind off her physical troubles, Jocelyn considered her mental difficulties. She told Mr. Fletcher about her meetings with Hammond, neglecting to mention her feelings on these occasions, as they were none of Mr. Fletcher's business. He immediately grasped the importance of the letter to Hammond's case.

"That explains a great deal," he said, nodding his head like the horse before them. "A letter like that will set the cat among the pigeons. Captain Hammond will rise very high in the opinion of our superiors."

"You as well, Mr. Fletcher," Jocelyn said.

"Yes, but the credit belongs to the captain. It's true he did fool me with all that talk about Fain's death. I can understand his reasons. It wouldn't be sportsmanlike to deprive him of his letter. Or his glory." Mr. Fletcher smiled and said loudly, "By God, I'd like to be there when he tosses the whole business in His Lordship's lap!"

"His Lordship?" Jocelyn asked.

Mr. Fletcher seemed to think he said too much and turned the conversation to Helena.

"Why did she run away? God only knows what is happening to her, out on the road alone. I've seen . . ." Mr. Fletcher recalled he spoke his soul aloud to a young, unmarried lady, who had lived a sheltered existence until her involvement with matters of national importance. "I am certain she will be waiting for us in Oxford," he finished lamely.

"I am also confident," Jocelyn said, patting his arm.

During the afternoon Jocelyn had time to reflect that at least the government seemed to have plenty of money, considering the way Mr. Fletcher spent it. The instant his horse tired, he exchanged it, lavishly tipping the ostlers to attend them before all the others waiting for service. Jocelyn saw them stare at the wagon, so ill-matched to the liberal coins in their hands. He also purchased certain comforts of the road for which Jocelyn was grateful. Arnold did not mind not being given the candy he asked for at each stop, for he soon remembered he kept the better part of his citron drops screwed up in a dirty piece of paper somewhere in the depths of his pocket.

CHAPTER TWELVE

HELENA'S EDUCATION, FOR ITS GAPS, HAD BEEN COMPLETE enough on one point. She often listened to tales of young girls setting out for a distant city, never seen again once around the corner from the places they had known. She knew enough to be careful.

Uncertain of how far Oxford was from Libermore, Helena walked slowly, not wishing to exhaust herself. Though foot-sore, Helena ignored several offers of rides from men, whether in a coach or a cart. She closed her ears to even polite invitations and continued on quickly after more inso-lent suggestions. Some of the men reminded her of Cocker. When those approached, she turned down the first lane that appeared as though it were her destination, and they drove on.

Only once did a respectable lady stop to aid her; the widow of a prosperous grocer, traveling in a high style with her servants and carriage. The woman asked so many questions and her maid looked at the girl with such narrowed eyes that Helena felt relieved to walk again. There was no doubt, how-ever, that this ride had saved her many weary, trudging hours, for she had traveled as far in two hours as would have taken her four or six or even eight hours to cover afoot.

Helena thought she should concoct some story to explain her presence on the road. Nothing came to mind. She found great difficulty in concentrating on any subject save one. The accusations of her friends repeated and repeated themselves in her thoughts. How could anyone think such terrible things of Nicholas? He could be difficult, especially as soon as he woke up in the morning. Grumpiness, even rudeness, was no crime. She would show the world what it meant to be a sister! By her brave and loving devotion, she would repay the good-ness he had shown her in bringing her to England when left destitute and alone in Switzerland.

As she walked, shifting her valise from hand to hand, He-lena embroidered this picture with brilliant colors culled from novels until the main figures no longer resembled either Mr. Fain or herself. Yet, she found a pleasure in it that distracted her from the growing discomforts of her self-ordered journey. She looked only at her shoes as she walked down the middle of the road, sparing them the worst of the mud in the ruts. The heavy cloak she wore, while stifling, at least kept her dress from the mire.

Her inner vision became more real to her than the day or the sky, which was boding rain. She did not hear or see the carriage behind her, drawn by four speeding horses. The horses' breath steamed as they bore down upon her. Their hooves cycled in the air. The driver fought to control them. She turned with a scream. A swirling darkness gathered around her. She felt herself slipping into it and tried to fight, uselessly. For the second time in a day and a half, Helena Fain fainted.

She awakened to voices that confused her. A heavy white-ness lay across her eyes but she did not feel frightened. Rather, she felt extremely comfortable, as if she never wanted to get up again.

"Jocelyn?" Her voice carried no louder than a whisper.

The voices abruptly stopped. "Here you are, then," some-one said kindly as the damp cloth was lifted from her brow.

"Where am I?"

"A cautious subject, I can see. Well, this is the Dog's Jug Inn on the Botley Road."

An elderly gentleman, tall and thin, stood over her, and Helena, realizing she was lying down, reached for the cov-erlet to draw up to her chin. Her fingers found only her cloak. However, she saw now she lay on a settee, fully clothed save for her shoes. A valet superciliously scraped them by the fire. She lay in a modest room whose heavily carved ancient furnishings and overall smell of spilled beer would have informed her this was an inn, if no one had told her so.

"Oh, dear," Helena said, looking up at the elderly man. "Were they your horses, sir?"

"Indeed, yes. Fortunately, you did them no harm, flinging yourself beneath them." The old gentleman drew forward an armchair and sat slowly down, motioning to Helena to stay prone. "You are not harmed, either," he said with a slow nod. "Only frightened and, I think, hungry."

He was old, quite the oldest person she'd ever seen, with skin like paper. His hair was completely white, and his hands shook with a fine uncontrollable tremor. Deep marks of weariness ringed his large eyes of pale blue, their expression unreadable. His clothes were quietly up to the fashion, though the body they covered was nearly fleshless.

The gentleman, seeing himself under such close inspection, smiled and became less remote. Helena, who had also heard of old roues pretending to be fatherly, was reassured by that smile. So might a grandfather look upon his favorite grandchild when she came in, singing, rousing him from some sad memory.

"What is your name, and why are you traveling alone and on foot?" The smile faded to be replaced by a look of censure, but Helena thought she saw the kindliness still.

"My name is Helena Fain," she said in a low voice.

"Is it? And . . . ?"

Her words were slow, and she stumbled often in the telling. And yet, she hid nothing from those eyes faintly washed with color as they traveled from her eyes to her lips to her hands. He remained silent, only nodding gravely from time to time as though something she said tallied with a thought in his own mind. His silence drew more information from her than questions could have done. She told not only all she had seen and heard the previous day but also half-realized thoughts and feelings. When at last she told of her escape down the small stair at the Luckems' house, the old gentleman nodded again in the slow, thoughtful way that seemed to be a habit with him.

"Were your friends so cruel to you that you felt you had to flee from them? This Miss . . . Burnwell, was it? She saved your life. And had you pledged yourself honorably to this tutor fellow—Fletcher, I believe you said?''

Helena said proudly, sitting up, ''My first loyalty must be to my brother, sir.''

''Then you still wish to go to Oxford? I happen to be traveling there myself, you see, to visit a troubled friend.''

''Oh,'' Helena said, mistrust mingling with hope. ''Are you certain you were going there anyway?''

''Yes, I only just heard of my young friend's presence in Oxford, and it is a visit I have long avoided. I wish now I had gone sooner. Beware of procrastination, Miss Fain. Always cure your faults at once. They only grow worse with age. All my life I have been cursed with pride. Many kinds of pride.''

''Is not pride sometimes worthy?''

''You have been raised among religious people, Miss Fain. What does the Bible say of pride? It is a very long time since I had cause to read it.''

The elderly gentleman turned toward his valet, who, some moments before, had accepted a large tray of food through the door and was now laying the meal out on the white tablecloth. ''Will you not join me? I do not wish you to imperil my horses again through hunger.''

He took very little, only a chicken wing and a glass of watered wine. However, he encouraged Helena to eat heartily. ''We are less than fifty miles from Oxford, and I will order my coachman to stop no more until we are safely there.''

''Thank you. You are very kind. What is your name?''

''I am Lord Ashspring,'' he said as he smiled sadly. ''I was raised to the peerage last month.''

''Oh! My congratulations.''

''Thank you,'' he said, summoning his valet to give him orders about their departure. Then he said to Helena, as he curled his thin fingers around the stem of his glass, ''Finish your dinner.''

At about the same time Jocelyn was trying to persuade Mr. Fletcher that they should stop. Their journey had lasted all afternoon, and now, as night drew in, Mr. Fletcher's exhaustion was such that he had twice nearly driven them into a ditch. But he was reluctant to stop. Before him always floated

Helena's face, whether transfigured by love or pale and cold in repudiation of him and his affection.

However, the second near-accident made him realize that his love would not be served by the delay, if no worse, of an accident. He drew up before a small inn of pale brick. The building had a homelike look to it with flowers planted by the drive and a garden to the side. Only the sign over the door gave it away as a public house. It depicted only the hind end of a dog, the tail curling over the back, for the rest of the animal was inside a pitcher of wine, presumably drinking.

The landlady of the Dog's Jug Inn, dressed in a plain brown gown with the white folds of a kerchief at the neck, greeted them cheerfully, though she was forced to apologize when Mr. Fletcher asked for a private room to take their supper in. "If you'd asked for anything else, sir, I'd have been better able to serve you. The only private dining room I have is occupied."

While Mr. Fletcher weighed the propriety of taking Miss Burnwell into a public room, the landlady's bright eyes observed Jocelyn shaking the creases out of her skirt. She noticed immediately the absence of a ring on her left hand when her gloves came off.

Operating an inn only fifty-five miles from Oxford, she saw a fair number of runaway lovers, for this was often as far as a girl cared to travel in one day. The one rule of her house was that no wicked goings-on of any nature were permitted. Mrs. Pierce drew herself upright, preparing to banish the travelers to another hour on the road.

Arnold ran in, slamming the big front door. "Legs all stretched?" Jocelyn asked.

"I jumped up and down twenty times," the boy answered. "That did it."

"So I should think." Jocelyn turned toward the landlady, her hand on Arnold's shoulder.

Mrs. Pierce said, thawing, "You can take supper with me and my boys, if you've a mind to it. The taproom can be a bit noisy now and again."

Jocelyn said, "Thank you. I for one will be glad of any chair that does not move."

The landlady led the way toward the back of the inn. With a nod toward Mr. Fletcher and Arnold, who were following behind, Jocelyn said, "My brothers and I are going to Oxford to visit my other brother Tom."

"Couldn't your maid come along?" the landlady asked slyly.

"I don't have one."

It is usually the first business of a young lady in an inn to try to impress the keeper of it with her consequence. She might brag about her servants, or her furnishings, or her family, in a mock-amused tone as if none of these things were important. Persons of innocence frequently think that this is the way to receive the best an inn has to offer when in reality it has the opposite effect.

That Jocelyn did not boast was a mark of favor in the eyes of the landlady, and she forgave her the obvious lie about her older companion being her brother. The landlady could not make out quite what the relationship was between these two new guests but was at least satisfied that there was no intrigue going on under her roof. No young man in his right mind would take a scampacious brat like that along during an elopement.

After showing them into her own private rooms, Mrs. Pierce set about getting the table laid. She was flustered but pleased when Jocelyn, after putting her coat and hat on a chair, began to help. "No, no, now, miss. You just sit down and let yourself be waited on. I must snatch a bite when I can . . . I'm half-run off my legs, usually. My boys give me what help they can, but there's no doubt a woman's better for the taproom. I was pleased to have boys, but one girl would have been a blessing."

"How many sons have you, Mrs. Pierce?"

"Oh, three or four. They'll be along in drips and daps as they find a minute to eat. Nothing but hard work when you run an inn." Swallowing a piece of ham and sipping at her ale, Mrs. Pierce left the three travelers alone.

Mr. Fletcher ate moodily, staring at the spotless cloth with which the table was spread. The fingers of his right hand drummed beside his plate. After a moment he reached into his right coat pocket and brought out a slender book, reading with frowning concentration. He didn't seem to cheer up, but at least his nerves were calming.

As Jocelyn cut slices of cake for herself and Arnold, a man

came in the back door. He kept his ragged straw hat on and
slouched against the wall. Jocelyn said, ''Your mother invited
us to sit here, instead of in the taproom.''

The man only grunted and reached for the bowl of beans
in front of Jocelyn. She saw that his hands, though beautifully
shaped, were quite filthy, and she looked away.

''Mark?'' she said brightly, as sister to brother. Mr.
Fletcher closed his book, leaving in a finger as a bookmark.
''Shall we walk? I'd be very interested in the inn's gar-
den. You know I'm not at all pleased with the one at home.
I'm afraid the soil isn't all it should be.''

Arnold groaned. ''Not the gardens!''

''Well, stay if you want to.'' She was certain Arnold would
not mind sitting while Mrs. Pierce's son ate his dinner. By
the time she returned, they would be the closest of friends.

Mr. Fletcher followed her as she walked through the inn's
spotless kitchen and outside. The sun had almost set, and it
was becoming difficult to distinguish colors. The garden she
had noticed was to the left. She opened the gate that sepa-
rated the garden from the open rear lawn and went in. Jocelyn
looked about her, admiring the neatness of the garden's plan
and stopping to inspect the tall beanstalks, the fat cabbages,
and the bridal bouquets of cauliflower.

''It was clever of them to put the garden here,'' she said,
looking toward the drive over a low hedge of viburnum, the
white flowers glowing in the pink light of sunset. A dark
carriage with a gold and green device on the door was drawn
up before the inn. ''If it were in the rear, they wouldn't know
if guests arrived while they were gardening.''

Mr. Fletcher glowered down at the dirt between his boots.
He didn't even look up when he heard a groom swearing at
a horse along the drive on the other side of the hedge. He
waved a hand past his cheek and said glumly, ''Let's go in.
There are flies out here.''

''Surely not so early in the year.'' Jocelyn still looked idly
over the hedge. The horse couldn't be more than two years
old and was mostly leg. He was backing and dancing on the
drive. The groom held the reins tightly, and his hand bobbed
up and down as the horse tossed its head.

He made a long arm and rapped at the front door. When
it opened, he said, ''Mum, tell the colonel his horse is ready.

And hurry him along. I want my supper.'' The horse play-fully jerked away, yanking the reins from the young groom's hand. There were several noisy moments until the groom captured them again.

The horse kept trying its tricks while the young groom listened to the coachman on the box of the carriage. All Jocelyn could see of him was the back of his tall hat, but his unhappy voice carried clearly to her. ''Never have I known Himself never to travel more 'n six hours a day, unless it should happen t'be His Majesty's busyness, which this t'ain't. Now here we are again, and changing hosses, an' all because some young minx don't have sense enough to stay out of the way of me coach. It t'ain't sensible, I tell ye.'' The landlady's son answered the driver's complaint with one of his own about missing his supper while having to hold a horse that couldn't stand still for two seconds together . . . Blast it!

Jocelyn turned to share her amusement with Mr. Fletcher. He had gone into the inn. She yawned and looked up to see the moon rising in the darkening sky. It would be nice when she could go to bed and draw the covers up to her chin. The viburnum breathed out sweetness.

The gravel crunched beneath booted feet. Looking toward the drive, Jocelyn saw a man with a valise in his hand enter the carriage. At first she thought this might be the owner of the splendid equipage but soon realized that someone who could afford to travel in such style wouldn't be carrying his own baggage. She watched idly to see who else would come out. Perhaps it would be a duke, regal and perfectly dressed. Or a general, uniform brilliant with gold lace and medals.

She yawned once more and was about to turn away when the door opened again, shedding a yellow rectangle of light onto the drive. A couple came out of the inn. The man wore a tall hat and a voluminous cloak. The girl who leaned on his arm was also wearing a cloak, the hood up. The groom let go of the saddled horse, which promptly began to eat the flowers in pots by the door, and leapt to open the door for the couple. The man, who Jocelyn now saw moved like someone who was very tired, stood back to let the girl enter first. He stopped to talk to the driver, who touched his hat with the handle of his whip.

"Right you are, sorr. We'll not stop for nothin'."

The groom offered his hand to the man, and he leaned heavily upon it to get up into the carriage. The carriage door closed.

The groom then saw what the horse was doing and caught at the reins. The horse moved cannily away at the last instant just as if it were playing with him.

The traveling chaise started forward with a great creak and many rattles from the harness.

The restive horse wanted to follow and the groom snatched again at the reins, alternately cursing it and pleading with it to stand still. Suddenly a hatless man emerged from the inn and leapt onto the horse. Even as it reared up, the rider snatched the reins from the air. The groom shouted wordlessly as the rider brought the horse under control.

As the horse leapt and curvetted, the rider shouted, "It was Helena! In the coach! I'll get her!" All four hooves came down at once. Fletcher's heels touched the animal's rounded sides, and they were away.

CHAPTER THIRTEEN

JOCELYN STOOD GAPING IN THE GARDEN. ONLY SECONDS HAD passed since Mr. Fletcher had come running out, seen the horse before him, mounted, and ridden off, seemingly all in one motion. Her first thought was to wonder if he left behind enough money to pay their bill. She walked quickly toward the garden gate, even as she heard the landlady's son calling his mother.

Inside, lamps blazed and everyone spoke at once, with the exception of the man who had joined Fletcher and Jocelyn while at table. He stood in the shadows under the stairs, Arnold close beside him. Jocelyn saw her cousin wore a wide grin, but she did not have time then to investigate what mischief he'd gotten into.

Quite a few men with ale pots in their hands created a general confusion, and more were coming out of the taproom to observe the commotion. Mrs. Pierce stood in the middle of the room, her hands beating the air as she begged for silence. "Please, Colonel! Please, Jack! Gentlemen, please!" No one paid her any heed.

"Just stole him, Mum! He just stole him, right outta my hand." Mrs. Pierce's son stared stupidly into his hand as if expecting to see the young horse there.

"My horse, by God! What's he done with my horse? I mean to say, can the fellow ride?" A very tall gentleman in a mustard-colored coat and gray riding breeches who seemed to be all arms and legs appeared more confused than angered by the theft of his horse.

145

"Can he ride? I should say!" A fat young man bounced up and down like a barking terrier. "Saw everything from the window. Jumped into the saddle like he was born to it." Several voices clamored in agreement.

Mrs. Pierce saw Jocelyn. "You!" she said, as if surprised to see her. The crowd followed their hostess's gaze. Though, all told, there were only ten observers, Jocelyn felt as if hundreds of fascinated eyes surveyed her.

"Yes, of course." She did not know whether to claim ignorance of what had occurred or to join in the discussion, which seemed to be divided between concern for the colonel's horse and admiration for Mr. Fletcher's horsemanship. She said calmly, "I wonder, could you tell me why my companion has left?"

"Your companion! I knew he wasn't your brother." Mrs. Pierce's mouth tightened to a thin line. One of her customers nudged another in his well-padded ribs. Jocelyn saw the men's expressions change from excited interest in the accomplice of a thief to another kind of interest. Her color rose.

Mrs. Pierce looked at their faces and said in a voice clear enough to penetrate the liquored minds of her customers, "Jack, tell Bob to hand drinks around to all our good friends. Free of charge."

At that there was a rush toward the taproom. Mrs. Pierce touched the colonel placatingly on the arm. "I apologize to you, sir. I don't know quite what to do about your horse at the moment but . . ."

The tall gentleman followed her words with jerky nods of his head as if they were written on the air before him. He interrupted her with an emphatic, "Nothing to be done . . . nothing, nothing. I mean to say, if the fellow can ride, it's all right, then. Isn't it, hey, isn't it?" He walked away into the taproom, arguing with himself, alternately nodding and shaking his head.

Facing the landlady, Jocelyn braced herself for an ugly scene ending in expulsion from the inn. The night that seemed so pleasant when viewed from the garden had an uninviting air when she thought of sleeping out in it.

Mrs. Pierce said, "I'm sorry, miss. I shouldn't have said anything in front of that lot. Give you and me both a bad repute. I think, maybe, you should tell me what kind of trouble it is?''

Jocelyn blinked at the landlady's magnanimity. "I will," she promised, "but first could you tell me what made my . . . friend leave so suddenly. And on someone else's horse?''

"Why, nothing in the world! I was merely chatting away to him, and he ran for the door like the bailiff was coming behind him." She seemed a little put out. As an innkeeper, and a woman, she was used to being treated with some respect.

"What were you talking of?"

"Nothing important. I told him of my business, bad though it's been, and then, to give him a hint, I told him about the young lady His Lordship brung in this evening."

"A young lady?" Jocelyn asked to prompt her. Could this really be Helena, or was Mr. Fletcher chasing a wild goose?

"That's right. This young lady, out on the road all alone, fainted right in front of Lord Ashspring's carriage. Well, it's a marvel she wasn't kilt outright. A regular beauty, she was, too. A good thing His Lordship found her instead of some I could name. A fine old gentleman, well known to the late Mr. Pierce's family. I told him—your 'friend'—about the girl in the hope that he'd do right by you. He should know the dangers a girl alone is heir to. A thing he's more than likely never thought of before. I know what these men are like, my dear, and my advice to you is to marry before you forget yourself.''

With a smile Jocelyn said, "It seems I'm forgotten already."

"No, now then," Mrs. Pierce said, patting the girl's shoulder. "The lad'll be back as soon as he recollects himself. Though it is strange, come to think of it, that he'd take off so after one girl when he's got another right here." She looked toward the taproom door, where two or three men, their tankards refilled, stared out at them. Giving them a cold glare, Mrs. Pierce said haughtily, "Let's go back to my parlor, where we can be private. You were going to tell me about your troubles.''

The landlady turned and then let out a little scream, pressing her hand to her white-swathed bosom. The grimy man moved out from the shadows in a lazy way Jocelyn instantly recognized from her own kitchen.

"Permit me to explain them to you, mistress," Hammond said, taking off his hat. His hair was matted with sweat and his face and hands were filthy. His clothing was a shade more disreputable than before.

"You!" Jocelyn exclaimed.

Hammond's face suddenly creased with a smile as bright as brass and twice as bold. She blushed anew with pleasure and embarrassment, a sensation of power tingling her nerve endings. Hammond only smiled like that at her.

Mrs. Pierce nearly burst with curiosity. "Another of them?" She looked at Jocelyn with renewed suspicion, mingled with new respect.

"No, indeed, ma'am," Hammond said. "I'm the only one."

Jocelyn suddenly remembered she was not overly pleased with Hammond even if she loved him. If he'd been sensible and brought Arnold and her this far, she would not now be in the lurch. "How do you come to be here, Hammond?" she asked with a lift of her chin, stepping away from his outstretched hand. "I thought you'd be in Oxford by now."

"Well, I would be," he said, his smile not fading a jot despite her reception. "If our friend's horse hadn't picked up a stone six miles back. You passed me on the road, you know."

"I didn't see you."

"I saw you, though. Our friend drives at a spanking pace. It's a pity he didn't choose better for me. Though the horse he picked up here seems to show he has some taste. I caught a ride with a carter, and counted myself lucky to get it, even if it wasn't of the quality Fletcher found."

"Heaven save us!" said Mrs. Pierce, following this conversation with a frown. "It's like a congregation!"

Just then Mr. Fletcher limped in, splashed to the eyebrows with mud. Arnold snortled and chuckled, finding the sight of his former tutor vastly amusing.

There was no time to speak before the colonel came striding out from the taproom. "Back, are you? Tell me, how far did you get? Come on, then."

Bewildered, Mr. Fletcher answered, "About a mile."

"Did he throw you?"

"Yes, sir," Mr. Fletcher said, shamed at having to admit to his poor horsemanship. The colonel came closer, his face working with excitement. Fletcher took a step back in alarm at these odd questions asked with such ferocious intensity by a man he had robbed.

"Aha!" The colonel slapped his long thigh. "Good on you, old man. Never got above half a mile, myself!"

"You mean that horse always throws people?" Jocelyn asked.

"Always, my gel. Always. Ha! My name's Tripp, old fellow, Colonel, Jordan's Cavalry, retired. Any time you feel like it, you come and stay at my place up the hill. Anybody'll point it out to you. Damn me, but you can ride!" The colonel smacked Fletcher smartly on the shoulder and said, "Good evening to you. A mile! Ha!" and left.

"Why—" Mr. Fletcher began to ask and found himself talking to a closed door.

"The colonel, poor man," said Mrs. Pierce with a click of her tongue.

Jocelyn asked anxiously, "Did you see Helena?"

"No, I rode as swiftly as I could and drew nearly even with the coach's window before that . . . beast took off in another direction. Then I was thrown." He rubbed at a tender spot on his anatomy. Looking up, he seemed to realize there was another person behind the two women. "Captain Hammond, sir! You'll help me, won't you?"

"With what?"

"With getting her back!"

"You seem to forget—" Hammond began to admonish Fletcher. Then the smile that made his face younger returned, and he said, "Well, at least she's on her way to Oxford, which is more than we can say. You *do* remember Oxford, yes?"

"Of course, but how are we to get there? Our horses won't make it without a change, and frankly, I'm about done."

The landlady said, "I can't give you horses. My last fresh pair went with His Lordship."

Turning to her, Jocelyn asked, "Colonel Tripp—does he drive as well as ride?"

"Yes," the landlady answered, relieved to be asked a direct question in the midst of so much confusion.

"Would he be willing to lend us the use of a carriage and horses?"

"I don't think he's ever refused anything to a man who can ride well."

"I'll go and ask him," Mr. Fletcher said as he sprinted for the door in a way that belied both his weariness and his bruises.

"I'll go, too," Arnold volunteered, dashing along behind his tutor before Jocelyn could stop him.

"Go along the drive to the right," Mrs. Pierce called after him. "It's only half a mile." She shook her head. "I don't know what it is that's happening, but I'll help all I can, if only to have a quiet night once the lot of you've gone."

Hammond thanked her. "Is there somewhere I can make myself more presentable?"

"Yes, you are a sight, aren't you?" she said, studying the interesting pattern of dirt on his lean face with the eyes of a mother. Mrs. Pierce again led the way back to her quarters. She showed Hammond to one of her son's rooms, and as he went along, she asked Jocelyn in a whisper, "Which one of them have you decided on?"

"I beg your pardon," Jocelyn said, unsure whether to be amused or incensed.

"Not sure yourself, are you?" Mrs. Pierce's sharp eyes saw the girl's mouth open as if in protest, only no words came out. "Or perhaps you do know. Now, take this water and soap along to him, and here's something to dry on. I'm going to start a cup of tea. It's over late for it, but I feel the need of it."

Jocelyn went down the hall and knocked timidly on the door. "Here's your water and a towel."

Hammond opened his door, shielding himself behind it. "Just a moment," he said.

When Jocelyn went in, Hammond stood with his back to the corner and held his ragged shirt in front of his half-naked body. Jocelyn saw the tear in the shirt's tail she had made under his direction. She set the jug down on a commode, hiding her smile.

"Are you feeling quite well, Hammond? Such a strenuous

evening. And it isn't over yet, I'm afraid. Oh!'' she suddenly exclaimed. ''I never made you that poultice I promised you. Please don't blame me for forgetting. I've had other things on my mind.''

''I know,'' he said softly.

''May I see your wound? I'd like to see if comfrey is the right thing to use. I think it is. It's very good for inflammation, you know.''

Hammond still held his shirt in front of his furred chest. ''There's no swelling to speak of and, well, dammit, I've been hurt before and gotten through it all right.''

''No swelling to speak of? Let me see.''

''Now listen, you're not dressed as a boy now so don't behave like one. It isn't right.'' His dark eyes traveled over her, lingering for a moment on her throat where the thin cambric of her chemise was gathered with blue ribbon above the square scoop-neck of her gown. With an effort he jerked his eyes back to her face, tinged now with a faint flush that echoed the sudden duskiness of his own skin. ''I . . . I think you'd better go.''

Jocelyn stood frozen, her body and mind both remembering with vivid sharpness the feel of Hammond's lips on hers. ''I quite see,'' she said, her voice under less than perfect control. She paused on the threshold to say, ''I shall make you that poultice regardless, but I shall send it by Mrs. Pierce.'' Jocelyn felt like skipping along the hall.

Mrs. Pierce kept comfrey in plenty and was very interested in Jocelyn's method of making the poultice. She sat at a table in the large kitchen, watching the girl while she sipped her tea from a thick mug. ''Salt?'' she asked. ''Doesn't that sting?''

''Yes,'' Jocelyn said complacently. ''It's very good.''

While Jocelyn worked, Mr. Fletcher came back. ''All's well,'' he said with a slight hiccup. ''Colonel Tripp's an excellent gentleman. He lent us a pair of bays and a coach.''

''Not the Glendening Bays!'' Mrs. Pierce said in wonder.

''I suppose so.''

''Will wonders never cease? You must have impressed him.''

Mr. Fletcher looked around. ''Where's Hammond?'' he asked with just a hint of suspicion.

"He's cleaning up," Jocelyn said. "Where's Arnold?"

"Out with the horses, I assume. He seemed fascinated."

"Bring him in, won't you? And see he washes. You might take a moment to do the same."

"Yes. Yes, indeed. I can't see Helena while looking like this," Mr. Fletcher said, looking down at his coat, encrusted now with drying mud. He brushed at it ineffectually and then repeated his statement. "No, I don't think she'd have much to say to me if I ask her to marry me again, looking like this."

"So!" Mrs. Pierce exclaimed. "I'm glad to have it straight at last. You're in love with the other girl, and the other man's in love with this one."

Mr. Fletcher looked at Jocelyn, placidly stirring some mess in a large pot on the stove. She didn't look to be in love. Mr. Fletcher thought about Helena and the glorious glow in her eyes when he caught her glance in the church. No radiance filled Jocelyn's eyes that he could see. Mr. Fletcher decided the landlady simply tried to make sense of the people in her inn, and a love intrigue or two was the best explanation for their admittedly odd behavior. Mr. Fletcher shrugged and forgot the peculiar idea.

Jocelyn, embarrassed, said, "Hammond's in the room down there to the right." Mr. Fletcher immediately set off to find him.

As soon as she spread the warmed, mashed roots in clean linen, she carried it, some strips of cloth, and another pitcher of water down to the men. The door was closed. It must not have been well made, for she could hear their voices.

Mr. Fletcher was saying, "I don't agree. Nobody has a higher opinion of Miss Burnwell than myself, but we should leave her here, where she's safe—or better yet, send her home. It's been easy thus far. I think it is going to be dangerous in Oxford."

Jocelyn expected Hammond to agree to leave her behind and so was surprised when he said, "No, she might be of use. I can't see walking up to a strange young man, especially an Oxford man, and coolly demanding his coat."

"Why not? Tom's quite likely to give it to you without asking any questions. I know this family, you see. Haven't I lived with them for almost a year?"

"You're forgetting about Miss Fain. Jocelyn will certainly be necessary when you find her again. I've no wish to sound like a prosy old woman—"

Coldly Mr. Fletcher said, "Miss Fain is my concern."

"And Miss Burnwell is mine. I can't send her home alone. *I* can't go with her, you can't go with her, and your Miss Fain cannot go wandering over the English countryside without somebody to lend, well, countenance. If you mean to marry the girl—"

"I do!"

"Very good. You can't, however, sprout up on your family doorstep with an unaccompanied female. Not if you want them to accept her. I've been out of the country a long time, but I don't think things have changed that much."

The weight of the pitcher grew by the moment. Jocelyn was reluctant to break in on this very interesting conversation. It was either that, however, or drop half a gallon of water in the hall. Her hands being full, she tapped lightly at the door with her toe.

Mr. Fletcher hastened to take Jocelyn's burdens from her. Hammond, completely dressed, his coat sponged clean, thanked her solemnly for the poultice. "I'm sure it's very useful."

"Can't I help you with it?"

Hammond said, "I'm sure Mr. Fletcher will be happy to help me." He caught his colleague's eye, and Mr. Fletcher made haste to assure Jocelyn that he would. A short silence filled the room. "Well," Hammond said. "Don't you want to freshen yourself? We have another four hours of driving before we reach Oxford. Once we're there—"

"I think we should rest here," Jocelyn said firmly. "If we leave now, we'll get to Oxford at midnight. You won't accomplish a thing by waking Tom up in the middle of the night."

"What about Helena?" Mr. Fletcher asked.

"There's nothing we can do for her now. Arriving exhausted won't make it any easier to find her. Let's sleep now and leave early. Before dawn if you like."

The men exchanged glances. "Yes," Hammond said. "What a reasonable idea."

"I'm glad you agree with me." She left them and went at once to Arnold. He was eating a large piece of cake under

Mrs. Pierce's indulgent eye. Jocelyn told her of the change in plans. The landlady bustled away to arrange a bed for her.

"Arnold, I want you to do something for me. We're going to be spending a few hours here. Can you stay awake?"

"Why?"

"I'm afraid Hammond and Mr. Fletcher may try to leave without us."

"They couldn't!"

"They might. You've got to prevent it. You're the only one who can. I can't sleep in their room to watch them."

Appealing to Arnold's sense of adventure, and his vanity, did not fail. It must also be confessed that the notion of spying on his tutor appealed powerfully to his baser instincts. He drew himself up to his full four foot eleven and all but saluted. "I'll sit in front of their door all night."

"I think you'd be more useful inside the room. There's a window."

"Right. I won't sleep a wink; I took a fine rest in the wagon." He dashed away. After a moment he returned. "Jocelyn? This isn't about my poaching, is it?"

"No," she said with a laugh. "If only it were that simple."

"Then what are we doing here? Who is Hammond, really?" he persisted.

That was what she wanted to know. "Everything's very complicated, Arnold. We're trying to . . . find Helena. She ran away. The shock of her brother's . . . death and . . ."

"Oh, don't tell me if you don't want to. I'm on your side, though. No matter what."

Before he could evade her, she kissed him on the forehead. "Thank you, Arnold. I don't know what I'd do without you." Hammond and Fletcher would find it almost impossible to escape with Arnold in the room. He was notorious for waking up at the slightest noise. Even a door shutting in the hall outside his room was enough to wake him at the priory.

CHAPTER FOURTEEN

━━━◆━━━

THE COLONEL'S HORSES PULLED THEIR CONVEYANCE AS IF IT and the four people in it weighed nothing at all. They seemed to enjoy the work, shaking their heads and lashing their tails as their hooves rang on the dawnlit road.

Jocelyn's head nodded almost as soon as they waved farewell to Mrs. Pierce, who seemed glad to be rid of them. Before sleep took her, Jocelyn reflected that they had at least given the Dog's Jug Inn a topic of conversation that would last for weeks.

When she woke up, she found Hammond's arm about her. His hand warmed her entire body from its innocent place on her shoulder. She kept her eyes tightly closed to savor the sensation. When she opened her eyes at last, the first thing she saw was Arnold snoozing on the opposite seat. Despite this vision, she at first felt so contented that she did not wish to move. Only a glimpse of her bonnet, hastily folded and shoved between Hammond's thigh and the side panel, brought her upright.

He smiled at her and lifted his arm from around her as she yawned and stretched. "I'm glad you had a second chance to rest. Didn't you sleep at the inn? Arnold kept good watch, you know," he said, laughingly. He passed her the now sadly crushed bonnet.

Jocelyn pushed at her hair. Her neck felt stiff. "I knew he would. It's just the kind of thing he does well." It did not take great insight to see he was laughing at her. All the same, she could not feel ashamed of her precautions. It would have been just like Hammond to leave her at the inn.

She put on her bonnet. The cool night air brushed over her skin, and she was glad of her duffle-cloth coat but wished she wore a warmer dress. "How far have we to go?" she asked.

"About an hour."

Once awake Jocelyn noticed Hammond's growing tension. No longer encumbered with her sleeping body, he leaned forward, his elbows on his thighs. His whole attention remained riveted on the tiny forward window, half-blocked by Mr. Fletcher on the box. Hammond moved restlessly, crossing and uncrossing his arms and legs, unable to sit still. He drummed his fingers on his knee and fiddled with his cravat. He did not look at Jocelyn, and he did not smile. She began to feel even colder.

As they crested a hill, she saw the gray spires of the university city in the distance. She felt nervous at entering a city of twelve thousand. Only three or four thousand people lived in Libermore. She sometimes thought she knew them all by sight. Her nerves were calmed by remembering she had only two purposes in coming to Oxford and both could be readily accomplished. The first was to find Helena before Helena found her brother, and that Mr. Fletcher would no doubt accomplish for her.

The other purpose was to get the coat for Hammond and then see him go on his way without saying any of the things she wished she could say. Cudgel her brain as she might, Jocelyn could think of no way to begin the conversation she wished to have with him. She considered saying, "Hammond, could you . . . ?" Or perhaps, "Would you . . . ?" Or even "Might you . . . ?" She could get no further.

Her task was the more difficult because Jocelyn could not even be certain herself what she wanted. She only knew they must not part without something said on her side or on his. Jocelyn was afraid that if she did not begin, he would not, and he would go, leaving this empty space inside her.

As they came up a hill, the horses slowing, they passed a great ruined building created of closely piled gray stones, tall and dour. Jocelyn looked up, fascinated. A square block with a mansard edge protruded from one corner of a long and high wall. Tiny windows peered blackly from the wall like old, blind eyes. Her spirits damp as wet gunpowder, Jocelyn dared to reach for Hammond's hand. He returned the pressure she gave it but did not cease to look forward. The light of the dawn spread out from beneath low clouds, like fingers lifting a drapery.

"The Castle," Arnold said sepulchrally, sitting up. "Mother's . . ." he yawned. "Mother's very interested in it, she said."

They came down the hill and clattered across a bridge. Jocelyn saw that the foundation stone date was 1771. Mr. Fletcher gradually slowed the horses. Stopping, the horses steaming in the cool air, he jumped down and came to the door. "It will be full light in a few minutes," he said to Hammond. "Shall I drive to Tom's?"

"It's early yet," Jocelyn said. "Tom's not one to rise first, I'm afraid."

"Breakfast," Hammond ordered, with a cheerful yawn. His eyes shifted right and left as he searched the streets. Few people were about yet, although apprentices were taking down the shutters on shop fronts. "I think our first action should be to eat. I'm hungry. Aren't you, Jocelyn?"

"Breakfast!" Arnold exclaimed eagerly.

"Breakfast!" Mr. Fletcher said in disgust. "I don't want to eat! I want to find Helena!"

Now Hammond smiled at his companions. "What better way to find her than to go to the most popular inn and order breakfast. Certainly the thought of food will occur to His Lordship. You're an Oxford man. What's the best inn?"

They ate their breakfast at the Marigold, a bustling inn near the turnpike. Every few minutes, even while the sun's beams were level through the narrow streets, fast coaches pulled up before the door. A huge shout would come through the noise of the gathered passengers as the driver called the coach's name.

"Who's for Bew's?" A rush for the door, ale half-swallowed, a piece of toast still between sticky fingers, crying babies in tow. "Burford, Witney, Oxford and Trane Fly! Ten shillings!" Coins rattled across the table toward the pot-boy, or barmaid, too many packages grasped in a single hand, and a coat only half on.

Jocelyn, Arnold, and Mr. Fletcher sat in the midst of this

manic activity, half-empty plates before them. Arnold still ate. Jocelyn watched the people as they entered or left, laughing at their folly or pursing her lips in sympathy over their difficulties. She looked on in amazement as a driver, huge in his many-caped coat, ate an entire breakfast, enough to feed the Luckem family, in the five minutes between pulling up and driving off.

Mr. Fletcher, however, never took his grim gaze off Hammond, who was trying to talk to a maid who stood behind the bar. She shook her capped head vehemently in answer to his questions, while expertly circulating trays stacked with mugs under a tap. Hammond touched her arm, acquiring for just one second the woman's full attention. Fletcher knew exactly the look on Hammond's face then. It would be compounded of an appealing twinkle in the eyes, and a debonair smile that said he wished there might be more time to talk. Fletcher often used it himself, finding it most useful when the woman wasn't particularly attractive. It was a common trick, and just then Fletcher felt it to be a cheap one.

He could see the barmaid's broad face turn pinker as she handed the tray over to another girl. Empty-handed for a moment, the barmaid ran her hands over the crisp white apron that outlined her firm figure. She licked her lips as she spoke, giving Hammond a sidelong look as good as an invitation. Hammond leaned forward, his elbows on the bar, nodding. Watching, Fletcher tried to hold his impatience in check for a few more minutes.

The other maid stood over him, and he looked up, surprised. She held the weighty tray easily on one hand and asked, "D'you or the lady want ale?" Smiling at Jocelyn, she added, "We got small beer." Jocelyn returned the smile but signaled refusal.

"No, no, take it away." Fletcher waved impatiently and tried to look around her to watch Hammond. The other man was gone from beside the bar. "Damn!" Fletcher said, slamming his hand onto the table, making the plates jump.

The maid sniffed and said clearly, "I wouldn't have him for nine hundred pounds," before walking away with a switch of her generous hips.

"What is it?" Jocelyn whispered across the table.

"Hammond! He's done us, again!"

"Done us?" Jocelyn said faintly. She glanced around for Hammond but did not see him. "Where . . . ?" she began to say.

Fletcher flew across the room, pulling his purse from his pocket. Jocelyn put on her coat and bedraggled bonnet, sighing. It seemed His Majesty's servants were never allowed a peaceful meal. "Come on, Arnold."

Coming back to the table, Fletcher said, "You're ready; good! Look, he can't have gone far. We'll see if we can follow him. Come on!" They forced their way through a press of people entering the inn from a large, muddied coach just arrived from London. The passengers, tired and hungry, did not take kindly to Mr. Fletcher's impatient shoving and curses burst in the air around Jocelyn's head. She felt like a beaten egg by the time she stood outside the inn. She settled her coat once more on her shoulders and tightened her grasp upon Arnold's hand.

The wheels of the numerous carriages rattled over the cobbles like dice in the hands of mad gamblers. Mr. Fletcher stood at her elbow, breathing hard. He looked up and down the street, Jocelyn's head turning to follow his gaze. She saw no sign of Hammond. Neither, apparently, did Fletcher.

He began to stalk up the street, his coat open and thrust behind him. People gave him strange looks as they passed. Jocelyn and Arnold could only try to keep up. Then he stopped, stared across the street in disbelief, and ran out into the middle of the road.

The driver of a dray packed with hogsheads stood up with the effort of halting his huge shire horses before they ran over the tutor. The driver called after him in wounded inquiry. People stopped and stared after him, and the consensus was that he was one of the insane men who belonged to the college.

Catching her breath, Jocelyn saw what Mr. Fletcher glimpsed through the crowd. A coach stood on the other side of the broad street. A coach with a green and gold coat of arms upon the door.

Jocelyn put one foot out to follow Mr. Fletcher off the pavement. But her waist was grasped by strong hands, and she was lifted and swung around. Only one man's touch ever filled her with such joy. Hammond, with a face full of laugh-

ter, put her down. "Come on," he said. "Fletcher's on his
way to his happiness. Now it's time for mine."

She and Arnold followed down a dark alleyway. The boy
copied him in vaulting a low wall. Jocelyn stopped. "Hammond," she said. "I have followed and will follow you nearly
everywhere. As you pointed out before, however, I am not
in boy's clothes now."

"I'd forgotten that," he said, coming back over. Gently he
picked her up and set her on the wall. Then he sprang over
once more and as gently lifted her down. "And very fetching
your dress is, too," he said. "What I can see of it in that
coat. Speaking of coats . . ."

"Oh, yes," Jocelyn said, her spirits falling from the high
level the touch of his hands around her waist had created.
She began to walk up the alley. "Yes, let's go and find my
cousin. I'm not at all acquainted with Oxford, so I don't know
exactly which is his college. I'll recognize it when I see it, I
think. Two years ago, at my birthday, he gave me a lovely
series of prints of views around the university."

They came out into the sunshine. Jocelyn gasped with
pleasure at the sudden change of scenery. Here grass shone
brilliantly green in wide lawns, and buildings of gray stone
rose in fretwork towers. As she hurried along behind Hammond and her youngest cousin, her head turned ceaselessly
from side to side. She saw many small gardens glimmering
through iron gates that she wished she could stop and investigate. Catching quick glimpses of quiet rooms through arched
windows, she sighed. "I didn't know Oxford was like this.
It's so . . . peaceful."

Hammond said, "I'm a Cambridge man, myself."

Up the road milled a large group of scholars wearing
sleeveless gowns of some material with a faint sheen. They
wore flat caps on their heads with tassels, some short, some
long, hanging over the edge. In the center of the group stood
an older man, stooped over, the light of great intelligence in
his narrow face. The front of his gown was faced with satin
of French blue.

The younger men around him were listening to an argument between two of their company. Jeers and taunts vied
with a chorus of acclaim after each statement of a particular
point of view. They created an incredible bedlam that did not

lessen when the two debaters escalated their argument into fisticuffs.

Arnold dived right into the midst of the crowd. Hammond took Jocelyn's arm as they approached and prevented her from making her way through.

"All universities, it seems, are the same. Wait a moment, and they'll finish."

Impatiently Jocelyn freed herself. In the shifting group, she saw a tall boy, his mortarboard pushed to the extreme back of his head, revealing bushy wheat-colored hair. She waved her hand and called, "Tom—Tom Luckem!"

Her voice went unheard in the animal roar that rose when the smaller debater again launched himself at the larger. The crowd of boys formed itself into a wide ring to give the combatants room. Her eldest cousin stood on the outside, quite near to her. She went over and touched him.

Tom looked around and down. "Oh, hullo, Jocelyn. Just let me get this wager down." He reached under his gown and brought out a wallet. Passing two coins to another boy, he said, "Put this on Arabin for me, would you? I'll collect in chapel. Course he'll win; look at him! Go to it, old fellow!" The short, plump boy had his adversary down and was pummeling him blindly.

Tom laughed and Jocelyn looked at him with affection. He was a handsome boy, very tall and broad. Not only the odds-on favorite in the annual horse race, but the students generally considered that if he rowed for Oxford, Cambridge would lose with considerable humiliation. Being a Luckem, he never lacked for self-confidence, but, unlike Arnold, he never pushed in where he was not wanted, and, unlike Granville, he never assumed more superiority than demanded by his rights as an Englishman. As a consequence, he had been well liked from his earliest days at the ancient university, and this added polish to a friendly nature.

Jocelyn drew him out of the crowd and introduced him to Hammond. Tom shook hands with a nod, then said to his cousin, "Let's get out of this." He led them up stairs through a Gothic doorway just as the other boys lifted the small debater onto their shoulders and began to carry him around the courtyard, shouting, "Arabin! Arabin!"

"What about Arnold?" Jocelyn asked, looking back.

"Is he here? Oh, somebody'll shove him along to my rooms."

The dim hall's silence was intensified rather than broken by a distant voice droning on somewhere else in the building. Jocelyn looked around with interest at the vaulted ceiling and the burnished wood before becoming aware her cousin regarded her with rather an odd, almost a calculating, expression.

"So," she said brightly. "What was the argument about?"

"I don't know. Something to do with the lecture we attended. Rights of Man, or the place of God in Society, I wasn't listening particularly."

Tom's manner became hesitant. His eyes wandered to Hammond, standing beside his cousin with an air of expectancy. "I say," Tom said. "I don't mean to play elder brother, and if I'm being rude, please tell me to bridle up, but have you—er—run away?" The quick glance he shot at Hammond made his meaning clear.

"Tom! What a revolting idea! Certainly not!" Jocelyn said, perhaps a little more emphatically than was flattering to Hammond.

"I thought not. That is, you'd hardly come running to me if you had. Just wanted to be certain. And yet, that is to say, I thought you were going to stay at Libermore with my brothers while Mother and Father were in London."

"I found it necessary to change that plan. We've a new housekeeper."

"Oh?" said Tom. "Er—?"

Jocelyn expected Hammond to demand at once the blue coat with the letter in it, but he seemed willing to lean against the wall and let this conversation continue at its own pace. Jocelyn decided to request the coat herself. "Have your parents come up from London yet?"

"Yes, they arrived yesterday. Father, as you might have guessed, has spent every minute in either Bod or Ash. Mother went right to the Castle, and I don't know if she's come down yet. If you want to see them, they're coming to my room before Hall."

"No. That is, of course I'd like to see them; however, we're more interested in what they brought you."

"They didn't bring me anything."

Now Hammond came to life. His arms uncrossed, and he pushed away from the wall. Jocelyn tensed, preparing to throw herself between him and her cousin if Hammond roared into violence as he had with her when balked in the recovery of the coat. Hammond didn't move toward Tom. He only turned his eyes on Jocelyn, and she hurried into her next question. "Didn't they bring you your lucky coat?"

"Oh, I thought you meant a present."

"Then they brought it? You have it?"

"Yes. Damned glad of it, as you can . . ." Tom stepped back as his plain cousin and the man she had in tow yelped with joy. The man picked Jocelyn up and spun around with her in a fashion never before seen in the peaceful halls of Academe. From the stair came the sound of footsteps. A gray-faced lecturer looked down upon them and said in a stern whisper, "Mr. Luckem, you are aware, are you not, that ladies are not allowed in the college? Kindly ask her to stop making that noise and then remove her."

"Yes, Dr. Randall," Tom said with a reassuring wave. "We'd better go," he said to the others. He did not fail to notice that the stranger Jocelyn was with did not release her hand on the walk to Tom's rooms.

Under his cap his brain seethed with questions, and not all the learning imbibed from the great university helped him in resolving them. He knew—for it was common knowledge—that his cousin was not a pretty woman. Why, then, did she seem so confoundedly attractive today? And why did this Hammond person look at her as if she were a pretty woman? Who was this Hammond, anyway? What reason could he have for holding Jocelyn's hand? Tom began to hope none of his friends would see Jocelyn appearing and behaving so.

After the brief walk to Tom's rooms, Hammond held the coat in his hands. He felt for the bottom seam. It crinkled as he touched it. He pulled his knife from his boot, at which Tom's eyes opened wide, and slit the stitches Aunt Arasta had sewed. His fingers hesitated above the open seam. "Who sewed it together?" Hammond demanded.

"My aunt," Jocelyn said.

"Then she *must* have seen the letter!" He groped for it with shaking fingers and stared at the pale cream paper. "Here," he said, offering it to Jocelyn.

It was in French. She could only understand a few words that were the same as in English. *L'Empereur, dangereux*, and, chillingly, *Les assassins del'histoire*. She scanned the signature and was about to return the paper when she pulled it back and looked more closely at the almost illegible scrawl at the bottom of the letter. The capital *N* was plain enough, and an *l* halfway down the word. She was a certain as she could be that it said *Napoleon*.

CHAPTER FIFTEEN

MR. FLETCHER HEEDED NO ONE AND NOTHING AS HE RAN across the High Street. He ignored the outraged shouts behind him as if they were unvoiced. All his senses focused on Helena, standing on the far pavement, her cloak open and her eyes bright.

On reaching her he babbled, "Please, Helena! Please listen to me. I understand how you feel, but I can't let you go to your brother. He's a bad man; you don't know." He seized her hands, pressing them to his heart, and received his first inkling of the change in her mood when she suffered him to retain them.

"I know, dearest," she said. "Someone's explained it all to me."

"Someone?" Fletcher asked.

"It is good to see you in such spirits, Lieutenant," said a voice Fletcher instantly recognized. He turned around with a guilty start that he tried, too late, to turn into the posture of attention.

Lord Ashspring looked out his carriage door. The long ride through the night had deepened the shadows under his eyes, but a smile rested on his thin lips. It vanished when he saw the way Mr. Fletcher gawked at him. "I am surprised at you, sir," Lord Ashspring said, his voice very dry. "I have gone to a deal of trouble to bring this young lady to Oxford for your express convenience, yet I receive no thanks. I expected better of a man in your regiment."

Mr. Fletcher bowed belatedly, forced to surrender Helena's

hands. But she willingly gave one back to him when he straightened, so he was none the worse for his courtesy. "I don't understand," he said, looking between his lady and his lord.

"Exactly what I should expect you to say," Lord Ashspring said. "Indeed, whatever induced me to think you could be taken from your horses, sir, I cannot guess. It is evidently their actions alone you understand."

"Oh, please," Helena said. "Don't tease him."

"Tease him? By the Lord, I shall give him every opportunity to prove me wrong." Suddenly Lord Ashspring snapped, "Did you or did you not read the file on Mr. Fain?"

"I did, sir. Before I left for my assignment."

"Then, if you read with any attention, you shall be able to tell me a simple fact. In what year did Mr. Fain's father first go to Paris?"

"Uh . . . 1797, sir! Just before Napoleon's return from Italy."

"And how old is Miss Fain?"

Mr. Fletcher's expression uncontrollably softened as he looked at Helena. He saw her lips move and, after a moment of stunned admiration for their loveliness, realized she mouthed a number. "Uh . . . eighteen, sir! As of November of last year!" Mr. Fletcher remembered Helena's birthday very well, for it had been the first time he'd seen her.

Lord Ashspring did not miss the young lady's signal and found it necessary to resort to hiding his smile in his handkerchief. After a lengthy cough he said bitingly, "I realize, sir, that you are only in the cavalry. Had you perhaps joined the navy, or even the artillery, where some basic knowledge of mathematics is useful . . . I see that light has dawned upon you."

Though it was obvious that Mr. Fletcher was otherwise occupied, Lord Ashspring continued. "It is not difficult for a man to father a child if he is not married to a woman. It is, however, impossible if they are nowhere near each other!" Lord Ashspring wondered if he spoke too plainly for the delicate ears of young Helena Fain. He reassured himself that kissing kept her too busy to notice any mere verbal impropriety.

Lord Ashspring was willing to wait an adequate interval, though it seemed the time required to kiss a girl had lengthened from the days he fondly recalled. He was obliged not only to clear his throat but to pound upon the floor of the carriage with his stick before Mr. Fletcher raised his head.

Still Mr. Fletcher could spare no attention even for his most superior officer. "Then you forgive me for . . . my profession?" he asked Helena, looking deeply into her eyes.

Her long lashes flickered and then lifted to return his gaze. "My . . . Nicholas has always been very kind to me. He sent for me when he heard of my mother's death and my desolate condition. I owe him everything. But now that His Lordship has explained it, I can see that my gratitude cannot be as important as the prevention of the crime my bro—Nicholas is intending. And . . ."

Now Helena's face became suffused with rose, and her eyes modestly dropped. Her voice was so low that Mr. Fletcher needed to strain to hear it, and Lord Ashspring missed her words altogether. She said, "I confess to feeling for you nothing but admiration and . . . love."

Lord Ashspring, compelled once more to attempt to rouse Mr. Fletcher from a most pleasant activity, soon surrendered the futile effort and sat back on the velvet seat of his carriage. Though his expression was sour, internally he began to feel as if a fountain of kindness, long stifled, began once more to flow. The feeling was not unlike indigestion, he thought, but pleasant.

At last the lingering and envious whistle of a passerby awakened the young people. Then it was Mr. Fletcher's turn to blush as he met Lord Ashspring's eye. This was definitely not the behavior to exhibit before the man whose acerbic comments were legend at the War Office. Mr. Fletcher paused before speaking, and Helena said, "You haven't even told us how clever we were to find you so quickly."

"Yes," Mr. Fletcher said, "I'm very surprised."

His Lordship said, "I merely assumed a young man after a hard journey across half the country would want his breakfast immediately upon arriving in his destination. I still have some powers of imagination and deduction, young man."

"I suppose Jocelyn was terribly upset by my foolishness?" Helena asked. She pressed her fingers to her forehead. "I think I must have had some kind of fever, to run away so from my dearest friend. I will make it up to her. We shall have her come to stay with us, almost at once, after we are married.''

Helena looked up at Mr. Fletcher to see if he would accept this extremely broad hint and renew his offers of matrimony. She was wounded to see him looking so absent. Perhaps, she thought, he has forgotten that our engagement was broken off. If that were so, she decided she would not add to her follies by reminding Mark she had been so stupid as to set him free.

After a moment that stretched an eternity for her, Mark said, ''I can do better than that. She can be present at the wedding, if Mr. and Mrs. Luckem can spare her. Oh, you don't know . . . they've a new housekeeper.''

''They do? How wonderful,'' Helena said.

''Putting domestic details aside,'' Lord Ashspring broke in. ''Is this Jocelyn Burnwell you are speaking of?''

''Yes, my lord. She's here, in Oxford. She insisted on coming with me, to help Helena if she wanted it.'' He looked vaguely off into the middle distance. ''I thought . . . she was with me a moment ago. Maybe I left her on the other side of the road.'' He turned toward Lord Ashspring. ''Sir, Hammond is here, as well.''

''Hammond! Go bring him immediately,'' His Lordship ordered.

Jocelyn cleared books and papers off her cousin's armchair by pushing them onto the floor and sat down. Now that Hammond had found the letter, she didn't quite know what to do. She was not looking forward to meeting her aunt and uncle some one hundred miles from where she was supposed to be. She felt she betrayed their trust by leaving their home in the hands of someone of whom, after all, she knew nothing. She thought of Mr. Quigg and felt comforted by the knowledge that he, at least, could be depended upon.

Nagging at her, too, was her certainty that Hammond would shortly be leaving for London. He said as much now, asking Tom which of the many coaches they'd seen that morning was the fastest. ''It's imperative I be in London as soon as possible.''

''Well,'' Tom answered, pulling at his chin. ''It's not so much a matter of which coach does the distance in the least time. It's finding one to take you. The term's nearly up, and everyone's trying to go home. I'm staying on, until my friends and I leave for Italy.''

"Tom!" Jocelyn exclaimed, surprised out of her gloom. "You're going to Italy?"

Her cousin nodded proudly. "Yes, Mother and Father gave their permission last night. Mackensie-Clarke and I have been wanting to go for years, and now that the war is over, there's nothing to stop us. Phillips, Munro, and Harbinson are coming along as well. We'd have left already if Harbinson's mother hadn't insisted he visit her before we go. We're only waiting for him to come back.''

"How marvelous," Jocelyn said. "If you don't write to me every week, I'll never forgive you."

"We've permission to stay away three months and perhaps longer. Maybe, once I know the place, we'll go back together.''

Jocelyn looked at him with approval. His generosity pleased her more than words could express. Two years ago he'd considered her almost as big a nuisance as Arnold now did.

Hammond waited impatiently for the cousins to finish speaking before saying, "What about the coaches?''

"Oh! Yes. Well, there's Bew's Flying Machine, the Worcester Fly . . .''

Jocelyn stopped listening. She did not want to know what decision they came to, for that would tell her when Hammond would leave. To stop from thinking about it, she took up a newspaper that lay on an oaken bookcase, scarcely serving its purpose, for the majority of the books were strewn about the floor. Jocelyn looked at the front page.

It announced in bold type that she held in her hand *Jackson's Oxford Journal* and bid all young men to remember their Maker in the days of their youth. The paper was divided between reports of the sinking of a coal barge, the visit by the Regent, a student protest against the new lecture system, and discreet advertisements. Moving her hands so that more light from the window behind her fell on the paper, she opened it, noticing that the pages were already cut and felt glad that Tom took an interest in the city. She read with great attention, yet the print blurred before her eyes.

Tom, remembering with a snap of his fingers that his cousin and her companion might appreciate refreshment, went out to yell down the staircase for his fag. Hammond took advantage of the boy's absence and approached Jocelyn.

He stood looking at her tangled swirl of dark hair, admiring the gleams of red where the sun touched it. Jocelyn, feeling his gaze, smiled up, and he looked into her gray eyes fringed with dark lashes. She laid the paper on her lap, and her lips curved into a calm smile of polite interest.

He did not speak. A look gleamed in his eyes that made Jocelyn's breath come short. Her smile faded, a faint frown between her brows. He opened his mouth to speak, and Jocelyn felt her heart catch. He said, "Good God, what's that?"

Hammond snatched the paper from Jocelyn's grasp and stood staring at the newsprint. Jocelyn's disappointment was tempered by curiosity and alarm. She stood up, touching his arm and looking over it at the paper. "What are you looking at?" she asked.

"The Czar! He's here!"

"Of course, I know . . ." She felt the room begin to spin as every drop of blood drained from her face.

Hammond threw upon her a look of savagery that consorted oddly with the utter deadness of his voice. "You knew!"

"Oh, Hammond," she said, her fingers tightening on his arm. "Everything's been happening so fast—Helena, Mr. Fain, Mr. Fletcher . . . you. I got muddled. I told Mr. Fletcher that Fain was coming here for that . . . to kill." Her voice dropped to an apologetic whisper. "I forgot to tell you."

Hammond nodded to everything she said, his teeth tearing at his lips. "You knew. You knew Fain was coming here. You knew the Czar and the Prince were coming here. And you forgot to tell me! What in God's name did you think I've been doing all this time?"

Jocelyn could only shake her head.

"Good God," he said again, staring at the words in smudged newsprint. "It's tonight. There's no time to prepare . . . no time to send a message to London for help. There's only me."

"I thought you wanted an opportunity to—"

"To what?" Hammond said, looking at her with hard eyes. "To play a lone hand again? I've had enough of that. One of the reasons I came back to England was to feel . . . I don't know . . . a part of something more than myself. I was going to take that letter straight to the Old Man. I wouldn't mind being in the forefront of the battle again, but alone? Oh, no." His wry smile came back to his face. "I want help, all I can get. But there's none to be had. So alone it must be."

"Not quite," piped a third voice. Hammond and Jocelyn looked around, startled. Tom and Arnold stood side by side in the doorway. "We'll help," said Tom. In their eyes Jocelyn saw with alarm that sparkle of recklessness that seemed a peculiarly Luckem attribute.

Tom said, "I'm sure to get plenty of others along. Just tell us where to go and what to do."

"Tom," Jocelyn protested. "You don't know anything about it."

"There's some sort of dustup coming, am I right? Well, my friends and I are always ready for that kind of sport. Horse racing and such is fine. I like it. I'm good at it. It's just grown a trifle old."

"All right, then," Hammond said. "I'll tell you the story."

The boys came in and sat by Hammond, watching the older man with fascination. An exchange of looks, the words "Is that so? Well, the old devil," and a low whistle were their only response to the information that the vicar of their community had turned out to be a thoroughgoing scoundrel. Inwardly Arnold rejoiced. At the very least, this meant no more boring sermons until Libermore found a new vicar.

When Tom again offered himself and his friends, Hammond asked for information about the building where the prince's dinner was to be held. Tom pulled out several books about the university, one of which contained a map of the Radcliffe Camera, a famous and unusual octagonal structure.

"Nobody's been allowed near the place since preparations began last week. Philly Munro told me he passed by the other day and saw crates and crates of gold plates being carried in. It's across from the Bodleian Library and All Souls, and Brasenose is right down the way so they can't keep students away from there altogether. Of course, they pulled all the books out of Radcliffe and piled them into Bod. Father complained about the trouble he was having finding what he wanted.''

At this Jocelyn made another effort to reach her cousins through their excitement. "Tom," she said. "What will your parents say?"

"Oh, that's a good idea. You should talk to them, Mr. Hammond. Mother's a bang at military tactics, from her studies.''

"I don't think we need trouble them."

Jocelyn sat down in the armchair again, defeated. "Won't it be dangerous?" she said, half to herself.

"Yes," Hammond said, not looking at her. "Fain could be very dangerous. That's why I'm going to use Tom to spot him and not you."

"What?" Jocelyn exclaimed.

"I've only seen the man from the far end of a church. I don't know him near to, and he may be disguised. Tom will spot him for me, won't you, boy?"

"Yes, sir." Tom's expression was mingled seriousness and delight in the fun of the thing.

"You can't!" Jocelyn exclaimed. "I've been beside you since the beginning. You can't push me out with a pat on the head now.''

"It will be too dangerous for you, and I want you to stay here. Please, don't argue, Jocelyn. I won't be able to do my duty if you're in danger."

Jocelyn found it difficult to press her point when the reason for his viewpoint was so flattering. She found herself left with nothing to say.

"What about me?" Arnold said, sitting up straight in an attempt to look older.

"You're to stay and protect your cousin." The boy looked as if he were about to explode in protest. A stern glance from Hammond silenced him.

Tom looked between his cousin and the stranger with narrowed eyes. It looked to him as if Mr. Hammond were flirting with Jocelyn. He didn't exactly disapprove, but he didn't want them to do it in his rooms. With relief, he heard a knock at his door. "That'll be Grassmore with the tea," Tom said, going to let his fag in. They couldn't possibly flirt and have tea, he thought innocently. "Mr. Fletcher!" he said, falling back into the room.

"Helena!" Jocelyn said, standing up and holding out her arms to her friend.

Helena released Mr. Fletcher's hand and embraced Jocelyn tenderly. "I'm sorry," she said. "I was wrong to frighten you so. I can't tell you what I must have been thinking. It was like some horrible dream where every friend is an enemy. Please say you forgive me."

"Of course. Please sit in this chair. Really, Tom," Jocelyn said, turning on her cousin and wiping away moisture from her eyes. "You should keep your room in better trim. Where are we all to sit?"

"This will do for me," Mr. Fletcher said, sitting on the worn rug near Helena's small feet. He took her hand, and she smiled down on him. Hammond cleared his throat.

"Then . . . all is well between you?" Jocelyn said hesitantly.

The look of pure happiness on both faces told her that their problems were settled. "I was so foolish," Helena said. "It's all been made clear to me now. My bro— Mr. Fain is no relation to me after all."

"No relation?"

"No. He is only my stepbrother. I didn't know that. I was only a baby when my mother married his father. I don't remember Mr. Fain, my stepfather, at all. He died when I was four years old. Besides, this is war, in a way, isn't it? Though I wasn't born here, I now feel English to the core." Mr. Fletcher kissed her hand passionately.

"How do you know all this now?" Jocelyn asked, much moved.

"Lord Ashspring told me."

"Who?" Hammond asked of Fletcher.

"You know," Fletcher said cryptically.

Hammond's eyebrows went up as his eyes opened wide. "The Old Man," he whispered reverently. "Thank heaven. Where is he? I have news to give him."

"He's down in his coach. The stairs were too much for him. Hammond, he doesn't look very well."

"He's all but indestructible, and you know it." Hammond started for the door.

"Oh," Fletcher added as an afterthought. "Remember he's a lord now." Hammond nodded as he went out.

Jocelyn said, "Is that the 'Lordship' you mentioned before, Mr. Fletcher?"

"Yes, Lord Ashspring. The man who has done more for England these last twenty years than all the army and navy blokes, for all their bombast."

"And more for us," Helena said gently, squeezing Mr. Fletcher's shoulder.

Arnold's eyes were nearly out of his head with wonder at the revelations before him. Tom, never Mr. Fletcher's pupil, tried to look blasé but only succeeding in appearing disgusted.

In the doorway stood a thin young man with broken glasses, a tea tray trembling in his hands. Jocelyn smiled at him and with another swoop of her arm cleared off the low table in the center of the room. "Set it here, dear," she said.

"Grassy," Tom demanded. "Get more cups."

"Yessur," his fag replied, his eyes never leaving Jocelyn.

"Show me where they are," she said. "I'll help you wash them out."

When she saw him on his way upstairs, three cups hanging from his hooked fingers, Jocelyn went outside. She crossed the green quadrangle and passed under an arched doorway. The dark coach was drawn up a short distance down the street, horses weary in the shafts. Hammond stood outside it, nodding at someone inside. She approached quietly. "Yes," she heard Hammond say. "That's best. Thank you, my lord, thank you."

He sounded very happy. Jocelyn sighed. He evidently was receiving the recognition and reinstatement he craved. She wished that the thing she wanted was so easily expressed and so readily granted. It was useless now even to attempt to make it clear. Hammond would be on his way shortly to defend Britain's interest abroad, and whether he went to France or the Kingdom of Peking, she would have no place in his life.

Jocelyn walked to the end of the street. She didn't want Hammond to think she spied on him. When she came back, passing the carriage for the second time, she heard a voice call from inside it. "Young woman." She paused, not certain if she heard correctly. "Young woman, come closer."

Approaching warily, Jocelyn stopped before the crested door. She could not see the occupant but remembered the tiredness conveyed by the single glimpse she'd had of him at the inn.

"What is your name?" the voice asked, rising a tone as if under some stress.

"Jocelyn Burnwell, sir." Jocelyn peered in the window and saw only an outline of her interrogator, as the curtains on the far side of the coach were drawn.

"So." That was all. Just one thin breath that scarcely reached her ears. Yet Jocelyn felt a shiver go through her at the sound. It was as if the man inside knew everything about her and was made unhappy by the knowledge. She wondered what Hammond had said and how she could correct the mistaken impression the man in the coach must have of her.

"Oh, please . . ." she began.

The man inside the carriage did not listen. He said, "Tonight I am to attend His Royal Highness at his festivities. There are few things I would dislike more. However, when a sovereign, or someone who might as well be a sovereign, singles you out for honors, it is best to seem grateful. Although no women are to be allowed to join the main party, I am given to understand there is to be a gallery arranged for spectators. If you would like it . . . if it would please you . . . I can arrange for you to be there. It will be tedious, I am certain, but women, especially young women, admire such spectacles. You may bring your young friend Miss Fain, if she wishes it."

"Thank you. I'd like that very much, my lord." She rarely did such a thing, but Jocelyn curtsied deeply to the man in the carriage.

"I suppose your mother taught you that."

"Yes, sir. She did."

"Some day . . . some day you shall tell me of her." A cane thumped the carriage floor. The driver shook his reins, and Jocelyn stepped back.

CHAPTER SIXTEEN

ABOVE THE CROWD ROSE THE VAST COLUMNED ROUNDNESS of the Radcliffe Camera. The people were waiting to see their prince and the foreign czar accompanied by his fierce, legendary guards, the Cossacks. Between the crowd and the building stood a circle of students, their strong young arms linked. Despite the eager pushing of the raucous crowd, the circle remained unbroken, for an arm that can lift fifty pounds of books can resist pressure for a long time. In their black gowns they looked like a circle of pre-Roman monoliths. At least, so remarked Mr. Luckem to Mrs. Luckem as they looked out of the library's windows across the bay.

The road to the Camera was open and empty. Occasionally a member of the crowd would be forced off the pavement and step onto the street, but he quickly rejoined the others. Anyone who wanted to approach the building more closely would have to walk up that single, unblocked street and pass the man and boy who waited at the head of the crowd. Spectators, the lucky few allowed to watch the royal dinner from inside the building, passed the stern-eyed monitors only after showing them an official invitation. Even with the cream-colored paper, each spectator underwent a gaze so intense the innocent flushed like the guilty.

Security was not lax inside the building, either, for two guards with a list of guests stood just inside the door crossing off the names of those who entered. It must, however, be confessed that those inside felt more concern for the golden dinner service than the health of the royalty about to arrive.

Though on occasion madmen shot at the Prince Regent, no one had succeeded in murdering a ruler of England since Richard III died on Bosworth Field. The stewards in the rotunda were not about to fuss over the outside chance that the future George IV would be next. They did not think about Czar Alexander at all.

Mr. Fletcher tried very hard to get them to think about the Czar. Polite bureaucrats kindly did not let him see that they thought of him only as another maniac. Between his exhaustion and their passivity, Mr. Fletcher felt as if he were swimming uphill in a syllabub. Even invoking the names of Lord Ashspring and the Lords of the Admiralty did not move the smooth faces of the officials. They seemed to feel that czars and such should take care of themselves.

"I mean to say," one gloriously uniformed and bemedaled individual said, "he's a foreigner or something, isn't he?"

Jocelyn did not ask Helena if she would go with her to see the royal party that evening. She could think of no polite way of asking if Helena would like to watch while Nicholas Fain was arrested. She knew Jocelyn wanted to go, for she overheard her friend telling Hammond of the kindness of His Lordship.

When Jocelyn came over to her, Helena said, her face hidden as she rummaged in her bag, "I'll help you to freshen your dress. I can pull the ribbons off this nightgown. We'll put them in your hair. You shouldn't wear a hat, I think. I'll brush my cloak and you can borrow that, too. Just don't take it off. That dress . . . not at all the right thing for such an occasion."

Jocelyn found it hard to concentrate on clothes while Hammond, Mr. Fletcher, and Tom made plans for the protection of the Czar. She tried once to tell them that Mr. Fletcher could identify Mr. Fain, though it might not be tactful for Fletcher to do it, considering the relationship he'd conceived with Helena. Tom was not necessary to their plan. The men only brushed her logic aside, Tom throwing her a glance that told her he did not appreciate her help.

When the men left to make arrangements, Helena went to work on her friend. "You must look your best. Someone important might take notice of you."

As Helena attempted the nearly impossible task of taming

Jocelyn's curls, she said, "I've been meaning to do this for
an age. I don't think your hair can be as difficult to manage
as you think." She tugged hard at a knot, and Jocelyn shrank
away from the comb.

"I shouldn't go, Helena. It's wrong to leave you alone.
Especially tonight."

Her eyes focused obstinately on the top of Jocelyn's head,
Helena said, "I shan't really be alone. Not with Arnold here.
I can't give way to self-pity and tears with him around, can
I?"

Arnold, lying on the floor with a large book spread open
before him, lifted his eyes at this mention of his name. Seeing
the two women employed on girlish matters, he kept reading.

Jocelyn reached up and silently patted Helena's hand in
sympathy. Helena went on more softly, "When Mark comes
back, he'll take me to the inn where Lord Ashspring is staying. He bespoke rooms for us. He's very kind."

"He seemed a little abrupt to me."

"I'm sure he has many things to occupy him . . . now."
Helena worked in silence for another moment. "There, that
is very prettily done." She looked around the small room.
"You can see yourself, more or less, in the window. Why
don't men ever have looking glasses? Oh, wait. Here's a knife.
It's covered with crumbs. Let me clean it off."

Jocelyn peered at the shining blade of the bread knife. Her
image wavered, here short, there elongated, but visible.
Rather than allowing her friend's hair to curl madly all over
her head, Helena had drawn it smoothly back from her forehead and set a peach ribbon to hold the massy waves behind
her small ears. A few errant strands escaped, springing
charmingly over Jocelyn's forehead. "Oh, that is nice! I look
almost . . ."

Arnold made a gagging sound and, wiggling over onto his
back, expired.

"You look lovely," Helena said defiantly. "And everyone
who sees you will think so, too." A nearby clock chimed the
hour. The girls listened, counting. "You'd better fly!"

On the street Jocelyn looked up at her cousin's rooms.
Helena stood, framed above her in the many-paned window.
Jocelyn waved her gloved hand and smiled, though she knew
her friend could not see the expression on her face.

"Jocelyn!"

She turned around. Arnold came toward her out of the arched door. "You can't come, Arnold," she said impatiently.

"I don't want to," he answered. "But . . . they said there wouldn't be anything to eat or drink for you. It might be hours before you get back, they said."

"That's right."

"Well . . . here." He shoved something into her hand. "It's the rest of the citron drops you gave me. You take them."

"Thank you." Jocelyn looked at the torn and dirty paper and then at Arnold. Perhaps he saw in her eyes that she wanted to embrace him, for he turned on his heel and bolted away. With a smile Jocelyn tucked the hard candies into her coat pocket. They were undoubtedly filthy from being in his pockets with dirt, objects of interest, and various livestock, and she could not imagine ever eating one. Still, it was kind of Arnold, and his kind impulses were rare.

Jocelyn took the opportunity to look more closely at Oxford. She did not want to walk through the streets which, after all, would not be so much different from Libermore. Therefore, Tom gave her simple directions on how to reach the Radcliffe Camera by passing through several yards and something called the Old Quad, although from Tom's description it did not sound so much older than the place in which he lived.

Jocelyn enjoyed walking at her own pace through the green courts. When she had come through with Hammond, he had been in too much of a hurry to permit more than hasty admiration. Entering what she thought must be the Old Quad, she could see at once the golden brick of a tall round building just over the ivy-grown wall. She began to walk more quickly, keeping her eyes on the Camera. A large woman, strangely familiar, walked past her on the graveled path, and Jocelyn nodded vaguely to her.

Through the darkly painted gate ahead was the building where, in less than an hour, the Prince Regent and Czar Alexander would be dining. Jocelyn wouldn't have felt more excited if she were about to meet the Prince Regent in person, her spirits only a little dampened by the thought of her former vicar. How she wished she and Helena could have shared this evening equally. It was just one more black mark against Nicholas Fain, that he'd made his stepsister so unhappy.

The noise of the crowd faintly penetrated the thick stone wall. She realized she'd been listening to it for some minutes before she'd known what it was. There must be thousands of people just the other side of the wall. For a moment they grew silent as a nearby bell began to toll the half-hour, answered by a faint chorus throughout the city.

With a cry Jocelyn fell to her knees, her head jerked back by a hand in her curls. A knife ground its teeth against her neck. Her eyes blurring with tears, she was forced to look up. A face appeared over her, upside down. Disoriented, she stared at it. It had no eyebrows and there was something else wrong with the bonneted head. She tried to understand what it was. For a moment, she forgot her hurts. That face! Greatly altered, it was still Nicholas Fain's.

Mr. Fain pushed Jocelyn to the ground. She landed hands first on the brick walk, small stones puncturing the palms of her gloves. Her mouth closed with a jar she could feel through her entire body. She was rattled. Turning onto her hip, she saw Mr. Fain. His head turned to either side, scanning the empty windows facing the quad.

Looking for witnesses, Jocelyn thought, and a fear indistinguishable from physical pain touched her. Her brain was paralyzed. She screamed. But the constant drumlike sound of the crowd beat on the other side of the wall, and she knew no one noticed one more cry.

Fain pulled her upright by the slack of her collar and ran with her into the shadows of the arch in the wall. She caught at his wrists as she strangled in his grasp.

"One more sound and I'll kill you." The words, grunted in her ear, froze her.

"I suppose you had a hand in planning this," he said, in a tone more like the one she was accustomed to hearing from him. A gentle sadness, like a reproof never quite stated, made him popular among the older ladies. Now his eyes were half-starting from his head in madness.

Fain shoved Jocelyn's head nearer the peeling paint of the gate, forcing her to look through a gap between two boards. The students had been joined by soldiers in red and blue, though Hammond still stood just before the entrance to the rotunda, inspecting every person that passed.

"I knew about it." In a rush she said, "You can't get in there. You can't—"

"I've gotten into more closely guarded palaces than this one. It's not even a palace. Just a library." Fain clicked his tongue against his teeth. "This plan must have been made today. I saw you arrive . . . you didn't know that! There must be a flaw in it."

Fain spun Jocelyn around. Within the rim of his ridiculous bonnet, his eyes burned in a whitened face. Their intensity contrasted with the gentle smile that curved his lips. "It's you, isn't it?"

"What do you mean?"

"You're my loophole. Why are you here?" He sniffed. "Perfume. Ribboned and gloved. You're going in there . . . to gaze upon Their Royal Countenances!" The knife once more pricked at her throat. "Get me into the gallery. I'll do it from there."

Jocelyn could not speak. She moved her head a fraction of an inch from side to side, feeling the blade like a sliver of ice under her chin.

"Take me in or I'll kill the dark-haired man where he stands. And your cousin." He bared his teeth in a smile like the grimace of a skull. Fain stepped back, holding his knife upright in the air. "Come now, Jocelyn," he said. "Who is more important? Tom and a man I think you perhaps care for? Or some wretched tyrant you don't even know?"

"I . . ."

He lunged at her again, pressing her against the gate with his body. She could not prevent a whimper of terror from escaping her throat. He chuckled and somehow that was worse than the threat that followed. "If you give me away, by a word, a look, a breath, I'll kill both of them before I'm stopped. Their blood will be on your head, Jocelyn."

Jocelyn walked up the street, her arm linked with that of the tall and heavy woman by her side. Jocelyn was laughing and whispering in the woman's ear, which was covered by a scooplike white bonnet, decorated with pinkish roses that clashed with the heavy red of her gown. The woman's shoes were clumpish and ugly.

A party of six, a harried father and five beautiful daughters, stood in line ahead of them, the father grumbling at the delay. Their chatter broke like the shrill cries of birds through the sea-sound of the crowd. Hammond let them pass.

"Oh, Captain Hammond," Jocelyn said, upon reaching the man who stood sentinel between the crowd and the Camera. "I'm sorry to be late. I met an old friend in the street on the way here. This is Mrs. Brewster. Imagine! She's a spectator, too!"

Hammond smiled. "I wish I were His Highness. All the beauties of England are here tonight." His eyes flickered over her companion, winced, and then went past her, to the next group approaching. "Go on inside, Jocelyn," he said, waving her in.

"Come, Mrs. Brewster." It was difficult to walk with a lump of lead sheathed in fear inside her and a knife pressed against her side.

"Mrs. Brewster" forced her along, with a squeeze of Jocelyn's arm that looked friendly but made the girl's eyes suspiciously bright. No one noticed.

The heavy door under the Grecian pediment stood open. Jocelyn sighed in relief and would have sagged from the release of tension. The knife in her side kept her upright. Whatever else happened, Tom and Hammond were safe.

Inside, the entrance was dark, save for shafts of light that fell through the windows above. Two guards were marking off names on a sheet of paper. Jocelyn could only perspire while three of the daughters in the party ahead searched themselves for their fans.

"Miss Helena Fain and Miss Jocelyn Burnwell," Mr. Fain fluted in falsetto upon reaching the man with the guest list.

"I'm sorry . . ." He began to say and Jocelyn breathed once more. The other one broke in. "Yes, they're here. Up the stair to your right, please."

Many people had already climbed the curving stairs to the gallery. Most of them crowded against the rail of marble running around the circuit of the rotunda, staring excitedly down at the scene below. The air was hot, for candles burned brightly below them. There were no chairs.

Mr. Fain dragged Jocelyn forward. The curses he used to get through the crowd sounded more horrible in Fain's parody of a woman's voice. The rest of the spectators drew away from Fain and Jocelyn as he pushed her up to the balustrade, her back against a marble pillar. Jocelyn's desperate eyes sought those of the men near her. They looked away or turned aside. No one would help her.

Fain looked down onto the main floor of the rotunda. "Look," he said, pointing down with one hand while the other kept the knife close against her. The rays of the descending sun struck flames from glimmering plates and brilliant crystal. Tables draped in white spread like a gold-chased fan across the circular floor. To her right she saw a more elaborately laid table with a scarlet cloth edged in gold like an altar in a church. Fresh flowers in a huge arrangement stood behind two large armed chairs raised higher than any other seats in the Camera. Fain stared at those two chairs. He smiled and began whistling tunelessly.

After a few moments he whispered hoarsely, "It is strange to consider, is it not, that you alone should be privileged not only to see but to understand my apotheosis."

"I don't understand," Jocelyn said. "How—"

"Softly, girl, softly, lest one of these brave English gentlemen come to your aid." Mr. Fain turned his head, but the people nearby remained pointedly oblivious to his presence. "You shall be my witness, you shall understand. Be quiet and patient only a little time more. You who have made a practice and an art of being quiet and patient."

Jocelyn said, "I don't know what you mean."

"I am not blind, Jocelyn. You are always meek, and yet I think you crave the excitements of a wider life. I did, at your age, and I achieved it."

"You're wrong about me, Mr. Fain."

"I should have said the same, then. I found a life in the service of a great leader. Today I shall prove that service is indeed my life."

Slowly, incautiously, Jocelyn said, "I think you are mad."

"I?" The knife against her shook. "You do not know me yet. Look down again and tell me who is madder. Those fretful popinjays worrying no doubt at this moment whether their sashes and furbelows hang to a nicety—or I. My master will with one final blow destroy these mean princes and set himself in his rightful place. I—I have been chosen to go before him to clear his way.''

Mr. Fain's eyes glittered as he looked down upon the elaborately dressed tables. His words rushed forth. Caution remained even as his blood grew hot. He never spoke above a confidential whisper. Jocelyn could only think his egotistical madness would have been worse if Napoleon's letter had ever reached him.

''I do understand, Mr. Fain,'' she said calmly.

''No! I can see that you do not. You shall be my witness nevertheless. I will make you famous. As famous as Corday or Judith. Yes, every bit as famous.''

Behind them the crowd swirled and parted. Mr. Fain pressed Jocelyn into the angle between pillar and balustrade, looking over his right shoulder. Two elderly gentlemen made their slow but insistent way forward. One carried a cane of polished black wood, the other stood as straight as a tree, old and hollow, that might topple in any sudden breeze. They made directly for the spot next to Jocelyn and the disguised Mr. Fain, urging one another on with word and gesture.

''To your left, Mr. Crowley. Between the woman in the bright purple dress and the fat man,'' the tall gentleman bellowed in the flat tone peculiar to the deaf.

''Indeed, Mr. McMasters. Slip ye along. Mind the female in the turban. Silly thing nearly put my eye out.'' The other gentleman was not above poking those in his way with his stick.

Jocelyn heard one woman say, ''The class of people here is not at all as I hoped it might be!'' Her husband tried to resurrect her pleasure in seeing the Czar and the Prince.

Another woman, more kindly, stepped forward to whisper and to point in warning against the foul-mouthed woman Mr. Fain appeared to be.

''What did she say, Mr. Crowley?''

The bent man shook his head and continued to press forward. ''Come along, Mr. McMasters, come along.''

Jocelyn felt her captor jump as the cane struck him on the elbow. The two elderly men pressed against the balustrade. ''Old fools,'' Fain said loudly in his hideous falsetto. ''Fall over the railing and have done.''

Neither man paid any attention. Jocelyn felt her heart sink. Out of the corner of her eye she saw the silver head of the bent man's stick. If only it were possible to hit Mr. Fain more effectively with it! She knew just where to strike, thanks to Regin. How long ago it seemed that he fell at her hands.

Somehow, as Jocelyn thought about her position, the sight of these two indomitable old men made her feel as if there were unrealized possibilities in the situation if only she could find them. She thought hard about everything she knew about Mr. Fain.

Brightly she said, "You will be pleased to know that I left Helena in excellent spirits. Of course, Cocker's setting fire to the vicarage was—" Mr. Fain grunted. "Fortunately, Helena and I flung ourselves out the window."

"What!" For the first time Mr. Fain forgot to modulate his voice. As though clockwork, every face in their part of the gallery turned toward him. He scowled around, and they once more turned their backs. "What do you mean, you fell out a window?"

"Not fell. Flung. Ourselves. We had no choice. It was that or be burned in the vicarage. I'm afraid they couldn't save your house."

"Cocker bungled it. I might have known I couldn't trust that— What were you and Helena doing in the house? I thought she spent the night with you."

"Cocker told us that you'd changed your mind, that she must come home. We went back, and while we were there, he burned the building."

"Cocker! I shall settle with him."

"That is what . . ." She hesitated, nearly but not quite mentioning Hammond. Somehow she felt she should not. "I thought you would say that. Why not now?"

"Don't be stoopid."

In the room below an increase in the bustling of the servants undoubtedly meant the advent of the royal presences. The people within the Camera fell silent as the building rang with the cheers of those standing in the street.

"They're coming," Mr. Fain said, breathing fast.

He stepped back from her, and Jocelyn, for the first time, looked at him without fear distorting his image. His costume was in the worst possible taste, every color clashing with another. She realized his bonnet was one she and Helena had trimmed the week before last.

With another look over his shoulder, like a woman checking for spies against her modesty, Mr. Fain lifted his skirt. Jocelyn saw he wore rough countryman's trousers beneath the worn red velvet of his gown. He sheathed his short knife.

With difficulty he reached into the pocket of his trousers and brought out a long-nosed pistol. It snagged on the material. He yanked it free. Jocelyn gasped and searched the crowd for help. They were all pressing forward, eager to see over the balustrade to catch the first glimpse of royalty. However, they were careful to leave a wide margin around the coarse woman and her young companion.

Mr. Fain held the pistol in front of his body. The pillar protected him from the crowd on one side, Jocelyn screening his hands from eyes across the rotunda. The two old men were close to him, arguing over some minor point of protocol. Jocelyn heard every word of their discussion as if she were in a dream.

"Your shoulder against the column," Mr. Fain ordered, pushing her into the cold pillar. "Put your hands in the pockets of your coat. Stand still."

Something hard passed between her left arm and the marble. Looking down, Jocelyn saw the black end of the pistol emerge. She tried to move but Mr. Fain's hand pressed against the small of her back, restraining her.

"You know, of course," he said conversationally, "that Judith saved her people by killing the Assyrian General Holofernes. You undoubtedly do not know, for the English are stupid about the rest of the world, that Charlotte Corday D'Armont killed Jean Marat. I did not agree with the lady's politics, but there can be no doubt she knew how to kill."

"Why do you tell me all this?" Jocelyn asked, although she felt she knew.

"Why, they are famous women assassins, and so shall you be. Or seem to be. I shall watch your future career with interest."

Below her Jocelyn could see large men in flowing trousers and tight pinkish coats entering and ranging themselves along the walls. They all carried long, heavy whips.

Mr. Fain said, "Those are Cossacks, the Czar's personal guards."

Jocelyn nervously toyed with something in her pocket. She felt it curiously, trying to recall what it was. Jocelyn said, "Don't you want to die for your cause, Mr. Fain? It can't be that you are afraid."

He chuckled. "An obvious ploy, Jocelyn. Every man is afraid to die, or he is a fool. I was willing to commit this great act and die a hero. I should much rather live as one. The moment I saw you today, I knew what a help you would be." His voice dropped, became soothing. "Stand still only a moment longer. I will soon be gone."

Now men who, by their dress, were gentlemen of rank and quality entered the vast round chamber. They sought out their places at the tables. A babble of voices rose and mixed with the exclamations from the gallery as various celebrities entered.

"General Blucher, there in the blue coat—good old Blucher!"

A cheer went up as the hero of the Prussian army was recognized. The white-haired general, already seated, stood up again, a glass in his hand, and waved it over his head, then sat down heavily, nearly missing his chair altogether.

"Drunk already, by God!" said one of the elderly gentlemen near to Jocelyn.

"Just a few more moments," Fain murmured, soft as a lover.

Her head spun. There was no help at hand. Fain was going to kill, and she could do nothing.

"Excuse me, madam," someone said on their right.

The assassin jumped, and Jocelyn nearly lost her footing. The old straight-backed man stood beside them, saying, "Your bonnet, madam, renders it impossible for my friend Mr. Crowley to see. Kindly doff it at once."

In answer Mr. Fain said something filthy and looked away. But the old man, with the tenacity of one who cannot hear a denial, insisted. Mr. Fain shook his head. Again, the loud flat voice demanded the bonnet be removed. His left arm still behind Jocelyn, the pistol pointing outward, Fain turned toward the old man to glare him into silence.

Jocelyn paid no attention. She frowningly concentrated on

the crunchy thing in her pocket. Almost laughing, she remembered it was Arnold's paper of candy. How trivial!

The sun through the upper windows shone brilliantly in
her face. Jocelyn turned her head away from the scene below
and began to pray silently. When she opened her eyes, she
saw the bent man, McMasters, standing behind Fain, nodding his head to the arguments of his friend. He did not lean
upon his cane but held it at an angle, more or less at Fain's
ankles. Jocelyn remembered Mr. Quigg and his pitchfork
handle.

She took the bag from her pocket, moving her hand a scant
inch at a time. She tried to picture the candies, whether they
were round and smooth or angular. It didn't matter. Half-
turning, she spilled the pieces down her coat, hoping they'd
fall silently. Mr. Crowley was booming noisily, protesting
Mr. Fain's reluctance to remove his hat. Jocelyn heard the
thumping of a band, and the cheers from the outside swelled.

Mr. Fain relaxed his hold on Jocelyn. She took one step
forward so the balustrade pressed against her middle. He felt
her move and grabbed at her while still looking at the old
man. Jocelyn hooked her foot behind his leg. Sliding on the
candy, Mr. Fain fell down. Tripped by his skirt and hers,
Jocelyn landed on him, her elbow striking his stomach. She
felt the pistol against her side. Then someone else was there,
forcing Fain's hand away. The cheers for the princes made
the inside of the rotunda ring like the bells chiming all over
Oxford.

The tall old man stooped and helped her to stand. "Terrible crush here, they shouldn't have allowed so many people
up."

"Stop him," Jocelyn gasped. "He has a gun."

He smiled and said to his companion, "If you wouldn't
mind, take his pistol."

Though the Prince Regent of England and the Czar of Russia were at this moment taking their seats, Jocelyn had eyes
only for the bent old gentleman. He grinned up at her, kneeling beside Mr. Fain's prone body. His face was less wrinkled
than she had thought and what looked like flour daubed his
hair and coat. One dark eye winked. Jocelyn grinned back,
all her troubles at an end.

Hammond said, "I can't search his clothes. Someone would take the wrong idea. Will you help me?"

"Miss Burnwell has helped you enough, I think."

Jocelyn looked at the other old man. He wore no disguise. His hands trembled, but he bore himself with an air of strength. He shuffled his feet and tottered on the citron drops. Jocelyn caught his arm to steady him.

"Thank you," he said with a slight bow. "I am Lord Ashspring. At least, I am now Lord Ashspring. For most of my life, however, I was Feldon Burnwell, a stiff-necked and obstreperous old man, as Captain Hammond made so bold to tell me today."

"Feldon Burnwell?" Jocelyn said in wonder. "My grandfather?"

Mr. Fain groaned and sat up. His bloodshot eyes shifted under the bonnet, right to Hammond, then found Jocelyn. "Is he dead?" he said to her.

"No, you've failed," Lord Ashspring answered abruptly. "And you'll hang."

CHAPTER SEVENTEEN

THE FORMER VICAR SAID NOTHING MORE, ONCE HE REALIZED his attempt had failed. Hammond hustled him away. No one paid any attention. The crowd in the gallery swallowed them up at once. Jocelyn could feel a certain pity for Mr. Fain, now.

"Lieutenant Fletcher is waiting for them," Lord Ashspring said quietly. "He'll spend the night in the Oxford gaol and in the morning be taken up to London for trial."

"Poor Helena. She will suffer the most for this."

"Yes." The man she now knew as her grandfather patted her shoulder rather awkwardly. "Look, His Highness is excusing himself."

Far below, a short figure in a formal, military-style coat, gold flashing from a sash around his considerable middle, bowed to his black-haired cadaverous guest, all in blue and silver. Quite merrily, so far as Jocelyn could tell, the prince regent took the arm of a person next to him and sauntered away.

"They'll have just told him about all this. Come, he'll be asking for me."

"But I can't . . . " Jocelyn protested, fluttering her fingers over her attire and bedraggled hair.

"Never mind," Lord Ashspring said. "Actually, I'd rather you looked the dowd when you meet him, than otherwise."

The main interior stair of the Radcliffe Camera circled grandly downward amid plaster reliefs. Hammond waited at the bottom of the steps, his hand on the ornate iron rail. "Fain's been taken away, my lord," he said, straightening.

"Very good. You might as well come along to meet His Highness. Or do you know him?"

"No, my lord. I've never had the honor. My father and he . . . but of course you know."

"Yes, and I've no doubt he'll remember as well. What a quarrel that was. Epic."

"My father has the devil's own temper. I believe he regretted it, later."

"He's regretted every argument he's ever had," Lord Ashspring said meaningfully. "But always too late. The prince and he are alike in that way, too."

They waited in an anteroom full of empty bookshelves. Her grandfather disappeared in a few moments, talking rapidly with an exquisitely dressed middle-aged man, who seemed on the verge of tears.

As soon as she and Hammond were alone, Jocelyn said, rather shyly, "I haven't thanked you yet for coming to rescue me. I didn't think you'd noticed anything wrong when I went past you."

Hammond looked up into a big gilded mirror hanging on the wall between two marble gods. His fingers adjusted his cravat, but his eyes went to her. "I didn't, truth to tell. Except you called me 'Captain.' I thought that was only because you were with someone from Libermore. Tom didn't know the 'woman' you were with, but he confessed he didn't know most of your friends. It wasn't until Arnold came running up—"

"Arnold!"

"Yes." He turned around, no smile lighting his face. "We owe him everything. He followed you, hoping, I think, to wheedle you into taking him up. He saw Fain throw you to the ground in the Old Quad."

"Oh, yes." She recoiled from that memory, the palms of her hands beginning to sting. She supposed they'd hurt all along; she'd just been too busy to think of them.

Hammond came to her. Looking inward, Jocelyn said, "I walked right past Mr. Fain, you know. I even nodded to him. He looked familiar and yet . . . really, the only thing I recognized was the bonnet he wore. Helena and I trimmed it, last month.''

"Don't think about it anymore. It's over." His fingers brushed her cheek. "I'm very grateful to Arnold."

"So am I. I shall have to buy him more candy. That's what Mr. Fain tripped on."

"Was that it? I'll buy out the first sweetshop I come to," Hammond promised.

He bent his head to kiss her, and she longed for him to. If he would only hold her, the horror of remembered danger could be kept at bay. The strength of his arms was the only weapon she required. All her love shone in her eyes as she raised them to his face. His expression sobered.

Before he could embrace her, the door behind them opened. A cough exploded. A short man, also beautifully dressed, said, "Please come with me, sir. Miss Burnwell."

As they followed him down the hall, Jocelyn noticed that his steps were oddly mincing. After a moment she realized his formal slippers had high heels.

Jocelyn caught Hammond's arm as they walked. "Did your father actually know the Prince Regent?"

"Is that all you can think of, at a time like this? Yes. But he was only the Prince of Wales then."

His Royal Highness's querulous tones penetrated the thick oaken door. Hammond and Jocelyn entered while their escort, actually the Pursuivant Herald Red, approached His Highness.

George, Prince of Wales and Regent of England, paid no attention. He breathed heavily, looking at his equerry with confusion in the depths of his flab-surrounded eyes. "Are you certain there are no more of these villains lurking about? Is attempt after attempt to be made on our life with no one raising so much as a finger to prevent . . . ?" He shuddered strongly.

The Herald murmured something to His Highness. "Yes, yes." He turned toward them, his head lifting nobly as he said to Hammond, "Our thanks to you, sir. A noble deed, done well."

Jocelyn, distracted from the prince's dyed hair and doughy skin, understood at once why, for all his faults, the Prince Regent commanded the ready affection of his friends, difficult though it might be for him to retain it. Those bright blue eyes turned next to her, and she dipped profoundly. He addressed no words to her, only inclining his head in response to her curtsy.

She felt Hammond take her arm, and they backed from the room. His breath went out of his body in a great sigh. "Not too bad, for a man who last year never thought to come to England again."

"What will you do now?" Jocelyn asked, no longer able to resist the question. She'd wondered about the immediate future from the moment he found the letter he brought from France, now in her grandfather's hands.

He stopped in the middle of a step and looked down. "Well . . . I don't know! I can't say I'd thought that far ahead."

Turning to her, he placed a tender hand on her cheek. Almost idly his thumb edged her lower lip. Words formed in his mouth. Words she did not want to wait to hear. Her eyes closed of their own accord. Swaying toward him, she heard the sound of booted feet along the marble hall.

"Sir!" someone said, close at hand.

Hammond chuckled ruefully as her eyes snapped open. A sergeant in a scarlet uniform stood at attention beside them, extending an envelope. "Orders, I expect," Hammond said. He read the paper. "Very well, sergeant. I'll come with you."

In the single moment they had, Hammond squeezed her hand. "I have to go to London. I'll see you there."

Alone, Jocelyn stamped her foot. It was always something! Constables, cousins, commands—the whole roster stood up and answered "Present" whenever she and Hammond stole an instant alone. She was sick of it. The very next time, she swore, he'd not have it so easy. One of them—and she feared it would be her—must make a plain, simple statement about their feelings, or she'd go mad.

Jocelyn and her grandfather returned to Tom's lodging, ill at ease in each other's presence. As soon as they entered, Helena bolted away and locked herself in Tom's room. Jocelyn's aunt and uncle, not at all put out by this abrupt termination to their conversation, greeted their niece with gentle kindliness. Lord Ashspring undertook to explain Jocelyn's presence in Oxford to them. He did not mention Mr. Fain, only saying that he requested Jocelyn come to see him in the hopes of making amends to her for his long silence and that Miss Fain and Mr. Fletcher accompanied her for modesty's sake.

Years of directing the clandestine operations of His Majesty's government had accustomed him to phlegmatic individuals, but he never knew anyone so calm as his relations by marriage. Mrs. Luckem, who seemed to do most of the talking, said, "I see. Of course, Jocelyn must visit you, as soon as you wish it."

"If you can spare her, I would have her accompany me now. Mr. Fain has given his sister into my care, temporarily. Mr. Fletcher wishes to take the responsibility permanently as soon as may be convenient." He was prey to the curious and most disconcerting feeling, one he had not known since his school-days, that he told lies to someone who knew the entire truth.

Helena said one evening during their third week in London, as they sorted through their new clothes, "If it weren't for Nicholas, I should be the happiest girl in the world!"

The two girls sat in the bedroom they'd shared since their second night in the city. The first night Helena had awakened with a nightmare, sobbing out a confused dream of separation and fear. After that she declared she slept better with someone else in the room. Jocelyn shared her room gladly, for she'd had her own nightmares. Sometimes, even now, she could feel Mr. Fain's knife at her side and would involuntarily jerk aside. She did not describe her dreams to Helena.

Jocelyn looked away from the mirror, letting her new promenade gown, fine as anything Miriam Swann could boast, fall limply away from her shoulders. "You're not letting him come between you and Mr. Fletcher, I hope?"

"I am trying not to let him," Helena said softly. Her hand darted out. "Look at this shawl!" she said, lifting a piece of gauze fine as morning mist. Jocelyn let her change the subject.

Nicholas Fain had been escorted at once to London, though he had not traveled in the same style as his sister and Jocelyn. Newgate Prison awaited him. Helena wanted to go to visit him, but Fletcher and Lord Ashspring had dissuaded her. "Better not to be connected with him, darling," Mark had

said. "This affair's made a lot of noise in the popular broad-
sides. You don't want to be bothered with strangers accusing
you of . . . complicity."

Jocelyn did her best to keep Helena's spirits high. They
traveled about London, seeing all the "lions," pleased by
nearly all they saw, and almost always unaware of the interested glances they acquired as they wandered, maid in tow.
If they did happen to notice, they behaved very coolly until
safely past and then giggled and teased, each insisting the
other was the object of attention.

Lord Ashspring did his part, insisting that each girl order
a new wardrobe, as they had come up to town with virtually
nothing. For once Jocelyn had another to do her sewing, and
she felt wonderfully guilty at her idleness. At first she enjoyed
ringing a bell and having someone come to take her orders
but, as she said to her grandfather, "I cannot be idle and be
happy."

By the second week of her arrival, she began to inquire
gently into the running of the house. A man tends to overlook
the minor details of housekeeping like dust under the stairs
and moldy closets that make the difference between a London
residence and a comfortable home. The servants were happier. His Lordship's chef produced much better dishes when
he knew Miss Jocelyn would care how they were cooked.
The butler felt he had at last someone worthy of his magnif-
icence. His Lordship never even noticed if the footmen's toes
turned out correctly. The only person displeased was the
coachman. "This," he said to anyone who would listen, "is
what comes a pickin' up femayles on t'road."

Slowly Jocelyn began to feel more at ease in the presence
of her grandfather. At first he seemed so cold and stiff with
her that she found it difficult to behave with less than complete formality. The two girls would have supper with him in
the library after he returned from the War Office. He spoke
kindly to Helena, making her talk about a variety of subjects
to keep her from thinking about her brother. But when he
looked on Jocelyn, his deep-set eyes frowned, and he would
be silent.

Late one night, after three weeks had passed, Jocelyn did
not feel sleepy. Helena slept soundly. Not wishing to disturb
her friend with a lamp, she brought a piece of embroidery

downstairs to sit in the library. Lord Ashspring had sent a message before dinner, saying he would be very late. The library was a dark, comfortable room, much like the one in the Luckems' house, only larger and missing the antique objects. She poked up the fire, always burning to warm her grandfather's old bones.

Half-hidden in a chair with great curving wings, she sat with her needle, brilliant floss spread over her white muslin knees. Embroidery did not take all her attention, and her thoughts turned inexorably to Hammond. He had never sent any word to her. Slowly she was becoming convinced, almost against her will, that his affection for her had been either illusionary or brought on only by the difficulties and dangers of their days together. She sighed and attempted to focus her mind on the dainty leaves forming under her hand.

Suddenly from behind her, she heard soft, slow footsteps. Her whole body tensed. A voice said, "Jocelyn?" and she jumped up with a little shriek. The threads on her lap drifted off, floating in the air.

Lord Ashspring woofed with surprise. "Damn, child, have you no better sense . . ." He saw her eyes were still huge and that she trembled. "It seems we have each startled the other. Sit down." He took her by the elbow and pressed her down onto the chair's cushion. Ringing the bell, he gave orders for two glasses of brandy, one large and another rather smaller.

"Drink that down directly. I know it tastes dreadful, but it will do you much good." Standing before the fireplace, he sipped his own glass appreciatively with a mental apology to the liquor. He deeply regretted denigrating the fine wine, recently brought over from France, but he knew it would taste worse than medicine to a young girl unused to the flavor.

Jocelyn made a face as the wine burned an acrid path down her throat. However, it did seem to help in getting her too-fast breath under control. "I don't know what I was thinking of," she said.

"Hmph! It's this Fain business, no doubt. I can't tell you what a fuss is being made. There's actually some talk about letting him go."

"Go?"

"They want to give him to the Russians. Let them take care of him. I'm against it."

"Why?" She leaned forward, looking at her grandfather with an air of grave interest.

"Their methods of punishing criminals are not as civilized as our own. We'll hang him, but they'd . . ." He closed his lips. "Never mind. What are you doing?" He looked at the embroidery hoop she held out to him. "Very pretty. Your grandmother, my Elizabeth, used to do crewelwork. Great Jacobite flowers to repair the bedhangings at the house."

"What house?" Jocelyn asked timidly. Though filled with natural curiosity about the rest of her family, especially about her father, of whom she knew almost nothing, she never yet dared to ask her grandfather direct questions about them.

"Our family home is at Acton Burnell, in Shropshire." He sat down on the chair across the fireplace from Jocelyn.

"Is that where our name comes from?"

"Yes, it's a corruption. Your father researched the question of how it came to be changed, but his investigations came to nought. He did not have time . . ." Lord Ashspring looked at Jocelyn, her face half-shaded, half-illuminated by the flickering firelight. "Sometimes . . ." he said so quietly she almost could not hear him, "sometimes you have his expression. And you laugh like Elizabeth."

Every evening thereafter, Jocelyn would go to sit near her grandfather as he sat reading in a circle of lamplight. He would read aloud to her, and then they'd discuss the subject at hand. He called her ignorant much of the time, and she supposed she was. On other occasions, especially when she agreed with him, Lord Ashspring would applaud her good sense.

Slowly they came to be more at ease with each other. Often he would mention something about the family she'd never known, and she treasured every word. He never went so far as to regret aloud the wasted years of proud silence, but she knew he sometimes thought it. Jocelyn began to picture for herself a new life, one in which the care of her cousins was replaced by living in her grandfather's house and being of help to him. Perhaps she could even take part in society in a small way. As the grandchild of a peer, even a recently created one, the wider world would greet her with some attention.

She mentioned these changed dreams to Helena, who looked at her in an odd, sidelong fashion. After a moment she said, "Mr. Hammond has not yet written to you? Did he not say he would?"

"No," Jocelyn said, trying not to let Helena see that his silence hurt her. "He only said he might call. I imagine he has many things to occupy his attention just now. He'd been out of the country so long."

"I wonder . . . I wonder if it was he Lord Ashspring sent to France."

"I doubt it." Lord Ashspring had sent to France to discover who Helena's real father had been, since it was established that Nicholas Fain's father was not hers. Jocelyn had told her grandfather that this mystery troubled Helena, as she did not want to marry Mr. Fletcher without knowing the kind of family she came from.

Jocelyn had gone with her friend to visit Mr. Fletcher's widowed mother, who lived in an elegant but small house in Chiswick not far from Sutton Court and the river. A short, plump, fair woman dressed in a gown of a fashionable cut but in the deepest black, she tended to sigh heavily when speaking of her late husband. Mrs. Fletcher hadn't any idea, apparently, what her son had been doing during the war nor the circumstances under which he and Miss Fain had met. "Where does your family live, my dear Helena?"

This, of course, was the worst possible question to put to her son's fiancée. Helena could not say anything without tears. Jocelyn mumbled for her, "Unfortunately, Helena is all alone in the world. My aunt and uncle . . . my grandfather Lord Ashspring . . . you understand." Jocelyn hoped she left the impression that Helena's family were long-term friends of her own somewhat more illustrious family.

Mrs. Fletcher had been very sweet and tender after that, inviting Helena to stay at her house rather than at Lord Ashspring's residence. "That's so very kind, but Jocelyn offered to let me stay until the . . . wedding." Only Jocelyn was aware that Helena had nearly said "hanging."

Two days after this meeting Mr. Fletcher suggested with a worried face that they delay posting the banns in his mother's parish until after the unpleasant epilogue to Mr. Fain's career was over. Helena agreed very calmly and then spent the rest of the afternoon sobbing in Jocelyn's arms. "If he doesn't want to marry me anymore, then he should tell me so. That would only be fair, don't you think? Don't you?"

Jocelyn did not know what to think. She sympathized strongly with Helena, who only wished to marry and put her relationship with her stepbrother behind her. Yet at the same time, she could understand Mrs. Fletcher's reluctance to take into her home and family someone whose background was not a matter for discussion. Jocelyn felt the most sympathy for Mr. Fletcher caught in the middle not only between his mother and his love, but trapped by confused loyalties to his career and Helena.

He couldn't even formally take up his regimental colors again, as the army found it had more officers than it knew what to do with. The navy was in the same state. The British government decided it was not necessary to keep the massive body of men they'd used as a sword against Napoleon now he was a tiger with every tooth drawn.

Jocelyn noticed Lord Ashspring's spirits seemed as low as Mr. Fletcher's. The secretive service to which he belonged was also being broken down. He would often, in their evening sessions, curse the short-sightedness of the Parliament, the Lords of the Admiralty, and the Regent's advisers. "No one remembers '02 when we took the navy down to peacetime standing, only to find it necessary to frantically rearm when Napoleon broke the peace."

"But we're safe now," Jocelyn said.

"Yes, safe enough. Until the next time. Napoleon's not the only enemy we have to fear."

Remembering things she'd heard, Jocelyn hazarded a guess. "The Russians?"

"Yes, and the Turks. Then there's noises of rebellion coming from India. And even . . . perhaps we shall soon be once more at war with the Americans. They've been meddling in European waters lately."

Jocelyn received three letters in the first three weeks of her London visit. Arnold wrote a short letter, badly spelled now that Mr. Fletcher was no longer there to correct him. It consisted largely of complaints against Granville and Miss Hargreaves, details of his speedy trip to London with his parents, and boasting about the events at Oxford. He seemed to feel this was a ripe area for exploitation.

The next letter came from Mrs. Luckem. Uncle Gaius had marched Arnold over to Lord Netherham's property, and an apology was duly tendered. Arnold had offered, under strong impetus, to perform menial tasks on His Lordship's property until his new school began in the fall.

Mrs. Luckem also enclosed news of larger doings. Libermore accepted that Mr. Fain died in the fire at the vicarage. General mourning was declared and a committee formed to petition the bishop for a new vicar. Cocker, she reported, was arrested on the charge of setting the fire, but he seemed to have lost his mind. He continually babbled of doing important work for the French government. At the next Assizes he'd undoubtedly be declared insane. The parish had paid for Mr. Hodges's funeral with the assumption that Cocker had killed him.

The final letter came from Tom, happily on his way to Italy. No others came to her. Though Jocelyn pretended to wait with patience, no word ever came from Hammond. No one seemed to know where he was or what he was doing, not even her grandfather.

On the fourth Wednesday of her visit, Jocelyn found herself alone in the house. Helena went with her Mark to tea at his mother's, to all appearances entirely happy. Lord Ashspring stopped at his club for his twice weekly afternoon of whist.

Jocelyn felt restless. She tried to stitch, tried to read, tried to look at the household accounts, but nothing occupied her attention for very long. Finally, exasperated, she threw herself into a chair by the window and concentrated hard on a book.

The butler entered, stately and portly. "Sir Erasmus DeReine," he announced.

Jocelyn looked around her chair wing, about to remind Jamison that her grandfather was not at home. Hammond walked in. For a moment Jocelyn did not even stand up. She simply gaped.

"I'm sorry," he said, pausing. "I thought I'd find Lord Ashspring . . ." Hammond looked around for the butler, but he had gone, shutting the door behind him.

"My grandfather went out," Jocelyn said, recovering her wits and her manners as she stood. "He has a regular appointment at his club."

"Odd," Hammond said, coming farther into the room. "He told me yesterday that this would be a convenient time to call." He glanced around idly, at the furnishings, the mirror above the mantel, her.

Jocelyn asked, "Won't you sit down and wait? He shouldn't be too long." She knew she spoke utter nonsense. It would be at least two hours before Lord Ashspring returned. Her lips and her brain, however, did not seem to be connected.

"Thank you." He remained standing, gazing at her as if she were someone whose name he could not quite recall.

He was not the same. It was not only that the tension she had always seen in his face was smoothed away. There were other changes. The old, rusty coat was replaced by a blue one of unimpeachable cut worn, however, with his usual carelessness. She wanted to reach out and tug the lapels into proper order. His shirt and waistcoat could not be improved, she felt sure, but if Granville were to see Hammond's cravat, he'd die of horror.

Hammond cleared his throat before saying, "You look well. A new dress?"

"Yes, thank you. I'm afraid my grandfather is spoiling me." She smoothed the pale green lutestring, taking innocent pleasure in the quality of the fabric. She was quite unaware that the color, which Helena had chosen for her, cast a green light into her gray eyes, increasing their size and luster. Jocelyn hoped her hair, which she now wore always in the style her friend invented, was not exploding into its usual untidy mass.

"Spoiling you? He must enjoy that."

"I don't know if he does," Jocelyn said. "He said he'd not have a pair of dowdy women in his house."

"Miss Fain is still with you then? How do the wedding plans progress?"

"Slowly I'm afraid. Yet, I feel confident that they shall come together in time." She shook her head. "I wish I could do more for her. Perhaps, in a few weeks, when Grandfather's business is concluded, we shall travel to his home in Shropshire. Mr. Fletcher and she may need time apart to

realize the true depth of their affection. I, of course, am longing to see it. Grandfather says his home is very beautiful.''

"I've never been there. I've just . . .'' He saw he did not
have her attention. "Jocelyn?''

She came back to herself with a start. "I beg your pardon,'' she said, a frown of puzzlement between her brows.
"What did Jamison say?''

"I don't know. Who is Jamison?''

"The butler. He announced you under a different name.''
She smiled. "Is it another of your subterfuges?''

"I have no subterfuges!'' he protested, stepping toward
her.

"Oh, no?'' She laughed. " 'Uncle'? Or is it 'Mr. Crowley'? Is Sir-whatever-it-is another one?''

"No,'' Hammond said, taking her hand and holding it as
if he did not quite know where he'd got it. "Rather the other
way around.''

"Oh, dear,'' Jocelyn said, standing up. Her hand fell from
his. Whatever dreams she'd been nursing burst like soap bub-
bles under a child's greedy hand.

"Why such a tragic face, Jocelyn?'' Why take a hand, he
reasoned, when a waist is so much pleasanter?

As his arm encircled her, warm and strong, Jocelyn felt
more nervous now than during those frantic minutes in the
Radcliffe gallery. She didn't know where to look or what to
do. Then her eyes met his, and she realized there was nothing
to fear. He would always be with her as he had been from
the first moment they'd met, regardless of his name.

Hammond kissed her so softly and gently that at first she
stood passive beneath his embrace. Very soon, however, she
slipped her arms about his neck and kissed him back in a
method she had never learned, but that he seemed to find
satisfactory.

He broke their kiss and chuckled warmly. When he spoke,
he seemed to be having trouble with his voice. "There, he'll
have to believe me now.''

Dreamily Jocelyn laid her head against his shoulder and
said, "Who will?''

"My father.'' He felt her start. "Didn't you think I had
one? I do, you know. We quarreled soon after my mother
died. As we are both slightly more stubborn than the devil,

we never made it up until now. I went home to make my peace. It was damnably hard, to be honest. He'd grown bitter, like me. He couldn't believe I'd changed until I told him about you and how I thought you'd civilize me."

"Civilize you?" Jocelyn asked, shyly meeting his dark eyes.

"Yes, that is the function of a wife." Hammond let her go just long enough to sit down and draw her onto his knees. After a few more bliss-filled moments, he continued, "We're an old family. The Hammonds . . . that *is* one of our name's, although we've got a few titles stashed about the place . . . we've always fought for the king, whoever he was and whatever he stood for. When Napoleon started up, I wanted to finish at Cambridge, and the old ruff . . . my father didn't understand why I didn't throw over the whole business and join our old regiment. We argued and he cut me off. He thought I was a coward, you see."

Jocelyn nodded. "I suppose he didn't understand that there are many kinds of bravery."

Hammond kissed her again. "What have you done to your hair? I liked it the other way."

Jocelyn reached up and pulled out the green ribbon, folded it and gave it to him. "Go on," she said when he allowed her to breathe.

"What? Oh, when I joined up, I went into the navy. I confess I did that to twist the knife, so to speak. We've always been army. One incident led to another, and I met your grandfather and entered his service. My father and Lord Ashspring knew each other but had argued. My father will argue with anyone, you see. You heard about him and the prince. I don't want you to think he's an ogre, mind. You'll twine him around your little finger, as you do everyone. One look in your beautiful eyes . . . did you know you have beautiful eyes? Soft and gray and loving. And your lashes . . . I don't believe I ever told you about them . . ."

The words were sweet to hear, but her curiosity was all on another subject. Still, she treasured his opinions. "You've made your peace with him, then?"

"Who? Oh, yes. I had to swallow a good meal of Southern County humble pie, but yes, I have. I think he was glad of it, though he couldn't admit it." His voice dropped. "The house and the lands have gone to ruin. I suppose he thought . . . I'm the only child. Between you and me, Jocelyn, we'll make it right.''

. "I know we will," she said, her voice trembling. "I love you so dreadfully.'' After that a long time passed before she could even think to speak again. Finally, lifting her eyes to him, she murmured, "Do you mind if I ask you a question?''

"Whatever you like.''

"What did Jamison say?''

Hammond blushed. He reached inside his coat and brought out a card case. She tilted the piece of pasteboard toward the window. "Erasmus? I suppose I should call you 'Sir Erasmus'?''

He nodded, a familiar scowl drawing down his lips.

Jocelyn reclined against him in a way that, though unorthodox, was very comfortable. "Hammond, let's have Arnold as our first guest. He and your father should get on wonderfully well. Don't you think so?''